MASTERS OF FATE

DARK STARS TRILOGY: BOOK 3

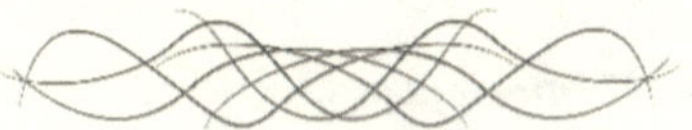

A K DUBOFF

MASTERS OF FATE

Published by Dawnrunner Press

ISBN-10: 195434418X
ISBN-13: 978-1954344181
Copyright Registration Number: TXu002121107

0 9 8 7 6 5 4 3 2

Produced in the United States of America

TABLE OF CONTENTS

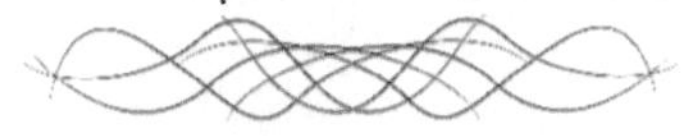

KEY TERMS, CAST & LOCATIONS

Key Terms

Crystalline network – A series of special crystals scattered across the known worlds; unique properties allow the crystals to record the physical state of reality at set moments in time, enabling "resets" to past configurations

Darkness – An alien weapon spread throughout the crystalline network, which transforms and shrouds the infected worlds in shadow

Hegemony – The collection of settled worlds in known civilization

Master Archive – A central repository of all backup data from the crystalline network; seems to exist outside of normal space and time, accessed on the planet Crystallis

Reset – A roll back to a previous physical state of reality from a past moment in time; resets can be on a local scale within a specific crystal's zone or on a universal scale

Dark Sentinel Team

Elle – Point-of-view character, wields the Valor sword artifact (strength focus); also exhibits traits from Spirit and Protector (magic and defense) focus areas

Kaiden – Spirit caster (magic focus) with Spirit circlet artifact, agriculture background; Elle's romantic interest

Toran – Protector (defense focus) with Protector gauntlets artifact, engineering background

Maris – Spirit caster (magic focus) with restorative and defensive spell specialization

Ship Crew

Commander Alastair Colren – Captain of the *Evangiel* and Hegemony representative

Chief Taminoret (Tami) – Head engineer and maintenance tech

Locations

Evangiel – Hegemony ship that serves as a mobile base

Capital – Seat of the Hegemony government and records repository

Crystallis – Planet containing the Master Archive, the backup for all reset crystals

Erusan – Elle's homeworld

Dunlore – Toran's homeworld

Falstan II – Kaiden's last world of residence

Yantu – Maris' homeworld

THE STORY SO FAR...

CRYSTALLINE SPACE: BOOK 1 RECAP

The unique crystalline network spanning the Hegemony's worlds records physical states at set moments in time, allowing reality to be reset.

Elle Hartmut was a regular teenager living on the backwater world of Erusan, getting ready to attend college in the coming months. She had dreams of going to Tactical School and becoming a Space Ranger for the Hegemony, but a childhood injury derailed those aspirations.

One afternoon, while enjoying her last summer break, Elle and her friends discover a dark cloud in one of the crystals outside their hometown. Before they can investigate, the mayor calls a town meeting and initiates what should be a routine planet-scale reset.

Instead of returning to the reset point, Elle awakens on a spaceship. Her consciousness has been extracted and synced with a new, enhanced body. She also has new abilities, granting her amazing fighting skills and the ability to cast magic, though she's not sure to what extent. Most crucially, she's told that she holds the fate of known civilization in her hands.

An alien Darkness is corrupting the crystalline network, threatening to destroy the Hegemony as it transforms the infected worlds into twisted wastelands. The only hope of saving the Hegemony's worlds is to seal the Master Archive, the backup record for the reset points of all known worlds.

Elle joins a team with Kaiden (a magic caster) and Toran (a fighter built like a tank). They begin searching for ancient artifacts that will allow access to the Master Archive so they can seal it. After retrieving the Protection artifact for Toran (a set of gauntlets), the team get a new member, Maris—another magic caster specializing in haste, protective, and restorative magic. The quartet then retrieves the Spirit artifact (a magic circlet) for Kaiden, and then the Valor artifact (a sword with magical blue flames along its blade) for Elle. Finally, they are ready to take on the last trials to seal the Master Archive.

The team enters the Archive and defeats a series of foes, using the skills they have mastered in their respective disciplines. Elle discovers that she has capabilities in all three disciplines, including the ability to cast magic. In the process, they each receive visions related to the Darkness: an invasion force is coming.

Upon passing the tests, the team is greeted by an ethereal voice who confirms that their visions will guide them in the fight to come. The team is then given a small shard of a Master Crystal. With the Archive sealed, it will enable them to control a universal-scale reset. They now have a means to fight back against the Darkness.

A LIGHT IN THE DARK: BOOK 2 RECAP

No measure is too extreme in the frantic fight for survival.

Elle and the Dark Sentinel team—Kaiden, Toran, and Maris—know the next phase of an invasion is coming, but they still haven't identified the origin of the alien menace. In an effort to get answers, they embark on a dangerous mission to Windau, the planet first infected by the Darkness.

While on Windau, they nearly succumb to the twisted vegetation and wildlife, though they are ultimately able to interface with the planet's primary crystal. They discover a strange signal may hold the clues they're looking for.

Once back on the *Evangiel*, Toran identifies a set of coordinates embedded in the signal, and the Hegemony prepares to confront their would-be invaders. Upon traveling to the indicated location, a hyperdimensional anomaly appears, and out of it comes the first of the alien ships. However, before the Hegemony fleet can mount an assault, a single alien ship destroys the fleet with a weaponized black cloud that disintegrates everything it touches. With the battle lost before it had rightly begun, Commander Colren orders a risky universal reset—the only chance to try again and avoid the devastating loss.

Elle and the rest of the Dark Sentinel team come to their senses the moment after sealing the Master Archive with a strange feeling of déjà vu. In time, they remember about the alien attack and take measures to ensure a more favorable outcome. However, when they arrive at the anomaly site, the alien fleet is already waiting; apparently, the aliens have clear memories the events from before the reset, unlike the Dark Sentinel's scattered recollections.

Before initiating a second universal reset, the team devises a strategy to carry over specific memories through the reset, hoping it will be enough to gain an upper hand next time; this time, Colren joins them at the locus of the event to hopefully make him remember, as well. They reset to a slightly later point and are able to remember enough of the previous encounter to devise a new strategy.

Knowing they only have one chance to try something new, the Dark Sentinel team boards the alien ship while it's still forming in the anomaly, to plant a spatial disruptor—a bomb capable of spanning dimensional planes. Using their magical abilities, seemingly augmented by proximity to the spatial anomaly, Elle and her friends fight their way to the center of the alien ship and deploy the disruptor.

With moments to spare before the scheduled detonation, the team retreats to their shuttle. However, before they can dock, the *Evangiel* is forced to jump away and leave them behind. The Dark Sentinels focus their magic energy on Elle's sword to create a bubble around their shuttle and ride out the spatial disruption wave.

The *Evangiel* returns to retrieve them, finding that the anomaly has been destroyed and the immediate invasion threat averted. Though shaken from this encounter, now they know how to hurt the aliens, and it's time to fight back.

THE STORY CONTINUES IN *MASTERS OF FATE*…

1

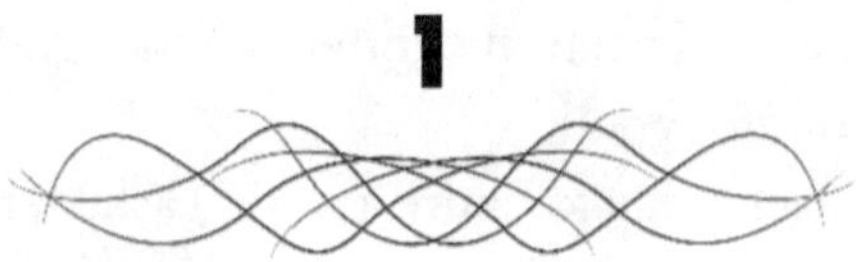

PRACTICE COMBAT WASN'T the same as a real fight, and I had a thirst for battle.

As I twisted and flipped around the mock battlefield with my three friends, I couldn't help but wish that we were on a world fighting creatures born from the Darkness rather than attacking rocks on an uninhabited planet.

Envisioning a shadowcat in my mind, I lunged to the side while swinging my sword in what would be a decapitating blow. I landed lightly on my feet then spun around to spot my next target.

"Nice move," Kaiden complimented.

I grinned back, still poised for action. "I can't wait to take them out for real."

The planet Commander Colren had selected for our exercises was one of the least interesting places from our travels to date. Rather, it was beautiful—impressive mountain peaks and expansive forests—but it wasn't... magical. I craved for the intensity of the crystals on Crystallis or the hum of the Darkness signal in the background. To be on a purely ordinary world felt like a part of me was missing.

Toran sighed, heaving his broad shoulders. He lowered his fists. "If our attacks are focused on individual creatures, we're going about the war all wrong."

"That's true. Any word on the larger strategy?" asked Kaiden, bringing his staff to a resting position on the ground.

Toran shook his bald head. "My conversations have been about the technical nature of the Darkness and the potential form of the aliens. We haven't gotten far enough to know how to take them out for good."

"Are you *ever* going to figure it out?" I asked, realizing only after I'd spoken that it sounded whiny. But, in the days following our engagement with the alien ship at the anomaly, Toran and the other scientists had concluded that the signal's origin wasn't nearly as clear as they'd once believed. It was coming from a specific location, and they knew where that place was, but there didn't appear to be anything there.

"It's a complex situation. There are forces here beyond our current understanding," Toran replied.

Maris tightened the ponytail holding back her dark hair. "Because it's *magic*."

"Just because we don't yet understand it, that doesn't make it magic," he retorted. "Frankly, some theories the Hegemony's science team has presented are pretty exciting."

"Because they're magic," Maris insisted.

"No, just higher dimensional sp…" I faded out, not remembering the term Toran had used yesterday.

"Hyperdimensional entities manifesting in our plane," Toran corrected. "But that's only one hypothesis. They just as easily could be beings that have learned to control matter using whatever mechanism the crystals use for resets."

"Regardless of what they are, we need to figure out how to

stop them," Kaiden stated.

Torn inclined his head. "Which is what we're trying to do. But, it's difficult when we don't rightly know what they're after."

"I still say it's matter—or dark matter," I posited. "All of the worlds infected by the Darkness were hollowed out."

"I still don't believe that's the case," Toran countered.

"Then what—" I was cut off by a chirp in my ear from the embedded comm.

"Dark Sentinel team, return to the *Evangiel*," Colren instructed.

"Is everything okay, Commander?" Kaiden asked.

"New information. Meet in the conference room," he replied, then cut the commlink.

I looked to my friends. "Good information or bad information?"

"That tone didn't *sound* good," Maris observed.

Kaiden let out a deep breath. "Looks like you may soon get your wish for a proper fight after all, Elle."

"We'll see what the commander has to say." Really, it wasn't that I desired to be at the center of the conflict, it was that I hoped for an end to the madness that had been our lives for the past several weeks. I wanted to put a face to the enemy who'd forced me away from my family and made so many people suffer at the hands of their planet-killing weapon. I didn't want to confront them because of bloodlust—rather, I wanted to end the war so we could return to our loved ones and once again have control over our own lives. Though my future path was now unclear, not having the threat of an alien invasion hanging over my head would certainly make matters easier.

The four of us hiked back to our shuttle in a grassy field

two hundred meters from our practice area. My chest was tight with eager anticipation to hear Colren's news. The commander had been strangely silent in the four days since our near-death encounter with the alien ship, so I looked forward to a face-to-face meeting to assess his current frame of mind. I could only imagine he was as anxious for the conflict to be over as I was—maybe even more so, having been in the thick of it for a longer time. However, he was our connection to the rest of the Hegemony, so I wanted to make sure he was still on our side. After all, he'd already left us to die once, when he jumped the *Evangiel* without us.

After a brief shuttle ride, we docked in the hangar and made our way to Central Command on the upper deck of the *Evangiel*. Colren rose from his seat at the center of the bridge and motioned us toward the glass-walled conference room.

"How was practice?" the commander asked as we took our typical seats.

"Good," Kaiden replied.

I nodded. "We feel prepared, if that's what you mean."

"It was," Colren said. "So, there shouldn't be any issue with carrying out our new orders."

Toran's brow knit. "The Hegemony has made a decision?"

Colren nodded. "We've been ordered to mount an investigation of the world where the alien signal is originating. Since nothing is showing up on long-range scans, we have no option other than to get closer."

My stomach flipped as I thought back to the last time we'd gone to an alien-controlled world to investigate the Darkness. I hadn't experienced it in this timeline, but my memories from the previous-future had become clearer with time. The multiple independent timelines with their own sequences of events wove through my mind; I couldn't tell quite how many resets we'd been through, but there were at least three clear versions of events where we hadn't stopped the alien fleet. In those timelines, worlds infected by the Darkness had proved almost deadly. I could only imagine a journey to their central hub would be the most dangerous of all.

Kaiden caught my eye from the seat next to me. He cracked a subtle smile, knowing how much I had been asking for a direct alien encounter over the past several days. However, in usual fashion, those aspirations sounded a lot crazier to me now that we were up against that reality. Our brush with death following the spatial disruptor had shaken me, and I suspected my friends had also been changed by the confrontation with their own mortality.

Still, sending the Hegemony's flagship into enemy territory… my own nerves aside, that sounded reckless.

"The *Evangiel* is going?" I asked in response to Colren's orders. "I mean, I know we're on board and our team is the most logical choice to check everything out, but isn't a ship this size a little… obvious?" Since Colren had always been surprisingly accommodating with answering our questions and us challenging his orders—at least when we were in good favor—I figured the best way to test his current regard for us was to needle him a bit.

The commander seemed ruffled for a moment by my question, but the cloud passed from his face almost immediately. "Yes," he admitted, "only larger vessels are capable of executing a jump of this distance. This crew has come closer to the enemy than any other. We're the best choice in a number of ways."

A thorough, on-topic answer. That was certainly a good indication that we hadn't permanently been relegated to cannon fodder status. "I'm up for the challenge," I replied, though my new nerves hadn't subsided.

"Good, because I mean it quite literally when I say that everything is riding on this mission," Colren continued. "The aliens could be back at any time with greater numbers. We got lucky you were able to get onto that ship and plant the disruptor, but those strategies only tend to work one time. To end this war, we need to go after the core of their civilization and do everything in our power to make sure they don't ever come looking for us again."

"No argument here," Kaiden said.

Colren folded his hands on the tabletop. "This will need to have a final resolution unlike any other conflict we've faced. If we're successful, it will mean that the war effectively never happened."

"We'll reset," Toran stated.

"Exactly," Colren acknowledged with a nod. "We need to figure out how to defeat them and then reset to before the Darkness ever arrived on a Hegemony world."

"Attack them before they can attack us," I mused.

"Yes, but they've demonstrated that they maintain awareness of other timelines through the resets," Kaiden pointed out. "Won't they be expecting us to do that?"

"Almost certainly, which is why so much is riding on this next mission," Colren replied. "The way I figure it, we have one shot to find their weakness and go in for the kill."

"That's not the right approach." Toran shook his head. "If we reset to before the Darkness arrived, there's no telling what will happen to *us*. We can't rely on deploying an end game strategy after a universal reset—though we got lucky last time, that was only going back a week. But months? To before we were transformed? I worry this whole mess would start all over again."

Colren frowned. "What other options do we have? We need to restore the corrupted worlds."

"Yes, but we should have full reset controls once we unseal the Master Archive," Toran countered. "We can initiate the reset *after* we've defeated the enemy."

"But then they'll just come back..." Maris said, casting him an exasperated glance.

Toran straightened in his seat. "Not necessarily. That's why we need to learn more about them. If the hypothesis pans out, then we won't need to go through yet another timeline to beat these guys."

Colren came to attention. "Are you talking about the hyperdimensional origins theory?"

"Yes, exactly. I've been talking it over with the research team at the Capital, and it's the only explanation that accounts for all of our observations."

I normally zoned out when the technical speak came up, but 'dimensional origins' sounded a lot more interesting than signals and frequencies. "Was this what you were about to get into planetside?"

He nodded. "The key bit of information we have about the aliens is that they seem to have remembered information from before prior resets. While it's *possible* they have a direct link to hyperdimensional storage that we don't, another possibility is that they're simply unaffected by time."

Maris raised an eyebrow. "Wait, what?"

"We might be dealing with higher dimensional beings—perhaps 5D, existing 'above' time, if you will."

I ran my fingers through my hair, brushing it back from my face. "Hold on a sec. If these are fifth-dimensional beings—assuming I remember anything from my physics class—then why in the stars would they have any interest in our measly spacetime reality? That'd be like us becoming obsessed with a stick drawing."

"Correct, which is where the transformed worlds come in," Toran continued. "You'd posited, Elle, that they were after matter or dark matter. I don't think that's precisely it, but they do seem to be after *something*. Perhaps they can only access it through this plane for whatever reason."

"Regardless of their objective, we're not going to learn anything more waiting around here," Colren stated. "It's time to see how they like someone pounding on *their* front door for a change."

2

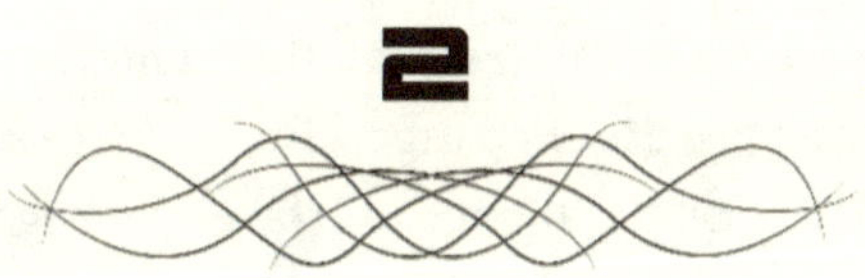

THE *EVANGIEL* DROPPED out of hyperspace beyond visual range of the alien planet. I was still nauseated from the jump when we reported to the bridge, the hyperspace transit having been a longer ordeal than normal. I had no idea where we were or exactly how far we'd traveled, but it was clear we were very much on our own.

Taking a series of slow deep breaths to try to settle my stomach, I turned my attention to the front viewport. Even with holographic augmentation, I still couldn't make out our target. "Is it like the anomaly site from before—a dark gravity well?" I whispered to Kaiden.

"No, we're just a long way from the planet," he replied. "I have a horrible feeling they're going to send us across the system in a shuttle."

"Great. Now that you've said it, it's sure to happen." Even the five-hundred-meter-long *Evangiel* was tiny compared to the vast emptiness around us. The notion of venturing out in a shuttle was downright terrifying.

So much for being ambitious and brave. I'd picked a great

time to let nerves get the better of me. Or, maybe I was just wising up to the bleak realities of the situation.

"Hey, it's going to be fine," Kaiden tried to assure me, seeing my worried expression.

"I liked our odds better before I knew we might be going up against higher dimensional beings."

"Nah, it's exciting!"

I cast him a skeptical glance. "Not quite the word I'd pick."

Colren rose from his seat at the center of the bridge, interrupting our private exchange. "Preliminary scans indicate no sign of activity on the planet's surface," he began. "If there's a civilization here, it's well hidden."

"Or beyond our means of detection," Toran said.

"Yes. So, I'd like you to take a closer look," the commander instructed.

"Alone on a shuttle," Kaiden muttered under his breath.

"I don't want to take the *Evangiel* any closer," Colren continued. "You'll travel on the *Sanctum*. Meet up in the hangar in fifteen minutes."

Kaiden pursed his lips. "I stand corrected."

"All right, let's go," I said to my teammates.

We stopped by our quarters to clean up. I waited for Toran and Maris to enter their cabins, hanging back in the corridor with Kaiden.

"I didn't think we'd head out so quickly," I told him as soon as we were alone, wishing there was time for more than a fleeting conversation.

He took my hands. "We can get all the time together we can stomach once this is over."

"That better be soon. I don't know how much more of this I can take."

"You're not alone." Kaiden pulled me into a hug. "We'll get

through this together."

We parted with a kiss and then went to our cabins to get ready. After a quick shower, I departed for the hangar with my team.

I'd recognized the name of the *Sanctum* as being the scout ship that rescued us following the spatial disruptor detonation at the anomaly site. The vessel was tiny by most measures, but our standard shuttle could fit inside its cargo hold. The first time I'd seen the *Sanctum*, it had been a welcome sight—a connection to what had become my home away from home during our fight against the Darkness. As we prepared to board the ship this time, however, I instead felt like we were taking a step into the dangerous unknown.

"Welcome aboard," a dark-haired man in his thirties greeted us at the top of the ramp.

"Try to bring it back it one piece, Richards," Tami called from the deck outside, her lips pursing into a worried pout.

"You know we always do, Chief," Richards replied with a slight smile. He returned his attention to us, his gaze pausing on our weapons and modified physical features—a common reaction among crew members meeting us for the first time. "So, you're the infamous Dark Sentinel team, hmm?"

"And you're Richards, it would seem," Kaiden replied with an equally evaluative look.

The man nodded. "*Sanctum* is normally Samwell's baby, but I volunteered to escort you instead—couldn't turn down the opportunity to see you in action."

"And Samwell was okay with that?" I asked, remembering the name of one of the officers who'd picked us up in our disabled shuttle.

"Let's just say that no one is particularly excited about heading into enemy territory like this. Didn't take a lot of arm-twisting," Richards responded.

"We've always liked living on the edge." A short-haired blonde woman poked her head out from the bridge and grinned. "I smell a promotion if we get you four back alive."

"This is hardly a time for career ambition," Toran stated.

The woman shrugged. "To each their own."

"To say Kess has a competitive streak would be a gross understatement," Richards said with a nod toward the woman. "Don't get her started."

"Hey, anyone willing to accompany us is good by me," I said. "I'm Elle."

My teammates introduced themselves in turn.

"Do you really have… magic?" Kess asked after the introductions, examining us.

"That's what we're calling it, anyway," Kaiden replied. "I know you want to see it, but if you do, that means things have already gone wrong."

Kess smiled. "Bring it on."

"Save it for the baddies, Kess." Richards paused. "Hey, what are we calling these alien bastards, anyway?"

I looked to my teammates. "You know, we haven't really been calling them anything."

Kess raised an eyebrow. "Seriously, you gave yourselves a team name and didn't name the bad guys?"

Kaiden shrugged. "I dunno. I guess we figured the Hegemony had a name for them, or we'd find out what they call themselves."

"It's always been 'the Darkness'," I added. "The beings themselves didn't come into it until recently."

Kess rolled her eyes. "Whatever. Strap in back there." She nodded toward a bank of seats along the outer bulkhead above the cargo hold.

"I'll get her fired up," Richards said, shimmying through the bridge entrance past Kess.

I took a seat next to Kaiden in the indicated seats and started to strap in. "You know, they do have a point about a name for these bad guys."

"Well, 'Creepy Alien Bastards Who Want to Destroy Us' has been working for me," Maris said.

"Yeah… 'cab-woo-du' doesn't exactly roll off the tongue or sound particularly menacing," I said.

Kaiden laughed. "Nor does 'cabbies' or anything else that comes to mind from that abbreviation."

"I suggest we table this issue for another time," Toran advised. "Personally, I don't care what we call them. Let's just focus on the not-dying part of the mission."

"I can get behind that," I agreed.

As soon as we finished securing our flight harnesses, a low vibration spread through the floor of the vessel, and the scene out the side viewport shifted as the ship glided through the hangar. We passed through the electrostatic field into open space, and the *Sanctum* boosted toward the destination world.

"All right, clear. We're looking at about four hours of transit time," Richards said over a central comm. "Get comfy."

Kaiden sighed. "I kinda miss being up front and in charge."

I swiveled my head, keeping a neutral expression. "This is my shocked face."

Toran chuckled. "It seems we've found our places."

"I feel all fancy getting transported around," Maris said with an excited shiver. "My mom always told me that you know you've 'made it' as soon as you have a chauffeur."

"Not your chauffer," Richards said over the comm. "You know we can hear you, right?"

I cracked a smile. "Just friendly banter. We can keep this

up for hours!"

"Have fun with that. We'll let you know when we're nearing the planet," Richards said. A chirp over the comm indicated that the channel had been muted.

I scowled. "Okay, on a scale of 'one' to 'annoying', I'd say we were only at a three."

"Yeah, I'm surprised they cut us off like that," Kaiden agreed. "Seemed friendlier when we met."

"They're soldiers on a mission," Toran reminded us.

I slumped in my seat. "So long as they don't ditch us on the planet, fine with me if they don't want to chat."

Kaiden nodded. "I have no doubt they'll come around once they witness our awesomeness firsthand."

"Not that they *will* see it. I mean, they aren't coming down to the surface with us, are they?" I asked.

"I'd hope not," Toran replied. "I believe they meant that they'd be monitoring the feed from the recorders on our packs."

"*Thrilling*," Maris said sarcastically.

"Hey, that footage is probably restricted access normally," Kaiden told her. "I guess I'd be pretty curious to see what allegedly magical abilities looked like in practice, too."

Maris got an excited glint in her eyes. "Well, guess we'll need to put on a show."

We made small-talk for most of the journey, comfortable in each other's company. I couldn't resist taking Kaiden's hand on occasion or giving him a pat on his arm or leg when he made a particularly eyeroll-worthy comment, but I tried to keep the contact to a minimum since I knew it made Maris and Toran feel awkward. I'd promised to make sure our team came before the relationship; I hadn't been able to keep that promise one hundred percent of the time, but I still tried my best.

For the final half hour of the voyage, Richards and Kess invited us to the bridge so we could watch the final approach to the planet on the holographic display overlaid on the front viewport. I appreciated the gesture, though I suspected it was a matter of practicality rather than them wanting us there.

"It really doesn't look like anything special," Kaiden observed as he studied the augmented image of a barren, brown-gray planet.

"Well, you have a breathable atmosphere, moderate temperature, and 0.9*g*, so it's pretty spectacular in the grand scheme of things," Richards replied.

"Hey, at least we won't die just from stepping outside the shuttle, so there's that!" Maris said with forced enthusiasm.

"What's more curious is the signal." Toran deftly moved his hands over the communications control panel at an auxiliary station.

"Still can't figure out where it's coming from?" I asked.

He frowned pensively. "You could say that… It's really like it's coming from everywhere. But it's not a signal, exactly, more like a… signature."

"As in, a radiological signature?" Kess asked.

"In a sense, yes, but not in that same core classification," Toran confirmed. "I believe this may be a sort of quantum echo—something I'd discussed with the Hegemony's research team. If that is the case…" he trailed off.

"Then what, Toran?" I prompted.

He took a slow breath. "Then that might indicate the presence of significant alien activity, only on a plane we can't see."

Kaiden frowned. "I don't like the sound of that."

Kess swore under her breath. "I should have known something was up with this whole op."

Richards snorted. "Yeah, like this info would have made you second-guess the assignment."

"Irrelevant distinctions," she replied.

"It's all speculation," Toran continued. "If we want to confirm that hypothesis, we'll need to get a closer look."

"Last I checked, we don't have hyperdimensional vision," Maris stated.

"Not exactly, but I believe we've been in contact with hyperdimensional access points in the past," he went on. "The Master Archive, for example, we agreed wasn't on Crystallis in a conventional sense."

I thought about what we'd observed. "That's true. There was also the weird tower on the Valor world."

"Exactly. There's a hyperdimensional connection between the crystalline network and the higher planes, so maybe that manifests in other ways," Toran said.

"What do the aliens have to do with that, though?" Kaiden asked.

Toran shrugged. "That's what we're here to find out."

Maris propped her elbows on her thighs and leaned forward. "Those other places had connections into the higher planes. Do you think there might be an access point on this world?"

"If there is, it's likely connected to a crystal," Kaiden said, twirling his pendant in his fingertips. "We already know how to find those."

Toran inclined his head. "Indeed, we do. Let's take a look."

"What's this, now?" Richards asked.

"Think of it as a sort of magical crystal-detector," Kaiden said.

Kess' expression brightened. "All right, now we're getting to the interesting stuff."

I raised an eyebrow. "The idea that a civilization might extend into another dimensional plane wasn't interesting enough?"

"But… magic-detector," Kess replied.

I couldn't argue with her logic. "Yeah, fair enough. Do you have everything you need for the interface, Toran?"

"Mobile setup should be in my pack, hold on." Toran disappeared into the cargo area of the ship.

"How did you come up with this tech?" Richards asked.

Kaiden gave a dismissive flip of his wrist. "Lucky guesses, mostly. Toran seems to have an instinct for this stuff."

"You've certainly won the commander's respect," Kess said.

"Didn't feel that way when he jumped without us," I mumbled.

Richards swiveled to face me. "You survived the disruptor wave, but the *Evangiel* wouldn't have stood a chance. Only reason we're here is because the commander made that call."

I knew in my heart that the soldier was right, but it had still distressed me to witness firsthand that we were disposable. "I know he didn't mean it personally," I muttered in an attempt to smooth things over with our escorts.

"This is war, not summer camp." Richards eyed me. "But," he took a deep breath, "you *have* made it this far, which is more than can be said for many soldiers. That's why I volunteered to come—to see you in action, and to help you see this thing through. I've heard some crew members say you're not up to it, but I think actions matter more than age or experience."

"After all, you survived a *spatial disruptor* detonation," Kess cut in. "Considering that's pretty much impossible, you have more than luck on your side."

"And, seriously, I've known the commander a long time.

You can trust him," Richards added, softer.

I nodded, dropping my gaze to my hands. "I know. I get why we were left behind. Just… made everything more real, I guess."

Kaiden rubbed my back. "And showed us we can do what we thought was impossible."

Kess smiled. "We're on your side. Anyone who doesn't have faith in you is an idiot."

Perhaps I'd misread the soldiers' intentions before when they'd relegated us to the cargo area for most of the journey; they were just focused on the mission, it wasn't about excluding us.

I wasn't sure what had been going on with me over the past few days—moodiness, paranoia. Ever since the incident at the anomaly I'd been on edge. Based on how Kaiden kept glancing over at me with his brow creased, it appeared he was concerned about me, too. I suppose it had just been a matter of time before the stress and pressure got to me. Maybe I was finally cracking. Considering what we were about to do, the timing could be a lot better. I took a deep breath and tried to center myself.

"All right, here we go," Toran said, returning to the compact bridge carrying a device the size of his substantial fist.

"What does it need to operate?" Richards asked.

"I can tap it into the communications console. It'll piggyback on the ship's sensor suite to identify the specific signature of crystals on the planet," Toran explained. "We'll see if any of those look like a key location and investigate accordingly."

"Proceed." Richards gestured toward the console. "We're under orders to remain on the *Sanctum* while you take the shuttle to the surface, so you'll be on your own once you know where you're going."

"Used to it, no problem," Kaiden said.

"It doesn't look like this world is infected by the Darkness, so at least we won't have to worry about contamination when we come back," I added while Toran began syncing the equipment with the shuttle.

"Thank the stars for that," Kess murmured.

We fell silent as Toran studied the data feeding into his specialized receiver, using the unique properties of Kaiden and Maris' pendants to identify resonant signatures on the planet's surface.

After two minutes of calibrating the equipment to the *Sanctum*, Toran sat back and frowned at the screen. "That's odd."

"What now?" Kaiden asked.

Toran sighed. "Well, every other time we've tried this sort of scan, specific crystal locations have been called out. On this world, though, it's like the entire planet is pinging. But that's strange, since we had difficulty getting readings on the Darkness-infected worlds unless we were close to one of the crystals."

"There's no evidence of the Darkness here," I pointed out.

"True, but I'd expect this planet and the others infected with the Darkness to demonstrate the same properties," he replied.

"Maybe there's something about this planet that isn't on the others?" Maris suggested. "An 'x factor'."

"I suppose." Toran examined the visual representation on the screen, illustrating a glow around the planet. "This does support the hypothesis that there's a civilization here we can't see."

"How are those connected? I thought this detected the presence of crystals," Maris asked.

"It's doesn't detect crystals precisely," Toran corrected, "more like it picks up a sign of their presence via unique signatures. But, it's possible that those signatures aren't unique to crystals and are actually signs of something else we can't see."

"Higher-dimensional energy?" I supplied.

Toran took a slow breath. "Perhaps, though I can't with certainty say it's connected to the aliens."

Worry spread across Richards' face. "Assuming there *are* higher dimensional beings, won't they know we're here?"

"Almost certainly," Toran replied.

"But, they haven't attacked us," Kaiden pointed out. "So, either they don't care, or they don't see us as a threat."

"Or, they're waiting for us to walk into a trap," I said.

"Regardless, we're not going to learn anything significant about this planet from here. We need to pick a site and investigate," Toran stated.

I nodded. "I'm not disagreeing, but I don't have a good feeling about this."

"Me either, but we don't have a choice," Kaiden said.

"Where do we target, then?" Maris asked.

"How about an old-fashioned visual survey?" Richards suggested. He modified the front viewport to display a holographic representation of the planet with augmented topographical features. Blue outlines appeared around specific sites, which contained signs of a built environment.

My brow knit. "City ruins?"

"Looks like it," Kess said. "Nature doesn't make straight lines like that." She traced her finger over a grid pattern on the largest southern continent.

"Any sign of a crystal?" Kaiden questioned.

"No, but the energy readings indicate there could be one at

that location, perhaps underground," Toran replied. "Since the city ruins are more intact there than anywhere else, that's my suggestion for where to begin our search."

"Works for me," I agreed. Ancient alien city ruins somehow upped the spookiness factor of the mission, but there was no turning back now.

"All right, let's get our stuff and head out," Kaiden said.

My friends and I climbed down to our shuttle berthed in the belly of the *Sanctum*, which completely filled the small cargo hold. Richards and Kess remained on the bridge in comm contact.

"We'll keep a low orbit, ready to rendezvous whenever you're ready," Richards said over the shared comm channel while we entered our shuttle.

"Shout if you need anything. We'll be watching," Kess added.

"And if the comms don't work?" Kaiden asked. "We've had issues before."

Richards didn't reply immediately. "Then we'll give you ten hours before we head back to the *Evangiel.*"

It sounded like enough time to give us a comfortable buffer. With any luck, we'd complete our task well before that. "Okay, see you soon," I acknowledged.

We got situated on the bridge in our usual seats and strapped in. Kaiden took the controls in anticipation of our release from the docking grapples.

"I have a lock on the destination," Toran stated from the seat behind me.

"Confirmed," Kaiden said. "Nav system is online."

"Safe travels," Richards wished us over the comm. "Releasing the clamps."

A shudder passed through the craft as the docking grapple

released, and a moment later the view changed to a starscape with the brown-gray planet below.

"All right, here we go," Kaiden murmured under his breath, aligning the shuttle for atmospheric entry.

I gripped my armrests as the shuttle reached the outer boundaries of the atmosphere. At the same moment, I became aware of a strange feeling in the air, almost like an electrical charge.

"Anyone else feel that?" I asked.

"Yeah, it's weird," Kaiden replied.

Maris grasped her pendant. "It feels like it did next to the anomaly."

"What's going on?" Richards demanded over the comm.

"There's a strange—" I cut off when my comm gave a 'disconnection' warning chirp in my ear. "Great." I leaned forward to try the shuttle's communication system; only static met my attempts to raise the *Sanctum*.

Kaiden let out a long breath. "Here we go again."

3

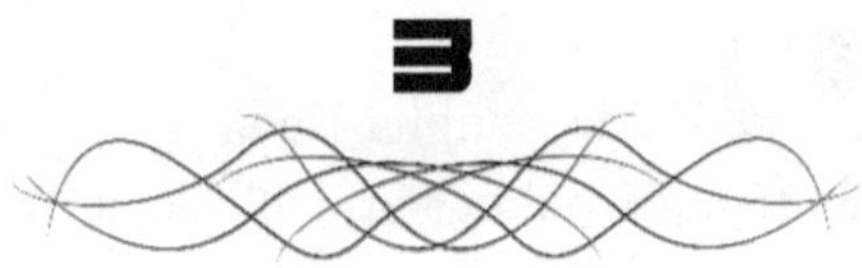

EVEN WITHOUT FUNCTIONAL comms, at least we weren't flying blind, unlike some past journeys.

Kaiden was able to maintain a nav lock on our target, and we slowly descended toward the city ruins, taking in the surrounding landscape.

The former city was spread out on the floor of a valley surrounded by mountains and rolling foothills. However, with no vegetation or snow, the landscape was lacking the kind of drama I'd expect from rocky peaks. What appeared to be a dry riverbed bisected the city ruins, the western side seeming to have weathered time better than the east.

"Land inside or outside the city?" Kaiden asked, circling around at a low elevation so we could scope it out.

"I like the idea of landing in the open," Toran replied.

I raised my hand. "Second that."

"Yeah, definitely," Maris agreed. "This place gives me the creeps even from up here."

There was something profoundly disquieting about the ruins. Only gray stone—possibly the remnants of cast concrete—and bits of metal support structures rose from the windswept landscape. I couldn't see any specific evidence of weapons fire or other attack from afar, but the irregular distribution of destruction around the city suggested that the damage wasn't simply from natural decay.

"What do you think happened here?" Maris voiced my own curiosity.

"Not sure, but whoever used to live here left a long time ago," Toran replied.

"Or *whatever*," Kaiden emphasized.

"If it's sentient, wouldn't it still be a 'who'?" Maris questioned.

I crossed my arms. "I'd rather not think about it."

Kaiden selected a landing area half a kilometer beyond the obvious outskirts of the city ruins.

I suspected that the area had once been a suburb, though only amorphous mounds remained where structures may have once stood. The sense of disquiet welling inside me intensified as the shuttle touched down. I unstrapped my harness and stared out the viewport at the desolate landscape. "I guess we should get to it."

"Yeah, the sooner we can get out of here, the better," Kaiden agreed.

The four of us shuffled into the common area to grab our packs. I hoped we wouldn't need any of the extra supplies stashed inside, but I'd rather have them than not.

Toran checked the readout next to the side hatch. "Atmospheric readings all look to be within tolerance, just like we observed from orbit."

"Minus microbes that will gestate inside us and hatch new baby aliens to take over the galaxy," Maris said.

I frowned. "Maybe we *should* wear EVA suits."

"If we get into a fight, that will put us at a serious disadvantage," Kaiden pointed out. "If our enhancements can withstand the Darkness, I don't think microbes are a huge concern for us."

"Yeah, good point," I conceded.

"Shall we go, then?" Toran asked.

I nodded. "Ready."

He released the seal, and the hatch folded down and extended a ramp to the ground.

I stayed in position for several seconds, waiting for the first wafts of the alien air to reach us. True to our equipment readings, we didn't instantly die. "Let's see how it is outside."

We descended the ramp and then re-sealed the hatch from the outside, not wanting to risk unseen rogue wildlife wandering into the shuttle. Standing on the grainy soil, I could tell the gravity was lighter than I was used to, though not enough to try anything too exciting.

"I say we head into the center of the ruins," Kaiden suggested. "That central square we saw might be a good place to start—probably the city center for a reason."

I nodded. "Likely a place to find an old crystal."

"Sounds good to me," Maris said, bounding toward the city.

We ran easily in the lower gravity, making quick time over the flat terrain. As we reached the first toppled structures in the ruins, I realized that I'd missed a crucial observation in our flyby.

"The scale seems strange with these buildings."

My friends studied the structures, slowing their paces along the former boulevard.

"You're right," Toran said. "Everything seems at least fifty percent larger than what we're used to."

"Not just that," Kaiden added, "but I'm not sure this was designed for a bipedal society."

I looked closer at the building he was studying. There did seem to be something off about the design of the stairs—like there were two sets of steps next to each other at alternating intervals. At first I'd thought that the steps had broken in half and shifted vertically, but they were intact upon closer examination. Though I'd seen designs like that on occasion in my own culture, for it to be everywhere was surprising—especially when coupled with the benches staggered along the strip between two flat roadways. The benches each had a distinctive slope at the bottom, joining to a ledge at the height of my shoulders.

"Maybe those are… sculptures?" Maris offered.

"I'm not so sure." My stomach knotted as I thought about the creature I'd seen on the alien ship four days before—an undulating torso, seamlessly transitioning from two to four legs as it skittered through the ship. I could picture the creature perched on the strange bench, as staggering as it was to think about those monstrosities being part of a society that would go for a walk in the park.

"Maybe we can find some art that shows what they look like," Kaiden said, picking up his pace.

"Yeah." I met his stride.

We encountered few other clues as we continued toward the city center, most buildings being too decayed to offer insights. I found it strange that there was anything left of the city ruins, but apparently the ravages of time weren't as harsh without vegetation or significant rainfall.

At last, the structures became larger and more elaborate, indicating we were entering a part of the city that may have once been the center of the economy. Most of the buildings were now piles of rubble standing three stories tall, but some rusted metal superstructures rose ten stories or more—the last remnants of what used to be. Unfortunately, it was impossible to get a proper sense of the culture's design aesthetic with so few intact elements.

"The town square should be just up ahead," Toran announced, breaking the eerie silence of the place.

"It's so similar to one of our cities," Maris murmured. "I thought it would be more… alien."

That did seem odd to me, too. While certain features did strike me as being designed for a different sort of creature, the overall layout of the place was bizarrely similar to what I'd expect from one of the Hegemony's worlds. It was almost like the city had been taken over and retrofit.

"Wait… what if this wasn't *originally* an alien city?" I said.

"Like, they invaded it?" Maris asked.

"Yeah, like they made some changes to suit them, but didn't change everything," I clarified.

Toran stroked his chin. "An interesting thought. I suppose this could have been a world they invaded before they mastered how to transmit the Darkness through the crystals."

"But if this is their homeworld now, of sorts, wouldn't they have gone back to transform it now that they *do* have that tech?" Kaiden asked.

"Not if they didn't need to," I replied. "Maybe the Darkness isn't for bio-optimization at all. Maybe we've been looking at everything the wrong way."

Kaiden frowned. "What happened to the native population here?"

I shrugged. "No clue. Maybe they enslaved them, or ate them, or transformed them in some way."

"Or they didn't need physical forms anymore." Toran

shuddered. "They're probably watching us right now, laughing at us feebly trying to put together the pieces."

Maris paled. "Yeah… maybe let's not talk about it anymore?"

"Wait, look." Kaiden pointed ahead of us. A distinctive tower was visible over the top of a nearby rubble pile.

"That's the monument in the town square," Toran said. "Come on."

We picked up our pace, eager to complete our mission as quickly as possible. I hated the notion that unseen beings may be watching us—creatures beyond my comprehension, existing outside the flow of time as I knew it.

As we rounded a bend in the street we'd been following, the central square came into view. Six roadways intersected like spokes on a massive wheel with a tower at its center. The top had appeared smooth from a distance, but I now saw that it was broken. It appeared that a statue had once been perched atop it, though the figure was now only broken shards around the base.

"I bet that would have given us some clues," I said with a sigh.

"There's still a lot to see." Toran peered at the tower's base. "I believe that may be a doorway."

I took another look behind the rubble, spotting the archway he was referencing. It did, indeed, look to be an opening. The tower itself was only five meters in diameter, so there couldn't be a chamber of any substantial size inside. However, if it went *down*…

"Do you think the crystal is underneath there?" I asked.

"As good a guess as any," Kaiden replied

Maris rummaged in her pack and produced a flashlight, grinning. "And, we're finally prepared."

Kaiden conjured a light orb in his palm. "Really, Maris? I thought more of you."

"Hey, if you want to serve as a living beacon of magical energy, go for it. Personally, I'd rather try to blend in."

He extinguished the light and swung his backpack forward over his shoulder to get inside. "On second thought..."

"I'm not sure how incognito we can be with these artifacts, but I suppose some precautions wouldn't be a bad thing," I realized. My instinct had been to draw my sword to have it in hand, but that might enhance its signature. I decided to wait until there were clear signs of a threat before I activated the weapon.

Toran and I also retrieved our flashlights as we approached the archway, climbing over small piles of debris. I kept an eye on the rubble for clues about what type of figure had topped the column, though I saw no remaining evidence of its form. The only hints were recesses in textured pieces of stone with an intricate organic pattern that reminded me of moss—or the fibrous webbing I'd previously observed inside the alien ship. The fragments were too small and eroded to tell for sure, so I decided to keep the observation to myself.

The archway was framed by an ornate rendering of twisting vines reaching toward stars and planets above. Maybe I wasn't reading too much into the other fragments after all. "Does that remind anyone else of anything?"

"Our visit to Windau," Maris stated without hesitation. "I'll never forget those horrifying vines that attacked us."

A rotted wooden door still hung in the recesses of the archway, but when Toran pushed against it, the remaining fragments turned to dust. "Looks like we have our way in," he said, shining his light into the blackness within. "There appears to be a path down."

I couldn't help thinking back to the Valor world and the strange staircase in the tower that didn't obey spatial reality as I knew it. It was possible that this passageway itself was a dimensional transition point. "I'll lead the way," I volunteered, figuring that my combined skills made me the best prepared to react to any threat.

"No argument here." Maris took a step back, allowing Kaiden to follow behind me and have Toran take the rear.

I steeled myself for whatever we might find and stepped inside.

The interior was adorned with similar motifs to the exterior carvings, with vines snaking along the walls and a celestial representation overhead. Rather than a staircase, as I'd expected, a ramp spiraled downward along a central axis, leaving clearance for even Toran's tall frame. Beginning the descent, I held my flashlight in one hand while keeping the other on my sword's hilt.

"You know, Elle," Kaiden began, "I think you may be onto something with that idea about the aliens conquering another civilization. This looks suspiciously like a temple."

"Do you think the people were… worshiping them?" I asked.

"I don't know, but if I saw evidence of a higher-dimensional being, I could see how it might seem to be a deity."

After we'd spiraled fully around the central column, the ornate carvings on the walls and ceiling transitioned to a single vine and star pattern along the outer wall. It continued in that manner as we progressed down three more stories, where the corridor opened into what appeared to be a natural cavern.

"Wow." I sucked in a breath, taking it in. The ceiling was at least three stories overhead, covered in shimmering crystal.

"All right, so I'm beginning to understand how your

pendants might be resonating with this entire planet," Toran said.

Kaiden couldn't take his gaze off the ceiling. "What is this place?"

"Clearly somewhere important to these people, considering the effort it must have taken to carve out that entry," I said.

"It's strange that so many of the images includes stars, yet their sacred place is underground," Maris observed.

"These crystals might be more to them than pretty decoration," Kaiden countered. "Maybe they understood that the crystalline network connects the planets."

"Do you think the vines represent those connections?" I pondered.

"Could be." He shrugged. "We may never know."

"Let's see what else is in here," I suggested, continuing into the cavern. However, I was only able to go a short ways before I encountered a four-meter-tall wall spanning the width of the cavern. A single archway to my right allowed passage through it.

"That's strange." Kaiden stopped behind me. "Why would they build a wall here?"

Toran approached the archway and looked inside. "Not a wall. I think this might be a labyrinth."

I frowned. "That makes even *less* sense."

Kaiden's face contorted. "Why in the stars would they build something like this?"

"Ancient culture, different philosophies," Toran said.

"Not that ancient, based on the state of the ruins," Kaiden pointed out.

"This labyrinth may have been down here for a long time before that construction," Maris point out.

"True. Labyrinths have been used throughout history for many things. Perhaps it's symbolic," Toran suggested. "Some ancient religions viewed mazes like this as a meditative exercise, or to represent a journey toward the inner self."

"Find peace and serenity with your evil alien overlords!" Maris jested.

"I'll pass." I kept my voice low, not liking how it reverberated in the chamber.

"How complicated do you think this maze is?" Kaiden wondered aloud.

"Depending on the value of what lies at its terminus, it could be anything from a simple exercise or a trap we may never escape," Toran replied.

"Not a great argument for going inside," Maris muttered.

"Agreed." Toran nodded. "This isn't what I expected to find in here. I suggest we look elsewhere."

"Come on! This is even more intriguing than what I thought might be down here," I countered. "This is way too promising a lead for us to turn back now."

"I really can't imagine us coming across a structure that might give better clues about what happened to this world," Kaiden seconded.

Maris shook her head. "I don't know…"

"Look, it's not like we can actually get trapped," I reminded them. "The top of the maze is open, right? We can just climb up and walk along the top—we'll see the path all the way to the end."

Toran considered the proposition. "I hadn't thought about approaching it that way. It could work."

"Might anger the evil overlords to outsmart them," Kaiden quipped.

Maris tsked. "Don't joke about that!"

"Relax, everyone. Let's just get to the end of this thing and figure out what it is." I searched in my pack for a coil of rope.

"I hope you're right." Toran took a steadying breath and then retrieved his own rope. He tied one end to my pack to use it as a weight, then hurled it over the top of the stone wall near the entrance.

I cautiously ventured through the arch to secure the rope. As I rounded the corner through the archway, I caught a glimpse of movement in the shadows deeper inside the labyrinth. "Is someone there?" I called out.

"Everything okay, Elle?" Kaiden peeked through the archway after me.

"Not sure. I thought I saw something."

"All the more reason for us to walk *on top* of the walls. Good thinking," he replied, coming to join me.

"Yeah." I went to where my bag had dropped and anchored it to the wall using the climbing gear in my pack.

Kaiden stayed with me while I finished, to my relief. Once the rope was secured, I grabbed my pack, and we ran back to the other side of the wall where Maris and Toran were waiting.

"All set?" Toran asked me.

"Yep."

"I'll go first," he said. "If it can hold me, the rest of you will be no problem."

I stood back to give him room.

Despite his proportions, Toran nimbly scaled the rope, bracing his feet on the wall. He hoisted himself over the top lip and looked around.

"The walls are nearly a meter wide, and the maze isn't too large," he reported. "I think we'll be able to find a way across, though it's difficult to see. I believe the maze terminates at the end of this chamber."

"And on to another cavern?" questioned Kaiden.

"Perhaps. I suppose we'll find out when we get there."

Since it was my idea, I climbed up next. True to Toran's assessment, there was no obvious break in the maze before us. I could barely make out the tops of the stones at the furthest edges of the chamber with my flashlight. "I'm not sure how well we'll be able to chart a path through here," I said. "We need something brighter.

Kaiden climbed up next to me. "I can fix that."

"Magic may draw unwanted attention," I reminded him.

"It's that or we waste time backtracking because we couldn't see well."

"All right, up to you," I conceded.

He conjured a light orb and released it into the center of the chamber. It hovered near the ceiling, illuminating the tops of the stone walls.

"Thanks." I flashed a smile at him and then turned my attention to scouting a path. "Okay, we should be able to follow along there and then take a left."

"Looks good," Toran agreed.

Leading the way, I took the proposed course at a quick but cautious pace. The wall was less than a meter wide, and while sufficient to provide adequate footing, it felt like a long way up to be walking on a narrow path. Despite my past jumps into the canyon on Erusan, I'd never liked heights. I especially didn't relish the prospect of falling here, not knowing what may be lurking in the shadows.

Occasionally, I shined my light downward to see if I could catch another glimpse of whatever I may have seen near the entrance. I sensed something nearby, though that may have been nerves getting to me again. Even though I tried to stay focused on my footing and following the path along the wall, my gaze kept wandering toward the shadows below. We were cheating by walking along the top like this. It's not how it was supposed to be.

"Elle, watch out!" Kaiden's strong arms pulled me back from the edge.

A section of wall had begun to crumble beneath my feet, throwing me off balance. Kaiden kept a tight hold of me, and Toran pulled us both backward away from the damaged section.

"That was close." Maris let out a shaky breath.

Kaiden released me, turning his attention to the path ahead. "It's not much further. Stick to the middle of the wall."

"I was, I—"

"You almost walked off the edge, Elle," he stated.

"I did?" I stared into the shadows. "There's something down there. I can feel it."

"Now that you mention it…" Maris wrapped her arms around herself.

"We need to stay focused," Kaiden said, though the words sounded forced.

Only Toran remained his usual, calm demeanor. "One foot in front of the other. We'll be back on the ground soon."

I still didn't *want* to be on the ground. All the same, I continued forward, watching my footing. We only had one more switchback of the wall to traverse before we'd reach the end of the cavern.

"Almost—" The wall gave way underfoot. I was falling, and the shadows were jumping up to greet me.

4

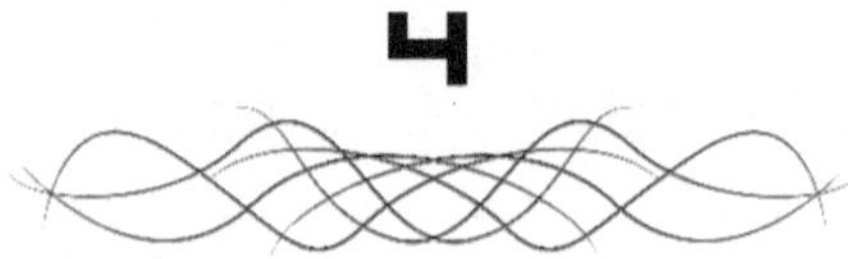

MY BACK SLAMMED into something hard, and I rolled over into a soft, sticky mass. Stunned, I lay motionless. It wasn't until I sensed tendrils coiling around my legs that I tried to react.

To my horror, my attempt to get up revealed that my arms were already wrapped in tendrils, as well. "Help!" I gasped, not sure where I was or if anyone could hear me.

"Close your eyes!" Kaiden shouted in the distance.

I squeezed my eyes shut moments before bright orange flames erupted around me. The tendrils loosened, and I jumped to my feet. "What the…?"

I was standing in a mass of writhing vines, similar to those I'd seen on planets infected by the Darkness. The vines were temporarily stunned, but I saw them slowly unfurling, preparing to lash out at me again.

A rope dropped down next to me. "Grab hold!" Toran shouted.

The end of the rope was tied into a loop, and I slipped my foot into it while holding on above with my hands. Toran pulled me up just in time to avoid another assault from the vines.

Their presence here made no sense, especially since we hadn't seen any other vegetation on the planet, and we were several stories underground. I'd always thought that the vines were a warped version of existing plant life, not... whatever was going on here.

"Stars! I don't know what happened." My heart pounded in my ears and my breath was labored.

Kaiden helped me up at the top of the wall. "I told you to be careful." His face was drawn with worry, seeming exhausted.

"I thought I was." I shook my head. "There's something about this planet—this entire system. It doesn't feel right."

"I know, I sense it, too." Kaiden took an unsteady breath.

"We need to get to the next cavern," Maris urged. "Learn what we can and then get out of here."

"It was a mistake to venture inside," Toran murmured.

"Too late now—" Kaiden cut off as the wall beneath us began to tremble. Dust rose into the air as chunks of stone tumbled down to the ground. "Shit, it's collapsing!" he shouted.

We dashed along the top of the wall, planting our feet anywhere that seemed remotely stable. Gaps opened in our path, and we leaped over the collapsing sections in our desperate race to safety.

Only six meters to go. The wall began to cave toward the opposite direction of the interior cavern. I grabbed Kaiden's hand, and we leaped together in the direction of the exit.

When I hit the stone floor, I bent my knees and rolled to the side, releasing Kaiden's hand. He popped up next to me, wincing, but otherwise appeared unharmed.

Maris and Toran were still running along the upper ledge four meters above us. A purple bubble appeared around them, and then Toran scooped Maris into his arms. He leaped down to where I'd landed, taking the full impact of the jump with only a slight knee bend. The moment he was on the ground, he set Maris down and resumed running toward the arch.

"Hurry! It's all collapsing," he shouted.

I couldn't see beyond the immediate cloud of debris, but I had no interest in waiting around to assess the destruction. Racing after Toran and Maris, I glanced behind me to see the vines lashing out after us.

Kaiden sent a blue fireball flying, enough to buy us the seconds needed to escape. The stone walls continued to fall, burying the dark vines in debris.

I dashed the final steps through the archway into the next chamber. The moment we passed through the archway, the vines stilled. The last remnants of the maze walls collapsed behind us, and then the chaos was over—a cloud of dust was the only indication that something had just happened.

Maris coughed. "I really hate this place."

I wiped dust off my face using my coat sleeve. "Was that a trap, or were the walls just old and ready to come down?"

Toran shook his head. "I could see it going either way."

Maris looked back at the destruction in the cavern. "Are we trapped in here?"

I evaluated the piles of rubble. "No, we can get over it." I waggled my fingers. "Besides, I have that fancy telekinesis magic."

"Too bad you couldn't have levitated us all the way here," Maris said.

"I don't trust my abilities enough yet to risk hurting you," I replied. "Besides, I don't think I can levitate myself."

"Have you tried?" she asked.

"No, but—"

"Elle, you might want to take a look at this," Kaiden interrupted.

I turned in the direction Kaiden was facing. He'd released a light orb into the center of the chamber, illuminating details I'd missed when I ran in. The chamber was easily the size of the previous cavern, but it was wide open space. Strikingly, the entire floor was glittering.

"What is that?" I stepped closer and crouched down. The sparkling sand appeared to be crystal fragments like we'd seen on Crystallis. "Are these?"

Kaiden squatted next to me, the glow in his pendant intensifying. "I think so, but these still have a charge to them."

I looked up at the ceiling; it was similar to the one in the first cavern and appeared to be intact. Wherever these crushed crystals had come from, it wasn't because they fell from the ceiling. "Could this civilization have been connected to Crystallis?"

"Or they pissed off the same group of hyperdimensional aliens and got wiped out." Kaiden stood up.

"Why shatter these and not scrape everything off of the ceiling, too?" Maris questioned.

"Not all crystals are the same," Toran reminded her.

"Well, this doesn't bode well for us finding a crystal to use as a dimensional transition point," I said. "Seems like whoever came through here had a grudge against the very thing we're looking for."

"That, or…" Kaiden trailed off.

"Hmm?"

He shook his head. "I was just thinking back to when we first came across the crushed crystals on Crystallis. At the time, we'd wondered if maybe there had been a war."

"Right." I nodded.

"Well, in war, a lot of strategy comes down to the territory you control, and access points. If there *were* battles being fought that spanned multiple dimensional planes, and if certain trans-dimensional interface points made it easier to move within the overall framework, it would make sense to restrict the number of those access points."

"Hmm, that's an interesting way to look at it," I said.

"I agree with that logic," Toran said. "And, if that's the case, perhaps there is a still a trans-dimensional interface access point somewhere down here."

"Hey, we've gotta have a shorthand term for that," Maris chimed in. "How about TDI?"

"Yes, much better," I agreed.

"That might explain where those vines came from," Kaiden said. "It's in here, too." He motioned toward the dark corners of the room. The black vines were barely distinguishable in the shadows, but they clearly recoiled from the light orb.

"Ugh, I hadn't thought of that." My heart sank. "That means that if we use a crystal as a TDI to the higher dimension, we'll be going through a gateway infected by the Darkness."

"Considering we're on the planet we think is the aliens' homeworld, it wouldn't be at all surprising if the TDI was connected to the Darkness," Toran pointed out.

"Doesn't make it any less disturbing," I replied.

"No, it does not." Maris looked around the chamber with distaste. Something caught her eye, however, and she perked up. "What's that?"

She jogged over to a low mound a few meters away, which was even shinier than the surrounding crystal powder. "Ooooo!"

We ran over to where she was standing over the object.

Partially buried under the crystalline gravel was a jewel-encrusted shield half a meter in diameter. The rainbow of stones was breathtaking, creating the image of a cosmic scene with a yellow star, blue and green planets, and purple-black starscape backdrop.

"This is totally mine," Maris declared, bending to pick it up.

I stopped her. "It might be a trap."

Kaiden looked around. "Yeah, this is literally the *only* object in this room that isn't a part of a structure."

"But it's so shiny!" She glared at us. "It's not fair—you all get special artifacts, and I have nothing."

"Three artifacts for three disciplines," I said.

"Doesn't mean there were *only* three," she pointed out.

I rolled my eyes. "Wanting the thing doesn't change the fact this is a super-fancy item in a destroyed, infected cavern under a ruined city. There is no way that *isn't* super-suspicious any way you look at it."

"It doesn't *feel* evil," she said.

"Maris, this is almost certainly a trap, come on," Toran urged, trying to motion her away.

"Or, it's a special thing that's been waiting for someone with special abilities to come along and find it," she countered.

"If you want to kill yourself, fine," I said flippantly, backing away with the hope she'd drop the matter.

Instead, she gave me a challenging look. "Fine."

Before anyone could stop her, she bent down to touch the shield.

I braced for an explosion or Darkness tendril to lash out at us. Instead, Maris simply picked it up.

"It's light," she commented, holding it in both hands.

I didn't let my guard down. "You're insane."

"No, just really sick of the three of you getting to do everything cool." She started to loop her arm through the strap at the back of the shield. "It fits—"

She cut off with a yelp of surprise as a shimmering silver forcefield appeared around her.

I jumped back from it. "Whoa…" The silver-hued bubble extended from the edges of the shield to make a protective barrier around her, moving as she moved.

"This is amazing!" she exclaimed. "See, told you!"

"You are so frickin' lucky," Kaiden muttered.

"I think you're envious." Maris grinned.

He only shook his head with exasperation in response.

"There's no telling what this thing does, Maris," Toran cautioned.

"I can sense it," she replied. Her fingers traced along the jewels with a contemplative expression. "It wants me to have it."

I sighed. "If you say so."

I couldn't explain how the shield came to be in that place, but I knew what she meant about the artifact feeling 'right' in her possession. I'd felt the same way when I first received my Valor artifact sword, and I felt like a part of me was missing whenever it wasn't at my side. As bizarre as it was, maybe Maris *was* supposed to find this shield here.

Or, it would slowly drive us all mad until we killed each other through some horrible curse. Despite us not instantly dying, I wasn't ready to take 'trap' off the table until I learned more about the artifact.

Either way, I didn't want to linger. The shadows continued to shift in the dark edges of the room, almost like they knew we were talking about them. I couldn't tell if my eyes were playing tricks on me, but some of them seemed to be moving independently from the vines.

"You have your thing now. Let's keep going," I suggested, returning my hand to the hilt of my sword.

Kaiden, likewise, tightened the grip on his staff. "This chamber is even more unnerving than the last."

"Speak for yourselves!" Maris practically skipped forward, the glimmering silver forcefield still around her.

I had to admit, a portable magic shield was a spectacular find.

I feigned confidence as I followed her deeper into the cavern, sweeping my gaze around the walls and ceiling every few seconds. I was certain there was something following us, even though I hadn't been able to get a clear look. Any kind of creature that had been locked in a dark cavern for stars-knew-how-long wasn't something I wanted to meet—especially not while I felt like I was losing my mind.

We continued forward at a steady pace. Halfway into the two-hundred-meter-long chamber, a breeze rustled my hair; I hadn't sensed any air currents since we descended the ramp. I spun around to check for signs of movement behind me. Before I'd pivoted a quarter of the way, a solid form bashed into my left side, knocking me to the ground.

Grunts of surprise sounded from my friends, and they collapsed next to me.

My combat instinct took over, and drew my sword in one swift movement while leaping to my feet. Kaiden's light orb still illuminated my surroundings, but there was nothing there.

"What hit us?" Maris asked, raising protective shields around each of us.

I felt a touch safer with the purple shell around me, though I was still on edge. "I don't see anything."

Kaiden jumped to his feet, hefting his staff. "It's like it came out of nowhere."

"I thought I saw something in the shadows, but I wasn't sure," Toran said.

"Same." I shifted my position so my friends were facing away from my back.

"Okay, so it wasn't just me." Maris gulped.

A dark mass passed across the corner of my vision. Without thinking, I sent a telekinetic disintegrating pulse from my focusing glove toward the movement. As if in slow motion, even without one of Maris' time-bending haste spells active, the creature dodged the attack and then disappeared, seemingly into thin air.

"What?" I tensed, looking around for it. "Where did it go?"

"You saw it?" Kaiden asked.

"Yeah, it was right—"

I cut off when Maris yelped. Her shield clattered to the ground and she lurched sideways with a cry of agony, falling—three bleeding claw marks raked the left side of her abdomen. She gasped in pain.

"Over here!" Toran ran to stand over her, his fists armored by their magical gauntlets, raised in defense.

Kaiden and I pivoted so the three of us formed a protective triangle around Maris.

"Are you okay?" I asked her.

"I'll live," she replied, pressing her right palm over the wound. Green healing light spread from her fingertips to the gashes, and the wounds began to close. "New rule: don't drop your shield when something unexpectedly slams into it."

"Also, I thought these clothes were supposed to be slash-proof!" Kaiden exclaimed.

"Yeah. They have been for everything else," I said.

"Shit, it was moving faster than I could see," Kaiden

murmured, a quaver in his voice. He picked up Maris' shield where she'd dropped it and handed it to her.

"Thanks." She looped her arm through the shield's back strap again, so it re-formed a forcefield around her.

"The creature is still out there, and there might be more." I scanned the shadows, looking for any sign of where it may have gone. I'd never seen anything move like it—lightning-quick attacks and then vanishing completely.

"We need a haste augmentation," Kaiden urged Maris.

Her wounds had healed, leaving bright pink scrapes down her side, but she still looked pale. "I'll try," she replied weakly. When she raised her hand, I didn't see the characteristic orange cast to my surroundings to indicate that the haste spell had activated. "I'm not…"

"Finish healing, and hold onto that shield," I told her. "We'll handle this." How, exactly, I had no idea. At the moment, I didn't even know *what* we were fighting.

My wonder didn't last for long—a sleek, black creature materialized in front of me, swiping a three-clawed limb toward my head.

I leaned backward just in time for the razor-sharp tips to miss my neck, simultaneously attempting to drive my sword into its belly. The creature arched its midsection to avoid my counterattack, then partially dissolved as it spiraled sideways toward Kaiden. He was ready with an electrical attack, sending a lightning bolt at the alien creature.

It froze in place, allowing me to get a proper look at it for the first time. The creature had elements of the other beings we'd encountered that were products of the Darkness. Its body was similar to the shadowcats from Windau, though it had a more elongated head and fanged jaw like the first creatures we'd fought on the Valor world. Its four, powerful limbs ended in what looked like a dexterous cross between a paw and a talon, with three retractable claws on the front and a shorter one facing backward; pads on the palm would allow for silent movement when it walked on either two or four limbs. A tail extended from its hindquarters—not entirely organic in appearance, but rather transitioning from apparently solid flesh to shifting, black smoke. Perhaps the most distinctive feature, though, was its red eyes positioned at the front center of its face, which sparkled with the depth of staring into the cosmos, mesmerizing me.

I'd seen those eyes before on the alien ship. And those limbs, the movements… it was exactly the kind of form I'd expect to occupy the modified city on the surface above us.

"Elle, get—" Kaiden had barely spoken before the creature disappeared again.

"Where—" The wind was knocked out of me as I flew forward, my back on fire where a paw had thwacked me. Next to me, Kaiden was toppling toward the ground.

As I fell, I glimpsed the creature lunging at Toran while he tried to protect Maris.

I realized the attack on me and Kaiden had been a distraction all along. The creature was going after Maris, our healer—who was also the weakest member of our team—and Toran—the physically strongest combatant—aiming to take both of them out of the equation first and minimize our chances to fight back. This wasn't a mindless assault like the shadowcreatures from the other world, it was demonstrating a smart, careful strategy to disable, not kill. It wanted us.

We'd finally come face-to-face with our real enemy.

5

TORAN'S EYES LOCKED with the creature's as it pinned his shoulders to the ground. It leaned in closer, eyes flashing.

"N-no," Toran stammered, trying to pull away.

The creature tilted its head while digging its front claws into his shoulders.

I wanted to yell at him to fight back, but I couldn't bring myself to move or react. It was as though I was frozen, somehow at peace with what I was seeing. The impulse to break free surged in my mind, yet I could do nothing.

Maris and Kaiden appeared to be equally frozen. Their gazes were fixed on the creature.

A series of percussive clicks sounded next to me and from behind. My pulse spiked, fearing another of the creatures had appeared to finish us off. However, I detected no physical presence, despite the sound seeming to come from multiple directions at once. It was then I realized that I'd only heard the sound in my mind.

The clicks repeated, morphing into a low trill, almost like a cat's purr. The sound sent a shiver through my body, pulsing in my head. I was transfixed.

Without stepping from where it had Toran pinned, the alien creature came to examine the rest of us while we were immobilized. Ghostly copies of the creature separated from its physical form, one gliding over to inspect each of us. I could see through the beast as it approached me, yet I sensed heat radiating from it. Dazzling red eyes bore into mine as the ghostly figure leaned in until it was only centimeters from my face.

Dark, nimble tendrils unfurled from where they had been folded against the creature's sleek torso. The dozens of tentacle-like tendrils attached to its lean chest and shoulders traced their way over my face and down my body, seeming to search for something. When they reached my sword, the tendrils recoiled, and a new series of clicks filled my mind.

My heart pounded in my chest. I could sense the creature was angry, but I didn't know why. I willed my mouth to work so I could yell at it to get away, yet I was still unable to move any more than was necessary to draw breath. It could kill me right now and there would be nothing I could do to stop it.

"Leave me alone!" I shouted in my mind. It took all the energy I could muster to articulate the words. Even then, I wasn't sure they would come through or if the creature would understand.

Another flurry of clicks sounded and the purr intensified. The tentacles quivered and swirled in what may have been nonverbal communication outside my frame of reference.

"Why are you doing this to us?" I tried to ask it telepathically, hoping that it could glean some meaning from my thoughts. The Hegemony had hoped to communicate with this race and find a peaceable solution without war; while I still didn't believe that was possible, maybe we could at least learn

their motivations and use that information to minimize loss of life on both sides.

The creature tilted its head, and a new chittering sound filled my mind. The clicks and tonal purr began to morph, turning into whispering voices. I couldn't make out what they were saying, but it sounded like it could be a language produced by my tongue, if only I knew what to say.

"I don't understand," I told it.

The whispers rose again. *"Steal."* The single word stood out from the din.

"Steal? Steal what?" I asked.

"Never enough."

I couldn't tell what the creature was saying. Did it want to steal something, or was it accusing us of being thieves? Everything we possessed we'd come by honestly, and I certainly wasn't about to let the alien take something from me, regardless of the reason.

"You can't control us." I tried to put force behind the words, but my present situation of being pinned in its presence hadn't given me a lot of confidence in myself.

The creature's expression changed into what I interpreted to be a sneer. *"So weak, so limited. Doesn't even know what it is."*

The last part of the statement caught me by surprise. Was that a comment about me, specifically? Did it know why I had a combination of abilities? *"What do you know?"* I asked it.

Its red eyes flared, and the whispers in my mind fell quiet. The creature pressed its face toward mine. *"Kill."*

Messages didn't get much clearer than that. I needed to break free—immediately.

The telepathic hold still had me pinned in place. I told my legs and arms to move, but the commands could never fully form in my head. I tried to scream, to cry out. Try as I might, no more than the faintest whimper escaped my lips.

I'd been a warrior only minutes before, able to leap and fight. Now, I was helpless, even though there was nothing physically holding me.

My friends still seemed unable to move. But, if we didn't do something, this creature seemed intent on killing us.

"*You can't control us,*" I told the creature again, believing it more this time. If the being was so strong, it could have ended us already. Either it was waiting to play with us more, or it knew we couldn't be taken out as easily as it wanted us to think. I chose to believe the latter.

"*Kill.*"

"*No!*" I shouted back in my mind. "*You can't stop us.*" More than anything, I wanted to break free. I willed myself, trying to believe it was possible. The only thing holding me in place was my own mind.

I still couldn't do it. I was trapped.

The creature extended its strange tentacles to surround me. "*Death.*"

Toran's fists shot upward from where he had been splayed on the ground, driving his metal gauntlets into either side of the creature's head. It reared, and the echoed versions of itself were sucked back into its body.

The paralyzing hold was broken.

Kaiden hurled a fireball at the creature from where he was lying on the ground, engulfing it in blue flames.

The creature leaped off Toran, unfazed by the flames, and rounded on Kaiden. Most of its tentacles smoothed back to form a protective armor over its body, but four remained at its side, which morphed into spearheads angled forward on the flexible tendrils.

While it was focused on Kaiden, I took the opportunity to jump to my feet and run toward it, sword in hand. It seemed to sense me coming, disappearing in a blink only to reappear behind me a moment later.

"Some haste magic would be great!" I shouted to Maris.

This time, my vision tinted orange in response to her magic. I rounded on the alien creature and found that my faster movements were now a match for the creature's abilities. It was trying to disappear again, but I could see the transparency beginning to form a moment before it transitioned. I could maybe reach it in time.

I lunged at it with my sword, going for speed over precision. The blade barely missed the top of its shoulders.

The creature disappeared and I paused, waiting to see where it would reemerge.

An electrical bolt cast by Kaiden clued me in that the creature was manifesting to my right. It was only halfway solid, the electrical assault apparently interfering with its ability to fully materialize in our spacetime. But, we needed to kill it, or at least wound it enough so it wouldn't want to come back. I assumed it would have to fully materialize for any physical damage to be effective.

"Hold it there," I told Kaiden, running into position.

I approached on its right and Toran ran over to the left while Kaiden continued to cast a continuous electrical bolt.

"I can't keep this up!" Kaiden warned.

"Let go!" I told him.

The moment he released the bolt, Toran pummeled it from one side while I sent a telekinetic blast from my glove. The creature bucked and undulated, its skin shimmering as the tentacles folded around its torso absorbed the blows. I sent another telekinetic blast, but the creature compressed and rose onto two legs, then bent over itself to turn the other direction.

"No you don't." Maris lobbed an electrical orb at it—weak compared to Kaiden's, but enough to get the creature's attention.

Clicks and trills filled my mind again, and the creature took a step toward Maris. Her face went blank, falling back into a telepathic trance.

"Maris, stay focused!" I ran after the creature in an attempt to distract it. I'd gone no more than two steps when the coloration of my vision returned to normal; the haste spell had been broken.

At the edge of my perception, the creature's body started to become semi-transparent, allowing me to see the world behind it. It was about to slip away.

I lunged forward and drove my sword through the broadest part of its torso. As the flaming blade passed through, the creature's body re-solidified. Its flesh disintegrated as the corpse dropped. Before it reached the ground, the entire body had turned to dust, leaving no trace behind.

I stood in shocked silence, working my mouth until I could form coherent words. "What in the stars just happened?"

"That was… an alien, I guess?" Kaiden replied. "I have no idea what's going on."

"Why did it disintegrate like that?" I checked my sword for blood, but there was nothing to clean. "Some of the other creatures we've fought did when they died, but this was instant—and it didn't bleed."

"It may have to do with it being a higher-dimension creature," Toran replied. "We've fought hybrids before, but a true higher-dimensional being… that's a different matter."

"It was in my mind. I couldn't move," Maris murmured.

"I've never felt so helpless." I caught myself. "Well, not

since we were modified."

"Yeah, no kidding. I couldn't even form a complete thought," Kaiden said.

Maris shuddered. "Me either."

"I tried to talk to it in my head, but I'm not sure it understood," I said. "I asked it what it wanted, and it just said 'kill'."

"How friendly!" Kaiden's attempted sarcasm felt hollow in the moment.

"I tried to communicate with it, too," Toran said. "I sensed it was frustrated with me."

"Really? How?" I asked.

He frowned. "I'm not sure. I believe it had hoped that I'd be completely submissive, and my ability to resist it caught it by surprise."

Kaiden scowled. "What was it after? If it was to 'kill', like Elle's encounter would indicate, why didn't it take us out when it had the chance. It was toying with us."

"We're different," I said. "We have abilities the rest of our kind don't. I think it was curious about us."

"But it also found us weak," Toran added.

"Yeah, said something similar to me, too." I nodded. "I think it figured it could take all the time it wanted with us and we wouldn't get the upper hand."

Toran's brow knit, but he didn't say anything.

"I could see why it was so confident. The way it moved... it was there, and then it wasn't." Maris shook her head. "How is that possible?"

Toran stared at the space the creature had occupied. "It never left."

"What do you mean?" I asked.

"I believe we were watching a dimensional shift. We

couldn't 'see' it when it moved through a higher dimension, but it was still governed by our spacetime rules when it existed in our 3D framework," he explained.

"It used those shifts to corner us," I said. "That was smart."

"Not *that* smart," Kaiden countered. "If it was, indeed, at least a fourth-dimensional creature— able to move across the fourth-dimension of time, or in an even higher dimension—then it should have been able to know our movements and avoided being struck."

I thought over the battle. "It did seem to always be ahead of us."

"But it's dead, we saw it dissolve. Wouldn't a creature residing in a dimension above spacetime be able to see the outcome and know how to avoid dying?" Maris insisted.

Toran smiled with wonder. "Not necessarily. To such a being, the past and present would be solid, but possible futures would still be foggy. All the same, it may not be dead—only the physical form existing in our spacetime destroyed. There's no way to know."

Kaiden sighed. "Anything we say here we're just making up. We have next to no information to go on."

"Our observations will help to reveal the full picture," Toran mused.

"You've gotten way too philosophical in the last few minutes," I interjected. "What went on back there? Were you communing with that thing?"

Toran's brows drew together. "I did feel strangely linked to it. It wanted to enter the deeper parts of my mind."

"I couldn't feel anything," Maris admitted. "I was trapped within myself. I didn't know how to have a thought of my own in that moment."

Kaiden nodded. "Yeah, it was like there was another

presence there, subsuming me."

The accounts were eerily similar to what I had experienced. I found it curious that Toran and I had been able to maintain a sense of identity during the encounters while Kaiden and Maris had been completely lost, but I didn't know what it meant. Toran had certainly fared the best of all of us, able to break free while the rest of us were helpless. I had to say that I really appreciated the span of skills on our team; it seemed like one of us was always able to come through for the others, regardless of the situation.

"I hope we never come across another one of those things again," Maris murmured.

"Don't count on it," I replied, trying to be realistic. "I still don't know if those are the alien masterminds or just a brand of their minions, but I can only imagine there are a lot more where that one came from. And, if we *did* kill it, the others will be pissed."

"Stars, pretty sure they're going to be pissed, regardless. If that thing was supposed to kill us but didn't, we're unfinished business," Kaiden said.

I frowned. "Speaking of which, why haven't we been swarmed?"

Toran was about to reply then hesitated. "That's a good point. If they can transition between the planes at will, then dozens of them could have come the moment the creature was in trouble."

Maris looked around the chamber suspiciously. "So why aren't they here?"

"The transition might not be straightforward for them," Kaiden suggested. "Maybe this one was already here and others can't just do it on the fly?"

I shrugged. "Regardless of the reason, I'm quite happy not

being attacked."

"I always get talked into going places, and then evil aliens from a higher dimension get involved…" Maris sighed.

"Didn't we say that the only predictable thing is unpredictability?" I said. "Or maybe I made that up just now, I can't remember."

Maris pressed the heel of her right hand to her temple. "My brain feels mushy."

"Well, we can either turn around and have the evil aliens come after us while we get nothing in return, or we can forge ahead and get what we came for, and hopefully figure out how to take them out in the process," I stated.

"Ahead," Kaiden replied.

Toran nodded.

Maris rolled her eyes and sighed. "You know my complaints never go anywhere."

I ventured a smile. "Forward it is."

6

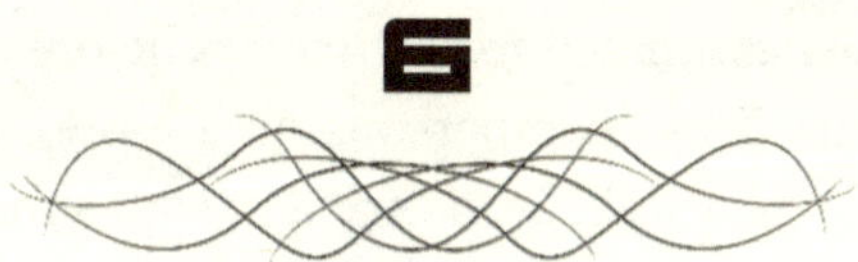

MARIS CAST ANOTHER haste spell now that she was healed, and we jogged toward the far end of the chamber. The dark tendrils still writhed in the shadows by the wall, but I saw no larger shapes lurking among them. I still wasn't confident if there had been more than one of the creatures in the chamber, but it either *had* been alone or the others had since fled. Either way, I was happy we didn't need to face another battle immediately.

As we approached the final quarter of the chamber, the volume of dark tendrils multiplied and extended further from the walls. By the time we were traversing the final meters, only a narrow path remained through the crystal dust on the stone floor, framed on either side by the weaving tendrils infected by the Darkness.

The ceiling and walls of the chamber also tapered, ultimately funneling us into a tunnel that was fully lined with the black foliage.

"Can't say I'm excited about going through there," I said, eyeing the two-meter-wide space. The ceiling of the tunnel would allow Toran to pass through without stooping, but only barely.

"I think we're almost to the end," Kaiden said.

"Might be wishful thinking," I replied.

"I don't know… there's a strong energy coming from the other side of this tunnel." He indicated his pendant, which was now glowing as brightly as it did when in the crystal canyon on Crystallis.

"I hope you're right." I stepped through the opening.

The tunnel continued for six meters before opening into another cavern. This chamber was on a more intimate scale than the two others we'd been through, with a four-meter-tall ceiling and approximately six-meter diameter. At the center of the space, a spherical crystal sat atop a carved stone pedestal. The dark tendrils wove around the base of the pedestal, seeming to merge with the crystal sphere at its base.

Despite the unnerving sight of the Darkness flowing out of the crystal, I was heartened by the sight of the sphere. I immediately recognized it as being a viewing device like the one in the secret room on the *Evangiel*. "That's promising."

"It is," Toran agreed, "though not what I was expecting."

I checked around the room to make sure there were no creatures lurking in the shadows. The spherical crystal at the center of the space was certainly the prize, and it wouldn't surprise me at all if it was guarded.

"Looks clear," Kaiden said, completing his own assessment with the aid of a light orb.

"What are we supposed to do with it?" Maris asked. "I kinda figured there's be, you know, a *doorway* somewhere. Don't we already have one of these?"

"This is one of the most powerful pieces of technology known to our civilization," Toran said. "If it's also here, I suspect we haven't been using ours to its full potential."

"Well, *we* haven't actually used it. Or, this version of us…" Kaiden faded out.

Maris raised an eyebrow. "Haven't we?"

Kaiden wilted. "You know, I've kind of lost track of what it means to be 'me' at this point, honestly."

"Doesn't matter." Toran stepped forward, focused on the device.

"Do you think we could use this to get information out of the Master Archive that we weren't able to get before?" I asked.

"I don't see why it would be any different," Kaiden replied.

"There are many reasons why it could be," Toran said, crouching down to look underneath the sphere. To my eye, it was suspended inside the stone cradle with no other attachments.

I crossed my arms. "You clearly have something in mind. Care to enlighten us?"

He frowned at the sphere. "There's no guarantee that this world is on the same crystalline network."

"Wait, *what*?" I gaped at him. "There are multiple networks?"

"We don't know for certain," he admitted. "I was talking through potential theories with the Hegemony scientists, and Lisa tossed that out a as a possibility."

"Lisa?" Kaiden questioned.

"A quantum physicist—at least, that's the closest field of study with a readily pronounceable name. She specializes in the subatomic mechanics we believe are related to the crystalline network's hyperdimensional links."

I stared at Toran. "You seriously either had no free time in your life before, or there's a lot more to being a maintenance tech than you're letting on."

He finally softened. "Why is everyone still so surprised I'm not illiterate in science? I majored in physics for a couple of years before I switched to engineering, okay?"

Kaiden eyed him. "If you say so. Now, what was that about multiple crystalline networks?"

"Well, the idea was that bandwidth would eventually tap out, as we've discussed before. While the hyperdimensional storage itself is theoretically limitless, there are still bottlenecks when it comes to retrieving data through the crystal interfaces. So, in an infinite universe, it may become impossible for a crystalline network to process all requests—it might need to be segmented," Toran explained.

"Different networks, but linked?" I asked.

"Yes, they would need to communicate with one another, such as to implement a universal reset. But, different sets of worlds may operate on different sub-networks from one another to streamline localized resets."

"And, what does that have to do with this device?" Kaiden prompted.

"Maybe if there *are* different subnetworks, that also means there are different Archives," Toran replied.

"But, the Master Archive is—"

"The only one that the Hegemony knows about," Toran cut me off. "That doesn't mean it's the only one in existence."

Maris pursed her lips. "If these aliens function on a different network, that might explain how no one has come across them before—at least not in recent history."

"That was my thought," Toran said. "But, keep in mind that this is all hypothetical. There *may* only be one network and the bandwidth issue is handled through other means. Decades more research will be needed to understand these systems."

"Could that explain how the aliens knew about the space

battle and were able to head us off after our first reset?" I asked.

"Yes, being on a different network could explain the difference in recollection. More likely, however, that was a product of residing in a higher dimensional plane. Given what we saw with the creature today, I'm still leaning toward that being the most likely scenario."

"Which, again, means that they're watching us right now," I said. "We shouldn't stand around here doing nothing."

"While I agree wholeheartedly, I don't think it would be wise to attempt to use this device without some careful consideration," Toran countered.

"If you want to study it, then study it," I said, unable to keep a touch of exasperation out of my tone. He'd already said it was impossible for us to know what the device did without direct contact, so staring at it wasn't going to get answers—we needed to just *use it* and figure out the rest later.

Toran sighed. "I know this is frustrating, but I don't want us to walk into a worse trap than we're already in."

"Noted, but leaping first and looking later is kinda how we roll," Kaiden said.

"In this matter, I highly advise against it," Toran continued. "The way I see it, there are three possible outcomes for interacting with this device. First, we might be able to use it as a viewer, either for the sealed Master Archive—in which case, we'd only get a 'no signal' type response—or we'd confirm the presence of at least one other Archive, thereby indicating that we're now under the influence of a separate crystalline network.

"Secondly, we might inadvertently trigger another universal reset. We know from experience that these devices are used as a control mechanism for those. Though I know we don't have a Master Crystal shard with us, there's no telling if there are other factors that could initiate a reset."

"That's a disturbing prospect," I said.

Kaiden frowned. "And this sphere has the Darkness vine-things coming out of it, and it might be connected to those beings. If we initiated a reset from this point, that might… I don't know what, but it seems like it would be bad."

"Yes, very bad," Toran said. "For all we know, it could be a master plan to trigger a complete restructuring of all the Hegemony's worlds at once, completing the transformation by the Darkness."

"That…" I didn't know what to say. It sounded like a brilliant master plan, in theory, except it was missing a crucial 'why' justification. I also had no explanation for how the aliens would know we would come here—aside from a fuzzy-future vision that we did—or why we would need to be the ones to activate the viewer rather than doing it themselves. Unless… I stopped trying to rationalize it. There were too many offshoots to chase; I needed to take it one thing at a time.

"And what's the third option?" I asked instead, hoping to complete the picture of likely possibilities before delving into the details of each scenario.

Toran took a deep breath. "This might open a dimensional doorway to allow us access to a higher plane—or multiple planes."

That was certainly the most mind-twisting of all the explanations. "Okay, let's table that one for a moment," I suggested. "Back to the idea about it triggering another universal reset. How would that be possible?"

"Well, different crystals have different properties," Toran said. "Colren spoke about Master Crystal shards being used in concert with the viewing devices to spark a reset, but there would be no way to tell if a shard was already inside one of the spheres, right? We used the shard at the same time as we touched it to activate the reset, but maybe we could have melded the two before and programmed it with special properties, so the next person to touch it—however far off in the future—would activate it."

I stared at Toran. "Not saying that you're wrong, but that sounds *really* paranoid and far-fetched for what this sphere thing might do."

"Normally I'd second that assessment, Elle, but we *are* talking about potential fifth-dimensional beings," Kaiden said.

"Regardless, it doesn't make sense," I insisted. "Why set a trap for us to initiate a reset?"

"They could just do it themselves," Maris said, echoing my own thoughts from earlier.

"Unless they can't, for whatever reason," Kaiden pointed out. "Maybe the interface doesn't work for higher dimensional beings."

I considered the thought. "Maybe, but still. What possible purpose would a reset serve? I don't buy the idea of them using a reset to transform all the worlds at once; they're already well on their way to accomplishing that end, and speeding up the process would be irrelevant for beings that aren't locked into a unidirectional flow of time as we know it. For that matter, what in the stars do they even care about spacetime?"

"I don't know," Toran admitted after a pause.

"Which probably means that's *not* what's going on here," I concluded.

"Yes, thinking it through, that does seem the most unlikely of the three scenarios," Toran stated.

"All right, so that leaves the option of it being a viewing device that may or may not work, or it being a dimensional doorway," I summarized.

"Or Option D," Maris said. "I'll just note that as 'unknown doom'. The letter even syncs up!"

"Or 'death'," Kaiden added.

I gave them each a horrified look and shook my head. "Moving on… The remaining options are either benign, such as the viewer, or going to turn our universe upside down as we know it."

"Sounds like it," Kaiden agreed.

"So, I say we just go for it," I said.

Toran shook his head. "Elle—"

I shrugged. "Yeah, it's probably dangerous and foolish, but what else is new with us?"

"I know I'll regret saying this, but I think we should do it," Maris said.

Kaiden let out a long breath. "I've got nothing else. Sure, why not? I always used to say how much I wanted to go sightseeing on another dimensional plane one day."

Maris eyed him. "You were a weird kid."

"I'm joking!" Kaiden rolled his eyes. "You in, Toran?"

The other man looked between us and the sphere. "I suppose that is the only way to find out."

"That's the spirit!" I drew my sword. "We should probably be ready in case this teleports us into some crazy alien fighting ring."

"I *wasn't* hoping for a dimensional access point, but I'll take that over an alien death pit," Maris said.

Kaiden chuckled, readying his staff. "Elle, you have entirely too active an imagination."

Something told me reality was about to get a whole lot weirder than whatever I could dream up. "Everyone ready?"

My friends nodded.

Weapons in hand, we reached out to touch the crystal.

7

MY SWORD RADIATED heat in my left palm as I made contact with the crystal orb. Reality distorted around me, appearing to unfold—or maybe *I* was unfolding.

For a moment, everything around me became blindingly bright, overwhelming my vision with white light. Then, there was only blackness.

I tensed. Had we initiated a reset after all? I searched around me, desperate to find a clue about what had happened. Nothing seemed to be there. My friends were nowhere in sight. Panic welled in my mind, but I had no physical form to respond to the emotion.

Reality unfolded around me yet again, almost like I was turning to the opposite side of a window and the blackness I'd floated in was the side edge. Forms slowly resolved, and I found myself standing next to my friends.

"What just—" I cut off when I noticed our surroundings.

If I didn't know better, I'd thought I had walked into a house of mirrors. Every surface was a semi-reflective window, as though I was inside a crystal prism looking at a cross section of moments in time. Catching the angle of the reflective windows just right, infinite variations of the events from that moment branched like fractals inside it. Past moments were clear, but branches toward the future were foggy.

The sight was beautiful, but the sheer magnitude of possibilities was enough to make me lightheaded. "How did we get here?"

"Through the crystal," Toran stated. "Well, not *through* it. We transitioned to a higher dimension. This is fascinating."

No wonder my head ached.

"If the devices are the same, why didn't this happen when we did the resets before?" Maris questioned.

"It might be a matter of intention," Toran replied. "We *wanted* there to be a reset before, took efforts to think of a specific moment in time when we wanted to reset to. In this instance, we wanted to gain awareness of the higher planes."

I stared around me in wonder. "The crystals really can read our thoughts."

"It's all energy," Toran said. "The network—and the viewing devices, specifically—are attuned to picking up on the subtleties in those energy patterns. The biomechanics of it are really quite remarkable."

Kaiden spun around, taking in our surroundings. "It doesn't seem possible."

I studied the images. "What are these?"

"Windows across time and space." Excitement filled Toran's eyes. "I can't believe I resisted touching the sphere—to miss out on coming here. This confirms everything."

Kaiden looked as frazzled as I felt. "What are you talking about?"

"Follow any one thread, and it could lead to any past time or place," Toran murmured. "Each dimension telling its own story, with paths intersecting across time."

I stared at the images around me. They seemed to only be of the chamber where we had been standing moments before. "That doesn't seem right, Toran."

"Just because we can't see it yet, it doesn't mean it's not there," he said cryptically.

"Did that creature mess with his head?" I whispered to Kaiden.

"Maybe. None of this is making sense."

I cleared my throat. "Are we… inside the crystal?"

"Not inside, no," Toran replied. "That was only a means to help us see what was already around us. The crystal is still here, see?" He pointed to a semi-transparent sphere. "We're just now aware of the levels that exist above that spacetime reality. Right now, we're outside—or, rather, above—the flow of time as we know it. Six-, seventh-, eight-dimension, maybe? It's difficult to say."

"All right, so the crystal *was* a hyperdimensional portal," Kaiden said. "Yay us?"

"Not a portal," Toran corrected. "A trans-dimensional interface—"

"A TDI, we know," I said. "But 'portal' is *so* much easier to grasp conceptually, Toran."

"But it's not accurate."

I sighed. "*Anyway*, I was right. You didn't think it was," I ribbed Kaiden.

"Can you blame me?" he replied. "It sounded nuts."

"More than us having magic?"

Kaiden groaned. "That can't be your retort for everything unexpected."

"Hey, we don't have our packs," Maris realized.

I reached for the straps on my shoulders and found them

suspiciously absent. "That's weird Why did our clothes and weapons come but not the packs?"

Kaiden shook his head. "I don't—"

"Quiet." Toran held up his hand, listening. "I'm not sure we're alone."

"Don't tell me this is where those creatures live," Kaiden said in a lower voice.

Toran listened for several more seconds and then shook his head. "Not to be pessimistic, but I suspect we're in a higher dimensional plane than those beings reside. What we may encounter here could be worse."

"Thanks, Toran. I feel *way* better." I tightened the grip on my sword.

"Wait, a *higher* dimension than them? How?" Kaiden questioned.

Toran ignored the question. "We shouldn't stay in one place."

"No, we're not going *anywhere* until we know what's going on here," I insisted.

"I told you," Toran began, "we're now, at a minimum, in the sixth- or seventh-dimension—"

"No, Toran, not just labels for things. That is completely meaningless to me right now as I stare through hyperdimensional windows into infinity! How does anything function in this place? How do we get *back*?"

Kaiden placed a gentle hand around my upper arm. "I'm freaking out, too, but *literally* freaking out isn't a good idea right now."

"I don't know, this does seem pretty freak-out-worthy," Maris said, though her tone was surprisingly level.

It seemed impossible that I was the one losing my composure. Maris was supposed to be the high-strung person on our team, not me. Was I overreacting?

I took a deep breath. It *was* a breath, right? There was still air in the higher dimensions? My head swam as I started to think about the bizarre mechanics of the world around me. Was I actually under the influence of gravity, or was this entire place a construct formed by my team's combined preconceptions about what reality was supposed to be? Would it all vanish if we were to suddenly stop believing in it?

My heart was racing. The clothes on my back were suddenly too heavy for me to bear. I panted for breath.

"Elle." Kaiden tightened his grip on my arm—firm, but still loving. "Elle, look at me." He stepped into my sightline, bending his knees to look me square in the eyes, leaning close to block out the dizzying views all around me.

His familiar face and touch took the edge off my anxiety, allowing it to recede enough for me to catch my breath.

"Hey, that's more like it," he said when my breathing normalized, offering a reassuring smile. "You're okay."

I swallowed, my cheeks flushing from embarrassment. "Sorry, I can't believe I lost it."

Maris waved her hand like it was nothing, flashing me a sweet, concerned smile.

"I don't think this was a random panic attack," Toran said pensively. "This is out of character for you."

"Heh," I grunted. "I thought it was." So much for being the calm warrior wise beyond my years.

Toran shook his head. "No, that creature we encountered—I believe that your… reaction may have been a result of its telepathic influence."

I did a double-take. "What?!"

"I sensed it in my mind, trying to introduce doubts," he explained. "But this wasn't the first time you encountered one of them, right?"

I thought back over the past week, recalling when my attitude had started to change. "True, I saw that one on the alien ship before we detonated the disruptor. Could that one have done something to me?"

"Perhaps. And, you said you've been feeling 'off'?" Toran asked.

I nodded.

"Maybe the creature we just encountered picked up on that kernel left behind by the other and exploited it, to mess with your emotional regulation. How are you now?"

"I dunno." My panic was receding and my thoughts were becoming more lucid. "Definitely getting better."

Toran evaluated me. "Well, it's possible that the dimensional transition may have broken its mental influence—we don't know what kind of changes our bodies may have undertaken during the transition, but it's clearly significant."

"Then why did I freak out *after* we got here?" I asked.

"Perhaps it was the sudden purging of the mental influence, bringing all of the subconscious thoughts they'd implanted to the surface at once."

"They had subconsciously re-programmed me?" I shivered. "That's a terrifying thought."

Toran shook his head. "That might be an overly dramatic characterization. It seems like they did little more than introduce some self-doubts—likely with the intention of making you easier to control. It seemed to want to subdue and study us."

"It also said 'kill'," I reminded him.

"Yes, but it could have easily killed us. I believe it wanted something from us first."

I swallowed. "I think that's actually *worse*."

He smiled warmly. "You've always been calm under pressure, Elle. This wasn't like you. I'd wager a small fortune those creatures had something to do with it."

The notion that I had been under psychological assault shook me even more than if I'd had a blade to my throat. What would have happened if I'd broken down in the middle of battle when my friends needed me the most?

"I might still be dangerous—" I started.

"Elle, all of us are probably just as mind-warped as you," Kaiden cut in.

"Very true," Toran agreed. "But, like I said, this dimensional transition likely disrupted any telepathic influence we may have been under."

"Regardless, you can't call yourself out as being the weak link here, Elle," Kaiden continued. "None of us are. The Dark Sentinels are a quartet, and we take care of our own."

It was funny to think of such fierce loyalty after only a few weeks together, but the experiences we had shared were more intense than what some people would endure in an entire lifetime. Even if I didn't fully trust myself at the moment, I did trust in the integrity of my companions. As long as we stuck together, we'd find a way to make it through each challenge as it came.

I took a few more slow, deep breaths. The nausea and dizziness were passing. "Thanks, guys. I hope it doesn't come up again, but I know I'm in good hands if it does."

"We'll watch each other. We're not in this alone," Maris said.

I managed a weak smile. "Thanks."

Toran froze again, listening. "I maintain that there's something else here," he said softly.

Temporary insanity or not, I remembered my original objection. “If we leave this place, how will we be able to find our way back?”

Our team’s resident scientist remained unnervingly silent.

“Toran…?” Kaiden prompted.

“I don’t rightly know how to get back from here, I’m afraid,” he admitted.

“Should we maybe test that before we wander out into the unknown expanse of a higher dimensional plane?” I asked, unable to keep a sarcastic bite out of my tone or wording.

“Back to your old self, I see,” Kaiden murmured just loud enough for me to hear, giving me a playful nudge with his shoulder.

I did feel a million times better, and I’d be on guard to make sure I didn’t crack like that again. Crazy emotional breakdowns didn’t work well with my image.

Image… Another wave of disorientation swept over me when I took the wrong moment to look into one of the windows. I squeeze my eyes shut and took a breath, allowing the feeling to pass. I could do this. I was in control.

When I opened my eyes again, Toran was standing at the sphere.

“Do we touch it like we did last time?” Maris asked.

“I’m not sure if the sphere functions the same way here,” Toran mused. “The sphere is here, but also everywhere.”

“What do you mean?” I shook my head. “Why wouldn’t it behave the same way?”

“What I should have said is that the sphere in our spacetime reality led here to the hyperdimensional plane—or ‘frame’, to be more accurate,” Toran replied. “The different planes aren’t sandwiched, but rather nested. So, accessing that same crossover point from here, though, doesn’t mean we’d return to spacetime where and when we left—it's not a one-to-one portal. We could find ourselves in an even higher dimension, or a lower one somewhere between home and here. Or… well, anything is possible."

"So, we *are* trapped," I concluded.

Toran didn't counter the statement.

"And you didn't think about that possibility *before* we came here?!" Maris squeaked.

"I was quite against the idea of activating the sphere without further study. You all overruled me." Toran sighed.

"Those possibilities aside, this access point is still our closest connection to getting back home," Kaiden jumped in.

I shrugged. "I guess if we got here once, we should be able to get back."

"That's what I was thinking," he replied. "Well, *hoping*."

"Perhaps only one of us should try, in the event it doesn't work in the intended way," Toran suggested.

"What happened to sticking together?" I asked.

"Given the potential for all of us to get *more* trapped, or just one of us, it seems like having people on the outside to help might be a good thing," he said.

"Does that mean you're volunteering as gateway-tester?" Kaiden questioned.

Toran nodded. "I, frankly, have a better theoretical understanding of where we are, so I'm the most likely to fare well on my own if we get separated."

It was the truth, and I had no productive counterargument to offer; knowing Toran, his mind was already made up. "If you're going to do this, then you should probably get it over with," I told him. "If something new is stalking us, like you said…"

"Right." Toran glanced at the sphere then gave us each a

heartfelt smile. "Hopefully I'll see you again soon." He reached out to touch the crystal.

Nothing happened.

"Toran?" I asked when he didn't react.

"I don't understand," he murmured at last.

"Yeah, have to say, I expected it to do *something*," Kaiden commented.

"It should have." Toran frowned. "Direct contact took us here, so reversing the procedure should have solicited a reaction of some sort."

"No finger tinglies, even?" I asked.

He cast me a look of admonishment. "Never a term I'd use, Elle."

"Hey, you just confirmed we're stuck on a hyperdimensional plane. Trying to bring a little levity to the critical situation here," I shot back.

"There has to be something else we can try," Maris said.

"I don't know what," Toran admitted.

"Well, at least we're together?" Kaiden's tone was still light, but I could see the worry in his eyes—on the verge of panicking just like me.

"I don't want to be trapped in a higher dimension forever," Maris whimpered.

We couldn't afford to feed into each other's worry and lose our heads. I'd given into that once already, and it hadn't helped anything.

While the three of us dealt with the news in our own ways, Toran seemed strangely calm about the entire situation. "I trust that we'll find a path," he said, breaking the silence. "We made it here because this is where we needed to come, and we'll find our way back when our task is complete."

The words caught me by surprise; this new philosophical

Toran was a little too much about going with the flow rather than action. "Yeah, sorry if that doesn't exactly set me at ease."

"Fate might be intervening." The end of Kaiden's staff glowed brightly as he spun away from me.

A moment later, I caught sight of his target. The creature—if I could rightly call it that—floated among the windows twenty meters away, though distance didn't seem to work the same way in that place. More like a blob than a living being, the semi-transparent form sparkled with a rainbow of light, bands of color rippling over its surface in complex patterns. Surrounding the central, transparent mass was a fine mist, giving the impression of a droplet of water evaporating in the sun—except, the drop of water was at least two meters in diameter and it could move on its own accord.

"Is that a jellyfish?" Maris whispered.

"We're not underwater," Kaiden replied. "I think it's more of a blob."

"Fine, a cosmic jellyfish," she amended.

"I was going more the 'cloud' route, myself," I said, not sure if the creature was friend or foe.

"Cosmic jellycloud," Kaiden offered.

Toran held up his hand. "What are you talking about?"

"There's a floating cloud-creature thing," I explained. "You don't see it?"

Toran shook his head.

"Weird. Why—" I cut off. "It's spotted us."

The nimbus, as I elected to dub it instead, glided toward us, its light pattern twirling and reversing every half-second. I wondered if the lights might indicate a sort of language or attempt at communication.

"It looks agitated," I said to my friends, then added louder to address the nimbus, "We're friends. We don't mean any harm."

The nimbus' lights stuttered and then initiated a new pattern of colored dots and zigzags.

"I suddenly wish I spoke Cloud," Kaiden quipped.

So did I—at least enough to know if the creature meant us harm. "Maybe we should get out of here," I suggested, backing away.

Four additional nimbuses glided from behind windows near the first, fanning out to frame us in a semi-circle.

"I don't like this at all," Kaiden murmured, his staff still glowing. "Three more just appeared, Toran."

"Stars! Why can't I see them?" Toran flushed.

I hadn't sheathed my sword since entering the higher plane, and I now wondered if I should. Perhaps if the nimbuses didn't see us as a threat, they'd leave us alone. On the other hand, I'd be at a disadvantage if they chose that moment to attack. I decided to try for the middle ground, lowering my weapon into what I hoped was a non-threatening position.

"What are you doing, Elle?" Kaiden hissed.

"We're the invaders here," I reminded him. "These things look like the opposite of Darkness. Assuming they're not connected to the other aliens, there's no reason for us to make new enemies."

Hesitantly, Kaiden lowered his staff.

Toran adopted a neutral stance with his gloved hands at his sides. "I hope they can sense our good intentions."

"They might not be dangerous at all," Maris said. "They're just big, puffy cloud things."

At first glance, maybe, but I disagreed with her assessment. These were intelligent, higher-dimensional beings, as far as I was concerned, and I didn't want to get in a fight with them. Now that we were on their turf, we couldn't rely on our experiences; we'd essentially entered a new reality with its own rules.

“Let’s just back away slowly,” I said, trying to stay calm. I made the first move and my team followed.

After we’d gone only two steps, violent pulse of light radiated from the four nimbuses, and they began to swell, electrical bolts of energy crackling inside.

The calm and steady approach was off the table. I spun on my heels. “Nevermind. Run!”

8

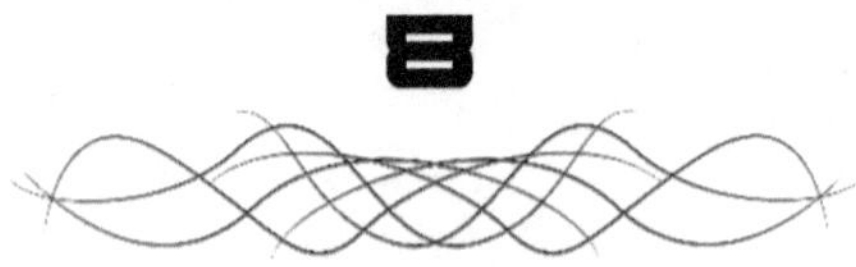

"SHIT, THIS IS *not* how I thought this was going to go!" Kaiden exclaimed as we barreled through the maze of mirror-like windows.

All of my thoughts about keeping track of our exit point were forced aside as the storming nimbuses chased us through the endless prism faceted corridors. I tried to keep track of the turns, but the strange angles made it impossible to maintain any frame of reference.

In that moment, I didn't care. We were being chased by angry cloud monsters, and I had no intention of finding out what their electrical bolts could do to me.

The view through the windows lining the walls changed from the ruined cityscape above the caverns to open plains. We couldn't have run far enough to have left the city in our spacetime reality, supporting my instinct that distance and scale followed different rules in that place. If we kept running for long enough, we could find ourselves near gateways to an entirely different planet.

Even though we managed to stay ahead of the nimbuses, they tailed us step for step. "How can we shake these things?" I asked, once it became clear they weren't going to stop following us.

"And why haven't they just jumped in front of us?" Kaiden questioned.

I'd been curious about that part, too. The other higher-dimensional beings we'd encountered had been able to glide through the planes and seemed to know everything we were about to do.

"I wish I could see what you're talking about," Toran said while running alongside me. "But I can maybe explain their movement—they're likely native to this plane."

"Native to here?" Maris said.

Toran nodded after we made another sharp turn through the maze. "Yes, seventh- or eighth-dimensional beings, wherever we are. They can't jump in front of us because they don't have access to a higher plane to use as a shortcut. I don't quite understand the rules of this place, but they are bound by them in the way we'd be back on our plane."

"Except with our magic," I pointed out.

"Yes, we do seem to be able to bend the rules," he admitted.

I had no clue where my abilities came from, ultimately, but I could sense that the hyperdimensional component of my consciousness that regulated my abilities was still above my present place in the dimensional hierarchy. That meant that we had an advantage with our abilities over the nimbuses—even if we were 'lower beings' in every other sense. If they wouldn't leave us alone, then we'd need to fight.

"Do you think they're a security guards of some sort?" Kaiden questioned. "Or, maybe they can recognize we're lower life forms and are trying to exterminate us like we'd kill ants in our house."

I wasn't crazy about those possibilities. Either way, it wasn't looking good for us.

"Let's take a stand," I said, preparing to stop so we could face our would-be attackers. "Try not to hurt them, but we can't keep running forever."

"I'm not even tired," Kaiden said. "But you're right, this is pointless."

Maris nodded.

"All right," Toran agreed. "You'll have to tell me what to do."

"Just hang back. We'll handle this." I looked to Kaiden and Maris. "Okay, now!"

I leaned back on my heels to stop my forward momentum and pivoted to face the nimbuses, raising my sword. They had expanded to more than twice their original size, now oblong four-meter-wide clouds with an internal lightning storm. Bolts of electricity struck the reflective walls, leaving no signs of damage. As my friends and I closed the distance between us and the nimbuses, the bolts lanced toward us.

Toran ducked and ran to the side. "Now *that* I can see!"

I gauged the reach of the bolts and halted just out of range. "Maris, haste!" I instructed.

"You've got it." She waved her hand in the usual fashion to initiate the spell.

My surroundings were unchanged. "What happened?" I took rapid steps backwards to keep myself out of striking range of the enemy electrical storm.

"Stars, of course!" Toran said. "We're higher than the fourth dimension—of course time manipulation wouldn't work here."

"Oh, that's bad." I ducked and dodged to the side as one of

the lightning bolts came dangerously close to striking me.

Kaiden retaliated with a wave of his staff, and the outer layer of the nimbus started to freeze.

"Good thinking with the ice!" I said.

The nimbus had slowed, but it was far from disabled. The others continued advancing toward us, the colorful light patterns taking on a decidedly menacing quality.

"There's has to be something I can do." Maris waved her arms again, and a purple shield appeared around each member of our team in addition to the silver forcefield around herself courtesy to her new shield.

Before I could wonder about if Maris' magical shields around us would stop the hyperdimensional creatures, I got my answer. One of the lightning bolts branched outward and struck the edge of my protective dome. The electrical current was reflected off the dome's surface, to my relief, and then struck one of the innumerable windows. I was surprised to see the reflected electrical bolts left singe marks—that hadn't happened when the nimbuses' bolts hit the mirrors directly.

"Their bolts are interacting with our magic!" I exclaimed.

"So they are," Toran concurred. "I wouldn't have expected that."

"Wonder later. We need to take these things out!" Kaiden urged.

"Killing them is a bad idea," I insisted. "We have no idea what they are. We're the outsiders here."

"I know, but *they're* trying to kill *us*." Kaiden dodged another bolt, then expanded his freezing spell to all four.

The lightning continued to bounce off the protective domes, striking the walls and ceiling. None of the bolts had yet hit the creatures. Given that the electrical attack had come from inside them, I figured it might not be a deadly blow, but maybe it would offer the kind of stun attack we needed to allow us to escape without killing the nimbuses.

"Maris, can you use your new shield to reflect their attacks back at them?" I asked.

"Yes, I'll give it a shot," she confirmed.

"Kaiden, keep that freeze ray going," I went on, moving forward now that I knew I was protected by the shield.

"Elle, what are you doing?" Toran asked.

"I'm going to provoke them," I said. "Stir up an electrical storm so they shock themselves."

"What should I do?" he replied.

"Be ready to grab me if I get electrocuted, I guess?"

"Careful, Elle," Kaiden said softly as I pass by him.

I flashed a daring smile. "I've got this."

"Ready with the shield when you are," Maris said.

"All right… now!" I raced forward with my sword while Maris simultaneously raised her jeweled shield so she could tilt the surrounding forcefield to the appropriate angle.

The nimbuses reacted just like I'd hoped, sparking a new electrical storm. The bolts shot out all around them, many striking Maris' shield and bouncing back. With Kaiden's freezing spell, the nimbuses' advance had slowed to a crawl, trapping them in the middle of their own storm.

Their external patterns shifted again to a chaotic display of colors and lights, which was undoubtedly a sign of distress.

"That's enough!" I called out to my friends, wanting to gauge the damage to the nimbuses before taking more aggressive action.

However, just as I started to back away, the nimbus in the right-center of the group broke free from its freeze and rushed toward me, releasing a flurry of electrical bolts as it ballooned to fill the corridor.

I dove for safety, my sword arm flailing as I fell.

As the nimbus expanded, a portion of it brushed against the tip of my blade. Light flared at the point of contact, then spread through the entire creature. With a bright burst, the nimbus vanished.

"Stars! Did I just do that?" I exclaimed.

"Your sword... why did it...?" Maris trailed off.

"The others, Elle! I can't hold them!" Kaiden shouted.

My stomach twisted with the thought of potentially destroying these creatures, but my friends were right—it was us or them. I ran forward and glided my blade over the other three nimbuses while they were frozen. The magical shield Maris had cast around me offering protection from their electrical attacks. They each vanished like the first, leaving us alone in the eerie corridor.

I lowered my weapon. "I didn't want to hurt them."

"What happened?" Toran asked.

"They came apart as soon as Elle's sword touched them," Kaiden summarized. "They picked the fight, Elle. We didn't have a choice."

"Still..." I stared at my sword. Only a graze from the blade had disintegrated the nimbuses—no other creature had been instantly destroyed with so little contact.

Toran followed my gaze. "That sword does seem to have some unique properties."

"Yeah, you can say that again." I watched the flames ripple along the edge of the blade before sliding it into the scabbard at my waist, not wanting to think about what else it could do accidently. "I wish we hadn't had to fight them."

"It might not be my place to speak since I didn't see both sides of the fight," Toran said in a fatherly tone, "but I can say for certain that our presence on this plane is about more than just the four of us right here, right now."

"*Why* couldn't you see them? That makes no sense," I replied.

"I'm sure there's an explanation, I just haven't worked it out yet," he went on. "What I do know is we have a mission to complete. To do that, we need to survive. More than that, we need to become masters in this place so we can use it to defeat the beings behind the Darkness. Other creatures may have been here first, but that doesn't mean we don't also have the right to be. We tried to leave them alone, they fought us, and you did what you needed to do for us to live. Maybe others of their kind will now regard us on their level so we can coexist. Either way, we need to establish ourselves as smart and capable—worthy of our place here. Sitting back and taking what we're handed won't get us where we need to go."

"I guess fighting and killing are the reality of our situation," I admitted, though I still didn't feel good about it.

Maris nodded slowly. "Those could have been highly intelligent, evolved creatures."

"Maybe so, but this team beat them," Toran stated. "Does that make us better? Not necessarily. Stars, I couldn't even see them! But, sometimes the little guy comes out on top, like a wild cat taking out a hiker. On the whole, survival of the fittest causes species to fall into an unavoidable hierarchy. The rest of our people may never glimpse this place, but the four of us…"

Kaiden nodded pensively. "What about the fight with the aliens behind the Darkness?"

Toran chuckled. "We're at an important juncture, aren't we? You could argue that being fifth-dimensional beings makes them superior to us, so maybe it would be fair to say that they should win. Personally, I think we have the right to fight for our survival. If we can overcome the odds, we will have proven our right to live another day."

"Considering the alternative is us dying, I have to agree," I conceded.

"There's this bizarre thing about being the more evolved entity in a scenario," Toran mused. "You can see everything the lesser forms are doing wrong, but from their own vantage, they're lost and helpless. It's like a bug getting trapped in the glass of an open window. You can see the path for it to escape—all it has to do is fly around the side and it will be free. But it doesn't—just keeps beating itself against the glass. We need to see that alternate path, to earn our right to survive. We're here in this place, we have the tools. It's up to us the seize the opportunity."

"I'd like to think we're more than bugs," Kaiden said.

Toran nodded. "Yes, but it's still up to us to fly around the side of the open window."

"Debating morality isn't important right now," Maris stated. "We need to get back to our home spacetime."

"I think this fight may have given us a clue," Toran said.

"Please share, because I have no idea," I replied.

He nodded toward me. "Your sword. I didn't make the connection until I saw how it affected those cloud beings."

"Let's call them 'nimbuses'," I interjected. "Couldn't get behind 'cosmic jellycloud', sorry."

"Stars, yes, much better!" Toran said

Maris looked a little miffed but said nothing. Kaiden shrugged.

"So, the nimbuses," Toran continued, "I maintain are native to this plane since they didn't just jump in front of us. However, since a brush with the sword disintegrated them, I believe the weapon must exist in a higher dimensional plane even than this—and that's also why it disintegrated the creature we fought in the chamber before making the transition, because it was a higher-dimensional being rather than something native to our spacetime."

I suddenly had to urge to rip the sword off me. "Are you saying this is, what, an eighth-dimensional object?"

"Possibly higher. I'm still not positive where we are now. I suspect our other artifacts may, likewise, be higher-dimensional items, though I'm not sure in what order."

Kaiden gaped at Toran. "What…?"

"It explains how we have been able to accomplish seemingly impossible tasks in the past," Toran continued. "For instance, opening the Archive, creating the shield around our shuttle during the disruptor detonation, entering this plane—Elle's sword is the common denominator. If she had been the one to touch the sphere, perhaps it would have worked, rather than when I did it alone."

My heart dropped. "But now we have no idea where that sphere is, relative to where we are now."

"I know, so that doesn't do us any good now. But, I think your sword might be the answer to us getting back to our usual reality. May I have a look at it?" Toran asked.

Despite our weeks of travel together, we'd never spent much time studying each other's artifacts. Once we each had 'ours', that had been it—we guarded our personal items loyally and only gave them up for decontamination cleaning when necessary. In particular, Kaiden and Toran had always seemed a little wary of my sword, and the one time Maris had asked to hold it during one of our practice sessions, she said it made her feel nauseated.

Even now, I didn't like the idea of handing it over to Toran. All the same, if it might help get us home, I couldn't decline. "Sure, here you go." I drew the sword and handed it to him by the hilt, careful to avoid the blue flames.

The moment it was in Toran's hand, the flames extinguished, looking just like any other weapon. "That's odd," he said.

Maris nodded. "Same thing happened to me. Give it a second."

Toran tilted his head questioningly, then his face contorted with discomfort. "Urgh," he moaned. "That's so disorienting—like I'm not connected to myself. Does this make you feel sick all the time, Elle?"

"Really, you too?" I shook my head. "Not at all. Makes me feel great, actually—like, supercharged."

Still wincing, Toran hefted the blade and gave it a thorough visual inspection. "It really doesn't seem that different, to be honest." He held it out toward me.

I took it back from him; the flames instantly reignited when it was in my hand. "Guess I just have a special bond with it."

"What are you thinking, Toran?" Kaiden asked. "Does this have something to do with our artifacts being on different planes?"

"Perhaps."

"Well, where does this leave us?" I looked between the faces of my friends. Since it seemed like Toran's inspection of my sword had hit a dead end, we were still trapped and directionless.

"I guess we should—" Kaiden cut off as a strange cry sounded, almost like a neigh. "Wait, did anyone else just hear a horse?"

"That can't be right," I replied, despite having heard it myself. Strange cloud monsters were the kind of oddity I'd expect to find in a higher dimension, but a horse?

"I think it came from over here," Maris said, her tone determined and excited. She ran to the left. "Come on, we have to find it!"

9

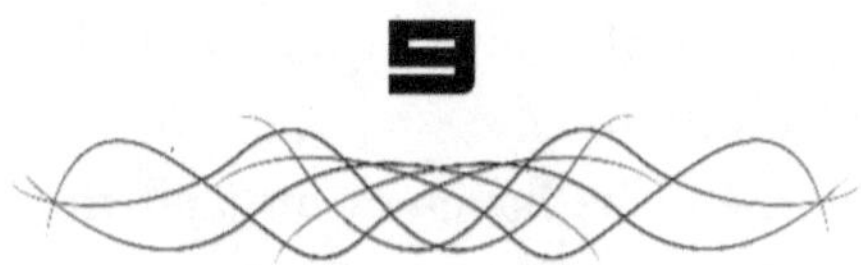

WE FOLLOWED MARIS through the twisting corridors of endless windows.

"I think I now understand why they built that labyrinth," I said. "Maybe someone glimpsed this place and it was a symbolic tribute."

"Could be." Kaiden nodded.

"Are you sure that sound was a call to us?" Toran asked.

"Yes," Maris replied emphatically. "It was so clear. I keep catching glimpses of it through the windows, too."

I wasn't as certain, but I had heard *something*, even though I'd yet to see any visual confirmation. Frankly, I wasn't keen on the idea of following the sound, since the last creatures we had encountered was far from friendly, but Maris was insistent. If this plan didn't work out, at least it wouldn't be on me.

While I recognized that I shouldn't look at things in those terms, I was still feeling drained and overwhelmed. The realization that my weapon was likely a higher dimensional object and our key to unlocking higher planes for our minds to access was throwing me in ways I hadn't expected. I'd barely gotten used to the idea of aliens, but this dimensional element was proving to be even more difficult to wrap my head around.

"I think I saw it again," Maris said, pulling my attention back to the present. She took a sharp right and paused, looking around. "I *know* I did."

Another soft neigh and a snuffle sounded in my mind. "Where is that coming from?"

"I don't hear it," Toran maintained.

"I think it's… in this one?" Maris examined one of the nearby windows, searching.

Toran seemed to be having a difficult time keeping his exasperation in check. "Why would there be a horse here?"

"Didn't say there *was* a horse, just that it sounded like one," Kaiden pointed out.

I sighed. "Fine, then—"

"Shh!" Maris cut in. "You're scaring it."

I froze and fell silent, trying to spot what she'd seen.

Maris approached a window to my right. "Hey, it's okay. We heard you. Do you need help?"

From my vantage, she was talking to herself. The sound was distinctive, though, so I gave her the benefit of the doubt.

"Why are you hiding?" Maris asked. "You can trust us."

Another soft snuffle filled my mind.

"What are you talking to?" I asked, coming toward Maris.

"Stop! You'll—" She drooped. "You'll scare it away."

Nothing was behind the window except a dim, indistinct landscape.

"What kind of thing is it?" I asked.

Maris shook her head. "Maybe he'll show you. Be nice." She held out her hands in front of her, palms up and cupped. "It's okay, they're my friends."

We remained motionless for nearly a minute. Then, a

white nose and snout came into view through the infinite planes fanning out inside the window. The tapered head led to an arched, muscular neck and long body atop four slender legs ending in crystal hooves. Its entire body was covered in tiny, scalloped scales that appeared as thin and light as feathers. A golden mane flowed from the crest of its neck and matching tail flowed almost to the ground. Though mostly solid in appearance, I could make out the faint outline of the backdrop behind it, and it shimmered with a soft, golden glow. Its most striking features, however, were its luminescent golden eyes and a spiraling, crystal horn at the center of its forehead.

"No frickin' way!" I exclaimed louder than I'd intended.

The creature bucked and quickly retreated into the shadows within in the window.

"Hey, it's okay! Come back," Maris soothed.

"What was it?" Kaiden asked, having been at the wrong angle to see.

"You wouldn't believe me if I told you. Come here." I motioned Kaiden to me and pointed toward where I'd seen it.

Several seconds later, after more gentle coaxing, the creature came close enough to Maris for it to enter our sightline.

Kaiden sucked in a shocked breath. "Is that a… unicorn?"

I'd been hesitant to call it that, myself, but the description was too close to lore to not call it like I saw it. "Yes, I believe it is."

To my eye, the unique coat gave it a touch of griffon or maybe dragon, but the overall impression was decidedly equine. I would have been more shocked by the discovery if I hadn't previously encountered decidedly dragon-y dragons on the Valor world, but the realization that there was truth behind the existence of legendary animals thrilled me.

"He's so beautiful," Maris murmured.

"How do you know it's a 'he'?" I asked, not seeing any distinguishing physical traits either way.

"He told me," she replied.

I'd heard some whinnying, but that was about the extent of my interaction with the unicorn. "Like, telepathically?" I clarified.

"I think so," she responded, a fond smile brightening her face. "I think he likes me."

Toran slowly came up behind Kaiden and me. "What are you looking at?"

I swiveled my neck. "You don't see it?"

His brow drew together. "There's a… unicorn?"

I nodded. "Yes, all white and golden and ethereal—inside the plane within that window."

"Maybe you need to 'believe'," Kaiden jested in a clear play on childhood fairytales. I knew he was joking, but I couldn't help wondering if there might be a measure of truth to the statement.

Toran shook his head. "It's just like before. I can't seem to perceive things on the same planes you can."

"You'll just have to take our words for it, I guess," I told him, trying not to sound patronizing.

"Has the unicorn told you anything else?" Kaiden asked Maris.

She was silent for several seconds. "He's… trapped."

"What? How?" I questioned.

Maris' brow furrowed. "I'm trying to piece it together. It's not words, more like a jumble of images. I think he… got lost somehow, separated from his kind. They used to take shortcuts through this plane using special routes connected to the plane below this one, where he's from. Except, when the Overlords came, their normal routes closed."

"Overlords?" Kaiden raised an eyebrow.

"The aliens behind the Darkness, maybe?" Maris shrugged. "Anyway, he got left behind and the rest of his herd were forced to go on without him or else also become trapped."

"Can he get back?" I asked, empathizing with the unicorn as I thought about how I was separated from my own family.

Maris hung her head. "Oh."

"What is it?" Kaiden pressed.

"He wasn't talking about the recent invasion of our spacetime. I think he's been trapped since whatever went down that killed this planet."

"Stars!" I couldn't fathom being trapped alone, with nowhere to turn, no one to hear my cries. It must have been terrifying.

"What can we do to help?" Kaiden asked.

"We need to try to get him out. He can enter this plane if we can open the doorway." She shook her head. "That's the best I can explain it. I don't know exactly what he means."

"I wish I could see what you're talking about." Toran grunted.

"You still might be able to help," Maris said. "Your gauntlets—you've been able to shatter other things. Maybe you can break one of the windows?"

"This isn't normal spacetime," he replied.

"Still, it might do something. Can you try?" she asked.

Toran sighed. "Very well. You said it was this one?"

"Yes, hold on." Maris leaned in close to the window. "We're going to try to get you out. Back up, but don't go far."

The unicorn pawed one of his crystal hooves and then backed up until he was only visible at the edge of the window.

"Okay, go ahead." Maris stood aside.

Toran stepped up to the window and raised his fists. He

pounded them into the surface in three rapid blows. The surface shuddered but didn't appear close to breaking.

Kaiden frowned at it. "Well, that doesn't seem to work. I'd suggest throwing some magic at it, but I'm afraid it would bounce back."

"No offense, but I don't think your magic is particularly effective here," I said. "It barely did anything to those nimbuses."

"Yeah, that's true." He stepped back. "Do your thing with your sword."

I smiled. "I swear I'm not trying to show off."

"You got the coolest artifact, we get it." Maris smiled back, clearly happier now that she had a special item of her own. Honestly, there were times when I'd rather have her new shield.

I unsheathed my sword, debating whether I should try bashing the window or take a more surgical approach. In the end, I decided to start with finesse, as I could always work my way up from there. I gripped the hilt in both hands and placed the tip on the center of the window.

The surface began to shimmer and flicker, fracturing the view through the window. As I pressed my blade deeper, each facet vibrated with increasing intensity until it was shuddering so fast that the view through the window once again became a single image. At the moment it coalesced, the pane dissolved.

I gasped, drawing back my blade from what was now an opening. The area beyond defied my expectations for a reality, with islands of solid-looking matter seemingly floating in a void. The unicorn was standing on one of these islands connected to the others by narrow bridges made from translucent filaments. "What is this place?"

"Another layer of reality above our own," Maris said. "He

doesn't know how long he's been here—time is fluid above the fourth dimension. But he said this isn't how it used to be—it should be filled with light. This pocket got cut off when the Overlords came, and it's been dark ever since."

"I'm so sorry he was trapped here. That must have been awful," I said.

"He thanks you," Maris interpreted. She stepped to the edge of the opening through the former window. "You're free now. Come with us."

The unicorn didn't move.

"He's scared. He's not sure he can trust us." Maris frowned.

"We want to fight the Overlords," I told him directly. "Can you help us learn about them?"

The unicorn snuffled, sounding in my mind. Slowly, he picked his way down the narrow path from the island toward the door.

Maris motioned us backward as the unicorn reached the opening. He sniffed cautiously toward where the window used to be and extended his nose toward it. When it freely passed through, he made an excited hop and leaped through the opening into the corridor.

As soon as he was through, I noticed tiny crystals forming around the edges of where the window used to be, joining together to form a single, smooth plane as they spread inward.

The unicorn backed away from us as he got his bearings, glancing between Maris and the rest of us as he danced on his four crystal hooves.

"You're free now," Maris said.

He met each of our gazes with his spectacular golden eyes. "*Thank you,*" I heard in my mind, though the words were a construct of my own imagination. I was wrapped in a warm mental embrace of sunshine, filled with joy and the thrill of freedom. The intensity of the emotion almost brought tears to my eyes.

"You're welcome," I told him. "Is there anything else we can do to help you get back to your family?"

The unicorn shook his head with another huff, which I took to be a 'no' as a dark cloud filled my mind. They were long since separated, and there was no going back now. However, new images and sensations of warmth embrace me.

Maris brightened. "He wants to help us!"

"We'll take all the help we can get," I told him. "What should we call you?"

A powerful, ancient presence filled my mind once more. Though it still didn't convey spoken words, I automatically translated into my native tongue. *"I am known as Huefneril among my kind."*

I winced. "Okay, fair warning, I sense a nickname coming on."

Maris crossed her arms. "Yeah, that won't do." She looked the unicorn up and down. "I'm gonna call you 'Hoofy'."

10

I ROLLED MY eyes. "Really, Maris, you're going to call this majestic being 'Hoofy'?"

"Only as a delightful term of endearment. You don't mind, do you?" Maris asked the unicorn.

He snuffled. *"You have freed me. You may call me whatever you wish in your tongue."*

Maris spread her arms. "Matter settled."

Kaiden pursed his lips. "Feels a little on-point to me."

Toran pinched the bridge of his nose and shook his head.

Exasperating nickname or not, I'd take it over 'Huefneril'; at least it captured the right spirit. "So, Hoofy, tell us about yourself."

"First, I am curious about you," he said in his telepathic language of images and emotion. *"How did you come here? Your kind are not ascended."*

"It's… kind of a long story," I replied. "When the Darkness came, our worlds were lost. We were able to escape to these new bodies." I held memories in my mind to augment my words, and I could tell that Hoofy was absorbing their meaning, feeling them as I did.

"They never stop trying." I sensed the fear in Hoofy's statement.

"You know who's behind the Darkness?" Kaiden asked.

"They call themselves the Overlords. They seek to control, to dominate."

"Are they the ones who trapped you?" I asked.

"Yes, but not intentionally. It was a side effect of their alterations to the crystalline network. I was young and inexperienced. I hesitated, and I was left behind." Hoofy shared his sadness and frustration.

"These beings… where are they? *What* are they?" I questioned.

"I have hidden from them so they cannot find me."

Maris softened. "I would, too. But we're friends. You don't need to hide from us."

Toran took in a sharp breath of surprise. "I can see him."

"Thank you," Maris said with an affectionate smile toward the unicorn. "How did you make him see?"

"I have hidden above them," Hoofy explained. *"They reside on a plane above time and thought, below this one. For years they have tried to ascend, but that is a place that cannot be reached by force."*

"Okay, so they're on a dimensional plane below yours and above our spacetime?" I clarified, trying to get back to my previous question.

"Yes, the plane beneath us. Once we used to commune with them on their level, but now we hide. Their ill intentions have corrupted the crystalline network."

I frowned. "Yeah, we've been seeing a lot of that."

"That's why I shied away at first—I could smell them on you. You were… changed."

I'd tried to forget how we'd come by our present forms—that we had been touched by the Darkness, and then our consciousnesses extracted and downloaded into modified bodies. I hated to think that any of the aliens or the Darkness was a part of me.

"We're not like them," Maris assured Hoofy.

"No, you have pure spirits. And you are more than them. Your kind is not ascended, but parts of you are. You can see what others cannot."

Toran brightened. "This is actually quite helpful—we can start narrowing down which dimension we're now perceiving. Can you help us understand?" he asked Hoofy.

The unicorn pawed a crystal hoof. *"There is time, and there is thought, then above that they dwell. We roam around them unseen, except when we pass through this place, over the bridges. They used to use them, too, but they started trying to change them and the bridges collapsed."*

These interpreted words on their own raised more questions than answers, but I probed the images and emotions that filled my mind, searching for the nuance of his messages. My perception expanded, and I saw what I knew as my reality flowing through time. Beyond that was an amorphous layer flooded by an infinite number of flashing thoughts; I realize this was the dimension through which Hoofy was communicating. Then, there was the dark plane where the Overlords, as Hoofy called them, resided. They manipulated matters of mind and time.

I recoiled. "That's how they were telepathically influencing me."

Kaiden pressed a hand to his temple. "Ugh, this is a lot to take in at once."

Toran grimaced. "It'd be really handy if we could transition between planes at will."

"Yeah." I paused. "I get it now—like, on a deeper level—what you were saying before about us having not actually *gone* anywhere. We're not stuck in a different place... our perception is just locked at a higher plane than what we're used to experiencing."

"Yes, but there is a spacetime component," Toran said. "Once we ran away from the entry point, our position in spacetime likely changed. Now I really *don't* know where we are."

"But, we *can* figure out which plane," Kaiden said. "Since time is 4D, that weird thought dimension must be 5D, making the Overlords on 6D, Hoofy and the other unicorns at 7D, and us presently at 8D, I guess?"

The eighth dimension—not a place I ever thought I'd experience.

"That count sounds right to me," Toran confirmed. "It makes sense, then, why telepathic influence broke down when we transitioned to 8D, since it's multiple planes away from 5D. Or, maybe that's a coincidence."

"I wonder where those dragons we met fit in?" Maris pondered.

"They live among us," Hoofy said in our minds.

"Okay, so sounds like the seventh dimension is the land of mythical creatures." I smiled.

Maris hopped giddily. "I can't wait to go there!"

"We have other things to deal with first," Kaiden told her. "Namely, figuring out how to take out those Overlord guys."

I frowned. "Okay, since it's come up a few times now, I guess I'll have to be the one to say it: 'Overlords', really? I mean, the ego on these guys!"

Maris laughed. "They clearly have some sort of 'lower

dimension' complex. Like, 'We're only 6D so we should call ourselves something grandiose to compensate'."

Kaiden smirked. "No wonder their spaceships were so big."

Even Toran chuckled. "You three are ruthless."

"Hey, they brought this on themselves." I grinned.

"I believe the four of you have been chosen to set things right," Hoofy told us.

My smile faded, remembering the graveness of our circumstances. "We want to continue in our quest, but we don't know how to travel through this place."

"I would like to help you."

Maris clasped her hands. "Really?"

The unicorn bowed his head. *"It is only right that I do."*

"No complaints here," Kaiden said. "Welcome to the Dark Sentinels."

Hoofy pranced to the side. *"Come this way."*

We followed the unicorn—I still had to check myself each time I thought the name—through the mirrored maze of corridors. Now that I was gaining a better understanding of our environment and what I was seeing, I paid more attention to the scenes on the other side. Each of the facets appeared to correspond with a specific location, and the fractal branches within each followed the threads of time for each of those places. Additional facets revealed the different planes of reality, not all of them visual, but each unique. They shifted as the interconnected threads intersected with one another, a woven tapestry spanning time and space of everything that had been, everything that was, and even the somewhat fuzzy things that might yet come.

I wished I could find one of my own threads and follow it to see how everything worked out, but I knew that was impossible—or, at least, ill-advised.

"What more can you tell us about these Overlords?" Kaiden asked Hoofy while we walked.

"They thirst for power. They live in the dark and seek to shape others to be like them."

"Do you know where they came from?" I asked.

Hoofy shook his head, fanning out his golden mane. A series of images filled my mind, not translating into words in the usual fashion. It was clear that the Overlords were outside of time in the same way as the other hyperdimensional beings, but they were obsessed with the goings-on in planes outside their own. They tied themselves to time by virtue of their meddling, and that would be their undoing.

"We'll try to make things right," I told Hoofy.

"There is a chance," he replied. *"They descended once before to go after the crystals, but they were ultimately driven back."*

"What do they want with the crystals?" Toran asked.

"To ascend," Hoofy replied.

My brow knit. "How? What does that even mean?"

"They wish to be able to exist on a higher plane. I cannot say by which means or method they hope to achieve this goal."

"Sounds like something a bunch of power-hungry over-compensators would do," Maris said.

Kaiden chuckled. "That it does."

"You know the destroyed crystals we saw on Crystallis and in the caverns here?" Toran began. "I wonder if that happened the last time the Overlords descended."

"Very well could be," I replied. "There was clearly some kind of conflict."

"I still don't get why they would descend if they're ultimately trying to get to a higher plane," Kaiden mused.

"We have the crystal interface terminals, so maybe that has

something to do with it," I suggested. "Considering that we jumped straight up to the eighth dimension from there, perhaps not all dimensions have clear methods to access them."

"Here." Hoofy stopped in the center of a particularly jumbled section of corridor with reflective windows arranged in odd angles. Even the gravity in the place seemed strange to me, though that may have been in my imagination.

The windows shimmered and seemed to tilt, revealing a landscape like the one where we'd seen Hoofy. The view through windows transitioned again, and I unconsciously moved backward.

Through the windows, there was a massive city spanning as far as I could see. Cylindrical towers rose from a nest of massive black vines at the base. The structures themselves were formed from the same latticework material I'd seen on the ships. Creatures similar to the one we fought in the cavern scurried through the alien city. The world was dark, only illuminated by a subtle, blue glow.

"Stars!" Kaiden breathed.

"I figured they'd have something like this, but actually *seeing* it…" I faded out, not able to find the right words.

At first glance, the activity reminded me more of an ant colony than anything I'd experienced with my own brand of civilization. However, as I followed specific creatures along their paths, I realized that they were actually interacting much like my own people would. They greeted some individuals as they passed by—acquaintances, but not everyone they happened to come across—and there appeared to be a brand of commerce. Certain areas were clearly designated social gathering places, which were adorned by organic pedestals that looked strikingly similar to the stone benches we'd observed on the planet's surface. Having made the connection, I even noticed that the black stairways bore a similar structural design to the modified steps retrofit in the ruined city.

I took it in with growing concern. "Did the aliens conquer the planet, or did the residents change into this new form?"

"Never satisfied, they always seek what they do not have," Hoofy said cryptically.

"There are a lot of similarities here," Toran agreed. "I could see it going either way."

"The point is, they're organized and have a lot of infrastructure," Kaiden said.

"And there must be even more than this, since they also have constructed and launched space ships," I said.

Kaiden frowned. "That's a good point. Why do they need ships at all if they can travel through dimensional planes outside of normal spacetime?"

"Assuming they're after something in our home plane, maybe that's a more efficient means to go long distances?" Maris suggested.

"Could be." I considered the information we had so far. "Maybe they could only create animals on the Darkness-infected planets but there was no way to get their own consciousness there?"

Kaiden nodded pensively. "They sent the Darkness through the crystalline network to prepare worlds, and then the fleet was to carry individuals to… do what?"

"That is the big question mark," I replied.

"I wish we knew the extent of their civilization." Toran stroked his chin. "Is there just a city, or are there multiple planets?"

"Do you know, Hoofy?" Maris asked.

The unicorn stamped one of its front hooves. *"This world*

is theirs, with the core at its heart."

"Only this world, this city? Or is there more?" I pressed.

"It is more than it appears to be."

Toran nodded. "Right, yes. It's not limited to three-dimensional space as we know it."

"Hey, what about the anomaly site?" Kaiden asked. "Remember, the gravity around the site was weird, like an entire system was there, even though we couldn't see anything."

"I bet you're onto something with that. It would make sense for them to build up infrastructure around a place where they could transition their fleet into our spacetime," Toran replied.

Maris brushed her hair back from her face. "I can't think about it too hard or I'll want to curl up on the ground."

"I understand the impulse," I admitted.

"I'm curious what location in our native spacetime corresponds to this city's location. Do you know?" he asked Hoofy.

The unicorn shifted uncomfortably on his hooves. *"This is their place."*

"Yes, but it would help to know *where* this is," Kaiden said. "Is there any way to tell if this is a planet, or—"

"Can you go down to a lower plane and find a location there that relates to this city?" Maris asked in a soft voice. "We can't do it ourselves yet, and it may help us get back to our friends."

Hoofy continued his agitated side-stepping. *"They might see me."*

"Oh, I hadn't thought of that." I realized the conundrum. To get a clear view of our three-dimensional reality in this place at our appropriate time, Hoofy would need to descend to that plane. However, descending would require him to pass through the Overlords' domain and then remain at a lower level as he assessed the surroundings, making him visible to them and vulnerable to their attacks. It was a huge risk—not one we could ask him to take.

"Is there a way we can see for ourselves?" I asked.

"Too dangerous," Hoofy told us.

"I know, but we need to," Maris said. "You don't need to come with us."

Hoofy snuffled. *"There is a place that holds the answers you seek. Follow me."*

11

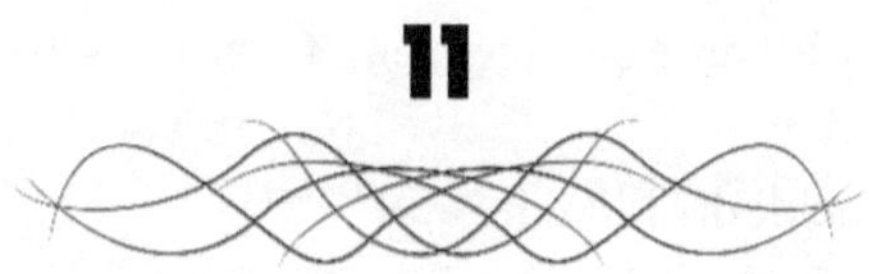

I FOUND MYSELF in even greater awe of the incredible eighth-dimensional landscape the longer I spent in the place. As we followed Hoofy through the corridors, I tried to peek through the windows to other planes, soaking in the wondrous sights.

"Now that I'm not on the verge of a nervous breakdown, this is amazing," I commented to Kaiden while we hung back slightly from the others.

"It doesn't feel as overwhelming now, does it?"

"No, it's just… wow."

He smiled slightly. "I'm glad to see you're doing better. I was worried about you."

"Yeah, unnerved me, too. I'm not used to being out of control like that."

"At least those Overlord guys can't get in our heads here."

I frowned. "You know, going along with the 'Overlords' thing is giving them too much credit. We need another name for them."

"That's pretty petty."

I laughed. "Oh, yes, I'm well aware."

He smirked. "And I like you even more for it. What do you have in mind?"

"Maybe the… 'Saps'. Create a self-fulfilling prophesy of them falling for whatever trap we set."

"You have a delightfully twisted mind."

"At least I use my talents for good."

"What are you two plotting back there?" Toran asked, looking over his shoulder.

"I propose a name change from 'Overlords' to 'Saps'. All in favor?" I asked.

Maris chuckled. "I like it."

Toran sighed. "Very well. 'Overlords' was too many syllables."

"Why do you find this new name amusing?" Hoofy asked.

I smiled. "Just a little word play. We mere lower-dimensional mortals have to entertain ourselves somehow."

We eventually reached an open area in the maze, which reminded me of a theater. Mirrors formed a dome overhead and down the walls in irregular hexagonal segments, transitioning to windows at floor level where they could be accessed. At the center of the space was a single crystal pedestal a meter tall, similar to the structure our Master Crystal shard had come from in the Archive.

"This is the infinity chamber. Here you may learn the ancient knowledge known to all ascended," Hoofy said. *"I cannot witness it myself, but if you can see, then you will know what must be done. You will be able to stop the menace."*

I swallowed. "No pressure, right?"

"Journeying to higher planes to glimpse the secrets of the universe—it's a regular Tuesday." Kaiden smiled.

"Yeah, hardy-har." Maris eyed the crystal pedestal like it was about to eat her. "How do we use this thing?"

Hoofy pranced with agitation. *"I will find you afterward. I cannot be here."* He galloped into the depths of the corridors.

I let out a long breath. "Totally reassuring."

"He'll be back," Maris said confidently.

"It's not that—what information is here that a being wouldn't want to know?" questioned Kaiden.

"I don't believe that's the issue. It's possible he *can't* access this information," Toran replied.

I raised an eyebrow. "How could *we* see something he can't? He's native to a much higher plane than us."

"And yet we're here now and were able to free him from a place he was trapped," Toran said. "I believe the four of us were changed more than we initially realized."

"Do you think our magic and abilities…?" I wasn't sure how to complete the statement, but I knew. Part of me had always known. Our powers came from somewhere, or *something*, and we were now close to understanding their origin.

Toran simply nodded in response.

"I guess we should activate this thing, or whatever we're supposed to do," Kaiden said.

"Do you think we just touch it?" I asked.

"Makes sense. All the other tech has worked that way," Maris said.

"Seems like a reasonable strategy," Toran agreed.

"Okay…" I approached the crystal pedestal. It hummed with the intense, sweet energy I'd come to associate with the crystalline network. I extended my hand toward it, and my fingertips brushed the surface.

The world fanned out around me, my senses richer and deeper than I imagined possible. I was surrounded by warmth and light amid an energy network connecting everything around me. At the edge of my awareness, I sensed my friends nearby. They glowed brighter than anything else in the vicinity—even more than the crystal pedestal at the center of the chamber—but there was still something even greater out there, just beyond my grasp.

As my awareness of my place within the energy network solidified, my consciousness expanded. The chamber, the eight-dimensional plane, were only one facet of my reality. At once, I was everywhere and nowhere. Darkness, light—it blended into a single sensory symphony. I knew that I was outside of time, yet I still had the urge to ground myself in a single place and moment from which to observe.

I searched around myself for some kind of foundation. However, there was only the color and light—beautiful, but I needed a connection to the familiar elements of my reality. Something, anything, to latch onto.

Beneath my present perception, I glimpsed a place teaming with life. I reached out for it, willing myself to pass through the dimensional veil so I could witness it for myself. As I descended through the layers of reality, I sensed my friends following me. Though we didn't bear the physical forms of our usual selves, I had no doubt it was them, visible or not. We gravitated closer to each other on the way to our destination until I felt like I could reach out and take their hands, if we had had bodies to touch.

The alien civilization we'd glimpsed through the window was now spread out before us, a fully populated planet and space dock beyond.

The scene spun backward. Now, a new world was forming before me. Signs of civilization formed and grew before my eyes, flashing at irregular intervals as physical reality was reset. Cities rose and fell, and then rose anew—bigger, more magnificent. They had achieved the pinnacle of development, and so the next phase began: to seek other life.

As I watched history play out in the spectacular cosmic time-lapse, the civilization learned to harness the crystal's power. They pierced the dimensional veil, to expand their consciousness to see everything that had been unseen. They found the other life they were looking for and welcomed the hyperdimensional aliens as gods.

However, the alien beings had aspirations of their own—to control the crystalline network and harness its power to regulate the unseen building blocks of our universe. All they needed was a direct link to the crystalline network: the interface crystals in our spacetime.

Blinded by ambition, the aliens tried to seize this power by force. In the end, their attempts to hijack the crystalline network backfired, shattering the crystals on many worlds. Interstellar society collapsed, with only a few scattered planets surviving to rebuild again. The aliens lost their gateway to the higher planes, but they knew that the keys to their ascension would emerge eventually. They would get another chance.

So, they retreated. They waited.

At last, civilized life in the lower planes—the reality my friends and I knew as our home—rebuilt enough to rediscover the keys that the ancient civilization had hidden for those worthy of gaining ascension to find.

The sword in my hand pulsed, and I knew it was one such key. The artifacts we now wielded opened access to the higher planes, and possessing them had forever changed us. Our time with the artifacts had enabled us to enter this dimension and to witness this ancient knowledge held within the fabric of the cosmos itself.

The aliens must not have realized our importance yet or

we'd already have been killed. They were on the cusp of completing their plan to ascend, and we were all that stood in their way.

In that moment, I understood my place. I knew what I had to do. And I was terrified.

My consciousness returned to my physical form, and the multi-faceted dome came into focus around me. My friends were standing exactly where they had been when I touched the crystal pedestal.

We stood in stunned silence.

"All right, that's going to take some time to process," I said eventually.

Kaiden nodded. "Wow. Not sure I have more than that to say at the moment."

Maris looked like she was on the verge of tears. "I don't think I can look at anything the same way again."

"We certainly won't," Toran said, still staring into space. "So, these invading aliens have always resided at a higher plane?"

"As far back as that little history lesson went, anyway," Kaiden said. "Were the people on this planet our ancestors?"

"Maybe, in a slightly different form," I replied. "They looked like giants compared to us."

Maris shook her head. "They mastered the crystalline network only to have it be their undoing. Makes you wonder if we should be messing with any of this."

"Too late for that," Kaiden said. "The Hegemony made that decision for us when they discovered the ancient civilization's tech and started hooking up viewing devices and interface consoles for the reset crystals."

"Crazy how cyclical it is, isn't it?" I murmured. "Civilizations born and raised only to fall into the same traps generations later."

"These hyperdimensional alien bastards really know how to play a long game," Kaiden said.

"To timeless six-dimensional beings, one civilization is just like another," Toran responded. "But we're different, because now we know what they're after."

I raised an eyebrow. "Do we? Because 'controlling the crystalline network' still feels like a pretty broad goal. What do they want to *do with it*?"

Toran hesitated. "That part I still don't know."

"Well, we have the keys to accessing the highest levels of the crystalline network," Maris said, patting her shield.

I nodded. "Yeah, I guess we do." The vision hadn't revealed how the artifacts were made or where they had come from, but I could sense the power of my sword in its scabbard. It was almost like it was pure higher-dimensional energy compared to everything around us, but I figured that was an after-effect of the whirlwind tour through space and time.

"Well," Toran said, "I suppose we have learned what we came to find out. The aliens are concentrated on this planet in the sixth-dimensional plane. We won't be able to do any more until we regroup with the Hegemony."

"I'm all for getting out of here," Maris said. "Once they learn about our artifacts..."

"Yeah, we don't want them to catch us on a lower dimension, that's for sure." My hand instinctively went to the hilt of my sword. While the aliens might not usually take much interest in lower-dimensional beings, eventually they'd figure out that we were the same team that had been thorns in their sides in recent weeks.

"About the getting back to our usual plane of perception..." Kaiden said slowly.

"Hoofy might be able to help us," Maris said. "Let's go find him."

We retraced our path into the chamber and found the unicorn waiting nearby.

"Have you found the answers you seek?" he asked, trotting toward us.

"We got some answers, but we also have a lot of new questions," Maris explained.

Toran nodded. "Do you know anything more about the crystalline network, and specifically the Master Archive?"

"The network is above all else. It is what bridges space, time, and the higher planes. To understand more than that is impossible for a being of my level."

"Surely you must have heard—" I pressed.

"It is not my place," Hoofy interrupted within my mind.

"That's okay, you've already done so much for us," Maris hastily cut in. "Can you help us find our way back to an access point where we can transition to our home spacetime?"

"That I can *do,"* Hoofy replied. *"This way."*

The unicorn led us through the confusing labyrinth of windowed corridors. Eventually, I spotted something recognizable. "That's the viewing-sphere!"

Maris breathed a sigh of relief. "Now we can go back home."

I drew my sword. "And this is the key, I guess?"

"Yes, I sense special strength in each of the artifacts you carry," Hoofy replied. *"That sword, in particular, holds great power."*

"We were discussing that right before we met you," Toran revealed. "Do you know anything more about it?"

"No, but I can tell you that it will facilitate your return home."

"Thank you for everything," Maris said. "You really saved us."

"It was you who saved me, truthfully," Hoofy replied. *"And in our short time together, I have become fascinated by your quest."*

Kaiden smiled. "Glad it's been entertaining to someone, because it's been pretty awful to live through."

"I was hoping I could journey with you," the unicorn went on. *"I will offer what support I can, but there are some things you must learn on your own."*

"That'd be great!" Maris exclaimed.

"No complaints here," I agreed.

Kaiden nodded. "Glad to get all the help we can get."

"Gladly. Will you be able to reside on our plane?" Toran asked.

"Not precisely, but now that you have witnessed the higher planes, I can make myself visible to you. Others of your kind, though, likely won't be able to see or hear me."

I chuckled. "Oh, this is going to go over *great* when we explain to Colren that we have a magical unicorn spirit guide."

"I *have* to be in the room for that," Kaiden said with a smile.

"Let's think that over before we say anything," Toran advised.

"All right." I looked between my friends and the viewing-sphere. "All together this time?"

We got into position and reached out to touch the sphere.

12

THE MIRRORED WALLS folded and warped, fading to black. When my vision focused once more, the underground cavern resolved around me. Our four backpacks were on the ground exactly where we'd been standing when we'd made the transition.

"Okay, that was officially the weirdest thing I've ever done," I declared, reaching down to retrieve my pack.

Maris scowled at our environment. "None of this feels right anymore."

"Yeah, I know what you mean." Everything around me seemed dull and lifeless after that amazing experience in the higher dimensions. It was simultaneously incredible and disturbing to know other beings could be observing me from a higher dimension without my knowledge. I tried not to dwell on it, knowing that it would be a path to madness, but I knew for certain that I'd never be able to look at anything the same way again.

"Hoofy?" Maris asked tentatively.

"I am here," he said telepathically to the four of us. *"I do*

not want to reveal myself in this place so close to the Overlords."

"Don't blame you," Maris replied. "And, remember, we're going to call them the 'Saps' from now on."

"They would not be pleased with this name."

I smiled. "Even better."

Kaiden headed toward the exit. "We shouldn't linger here."

I followed him. "Yeah, more of the Saps might be ready to transition to this plane now, however they do it."

Toran took up a position at the rear of our party. "This is not a place we want to find ourselves in another engagement."

I shared his concern. Now that we knew our artifacts were more than the weapons and defensive tools they appeared to be, we had to take extra precautions, lest they fall into enemy hands.

"Stars, I hope the *Sanctum* is still waiting for us," Kaiden realized. "How long were we in there? Or, sorta there. You know what I mean."

"I didn't check the time before," Toran said. "And, I don't know if we could trust the time readouts on any devices with us, anyway."

"I guess we'll see when we get back to the shuttle," I replied.

"Yes, no reason to delay," he concurred.

We jogged toward the exit, passing through the large cavern with its crushed crystal ground as quickly as possible. I kept a close eye on the black vines writhing near the walls, but no creatures came forward. I wasn't sure if they were wary of us after we took out the one earlier or if they had another reason to hang back, but it almost made me more nervous that we were able to pass through without incident.

Despite the amount of rubble in the chamber which formerly held the labyrinth, we were able to hop along the tops of the fallen wall slabs to quickly traverse the space, careful to avoid the shadowed recesses where the tainted Darkness vines may still remain. Beyond that, it was a quick journey up the spiral ramp to the surface. Passing through the corridor with its mosaics, this time I clearly saw the story depicted in the images, telling of the civilization welcoming the hyperdimensional aliens, only to be betrayed. The temple, the city, everything in their society had been changed to revolve around the Overlord's demands. I still didn't know exactly what had happened to bring about the society's ultimate demise after the crystals were damaged, but I was certain the Saps were to blame.

We hurried through the city ruins to our shuttle and took off as quickly as possible. As we reached the upper atmosphere, our comms chirped.

"Headed back already?" Richards said over the shuttle central's intercom.

"Good, you're still here!" Kaiden exclaimed from the pilot's seat.

"Yeah, of course we are. We agreed to wait ten hours," the ship captain replied.

Kaiden exchanged glanced with the rest of us. "How long has it been?"

"You only dropped out of comm contact about an hour ago," Richards revealed.

"Wait, that can't be right." Kaiden went into the flight record to see when we'd landed. The flight logs he overlaid on the front viewport clearly indicated that only a short time had elapsed—barely enough for our walk from the shuttle, to the sphere, and back again.

"No time passed while we were in 8D?" I asked.

"Fascinating," Toran murmured.

"I'm getting the impression that you have quite the story

to tell," Kess chimed in over the comm.

"Oh, you have no idea." I let out a long breath.

"You can tell us on the way back," Richards said. "We'll open the cargo doors for you."

"Anything we say will have to be over the comms," Toran replied. "We came into contact with some of the Darkness. Best to follow contamination protocols just in case."

I slumped in my seat. "Stars, that's right."

"Does that mean we're heading back to the *Evangiel*?" Richards asked.

"Yes, we have what we need," Kaiden confirmed. "Trust me, we don't want to be around here."

"Roger that," the captain said.

Kess sighed. "I'm just bummed I didn't get to see your magic."

I chuckled to myself. "It's been a crazy day."

We flew the remaining distance to the *Sanctum* and docked in the belly of the ship. As soon as the docking clamps were in place, I felt the telltale rumble of engines as the *Sanctum* accelerated toward the rendezvous point with the *Evangiel*.

"Thanks, guys. Talk to you in a few," Kaiden said into the comm then muted the channel. He turned to us. "What are we going to tell everyone?"

"That's a very good question," Toran replied.

We moved from the shuttle's small bridge to the compact common room amidships and took seats in the dining table booth.

"We need to be honest about what we experienced," I said as soon as we were situated, "though I expect a good deal of skepticism."

"Agreed." Kaiden nodded next to me. "Between the

hyperdimensional planes and time passage, a lot will come as a shock."

"They have no reason to doubt our word," Toran said.

"Yeah, but believing what we say and knowing what to do with that information are two different things," Maris pointed out. "Like, no matter what we say, telling them about Hoofy is going to raise eyebrows."

"You need not tell them about me unless you want to," the unicorn said in our minds.

"I suggest we keep to the most critical information about the Saps and their capabilities and play the rest by ear," Toran stated.

"Yeah, that works," I agreed. "The other major thing is regarding our artifacts."

Toran nodded. "They have become much more important than I initially realized."

"I'm not sure what we *can* say about them, other than they seem to be able to enable the sphere to act as an interface to higher planes," Kaiden said.

"But it's not just our original three," Maris pointed out. "My new shield seems to have an extra bit of fancy, too." She admired it. "And I don't just mean the bling."

"It does indeed hold great power," Hoofy confirmed.

Maris beamed with pride about her new possession. "I've always had exceptional taste."

"It is very 'you', no doubt. But, why didn't the Saps take the shield?" Kaiden asked. "If it's so powerful, why leave it down there in the cavern when the crystals shattered?"

"I think we've been very lucky," I said.

"That doesn't seem like a matter of luck, Elle," Toran countered.

"No, I mean, the Saps have huge egos, right?" I went on.

"Well, a shield like that is defensive, which suggests the user has a vulnerability. I wouldn't put it past them to have looked at it and decided anyone carrying a shield must be weak, and therefore dismissed it. After all, what could possibly harm an 'Overlord'?"

Kaiden chuckled. "That's just ridiculous enough to be true."

"More likely, they can't wield the items," Toran pointed out. "After all, they are harmed when we touch them."

"True," I agreed. "In that case, we don't have to worry about them being stolen."

Toran shook his head. "Not necessarily. The items still hold great power, and the aliens—er, Saps—seem driven to tap into the crystalline network using any means necessary. I don't think we can assume our safety."

"And, are some items more valuable than others?" Maris mused.

Kaiden was silent for several seconds. "Okay, random thought: could the disparities we first experienced in our perception have something to do with our artifacts being at different dimensional levels?"

"Could be." Maris nodded. "Each of us, aside from Toran, did seem to see the cosmic jellyclouds—"

"Nimbuses," I corrected.

"—in slightly different ways," Maris continued without missing a beat.

"What if all of those visions were valid, just perceiving the creature on different planes?" Kaiden posited.

"But we were all in the same plane," I countered. "How could we not see a being native to it?"

Toran took on a pensive expression. "Just because we were in the same environment, that doesn't mean we'd be able to perceive everything in the same way—the more layers are added, the more complex the environment for our minds to grasp. Perhaps the artifacts assist with that mental evaluation in some way." He paused in thought. "You know, there really might be something to that, Kaiden. Just because we all have 'artifacts', that doesn't mean they're all attuned to the same dimension. Maybe spending time with each of them has made us particularly sensitive to perceiving the plane where they're based."

I considered it. "Could we figure out the dimensional order of the artifacts based on what attributes we saw of the nimbuses?"

"Yes, this hypothesis would suggest that perception would be layered—if part of the creature was in one plane, those with a higher plane of perception would see the parts on their plane and everything lower," Toran confirmed.

"Sorry, Toran, but you seem to have drawn the short stick for the artifact lottery," Kaiden said with a sympathetic smile.

"I already figured as much," he replied. "Now, what did each of you see?"

The three of us relayed the traits of the nimbuses we'd observed. Kaiden clearly had a less-formed vision than Maris and mine—little more than amorphous blobs that shot lightning. After some back and forth, I determined that Maris and I had actually seen the same cloud-like creatures, though the terminology we'd used initially was different.

"Does that mean our artifacts would be on the same level?" I questioned.

Toran shook his head. "No, Maris was only able to fight back against them, but your sword instantly destroyed them, Elle. That would suggest your sword exists on a higher plane than we were in at the time, and Maris' shield is native to their plane."

"I guess that's how it was able to cut through the window, too," I realized.

"Yes. That really does explain a lot."

Kaiden's brow knit with concentration. "Okay, so to summarize: we're normally living in 3D, traveling through time, 4D. The Overlords are 6D with the ability to manipulate 5D, thought. Toran's gauntlets are 6D, my circlet is 7D, Maris' shield is 8D, and Elle's sword is... 9D?"

I laughed. "I don't think all of that should be stated in a single sentence unless you want someone's head to explode."

Maris spread her hands. "All I got out of that is that we have a lot of stuff that's on the same or higher level as the baddies, and that means we can take them out."

Kaiden smiled. "I like that summary much better."

We spent the remaining hours of the voyage relaxing as best we could, thankful to be temporarily out of harm's way. Hoofy remained quiet and invisible, though I could sense his presence at the back of my mind, listening with fascination to our banter. I remained on edge as the time passed, still concerned that the Saps were somehow watching us.

It wasn't until we were within visual range of the *Evangiel* that I finally started to relax. "I'm looking forward to a hot shower and some sleep."

Maris glanced between Kaiden and me. "Yeah, I'm sure that's the *only* thing."

I flushed in spite of myself, hoping the low lighting in the shuttle hid it. I really *hadn't* been thinking in those terms, but snuggles did sound amazing after the day we'd had.

Kaiden brushed his foot against mine under the table. "I'm sure we could all use some downtime," he deflected on my behalf.

"Don't get too comfortable," Toran warned. "We still have

quite the debrief to go through."

I sighed. "Oh, can't wait…"

After docking and completing the standard decontamination procedure, we headed for Central Command.

"Now I *really* hate leaving my sword behind," I whispered to Kaiden as we exited the hangar.

"I know, I was just thinking the same thing. But, if we can't trust Tami, we have bigger issues to worry about—she could kill us in a hundred different ways every time we step onto one of her shuttles."

"Good point."

Maris seemed miffed. "I wanted to show off my new shield."

"You'll get the chance soon enough," Toran assured her.

When we reached Central Command, we were immediately buzzed inside to find Commander Colren waiting for us. He looked us over expectantly. "Well, what did you learn?"

I took a deep breath. "Boy, do we have a story for you."

13

COLREN STARED AT us from the other side of the conference table, dumbstruck. "That isn't how I expected this recon mission to go."

"We didn't either, but there you have it," Kaiden replied. "The question now is… well, everything."

The commander steepled his fingers. "I wish there had been a clearer indication about what the 'Saps'—as you now call them—are after."

"Yeah, that's been a sticking point for us, too," Toran admitted. "It seems to have something to do with the properties of the crystalline network, which appears to function on a higher dimensional plane than we 'visited', if you will."

"Do the scientific models point to anything?" Colren questioned. "I know you've been in contact with the Hegemony's research team."

Toran shook his head. "We hadn't discussed anything beyond the idea that the aliens might actually be hyperdimensional beings. Guess that's been confirmed."

Colren gave a disbelieving chuckle. "I still can't wrap my head around what that means—the notion of a sixth-dimensional being existing above time."

"I assure you, it's even *more* disorienting to spend the better part of a day walking around somewhere only to discover that no apparent time has passed in your home dimension," I said.

He leaned back in his chair. "Yes, I could see that."

"So, Commander, we're at a bit of an impasse here," Kaiden said in the intervening silence. "We know *where* the aliens are—sort of—but the new knowledge about their hyperdimensional position means the previous attack plan won't work."

Toran folded his hands on the tabletop. "Yes. Unfortunately, the spatial disruptor is only a 5D weapon, and the Saps are 6D."

"What does that mean for the anomaly site we attacked?" Colren asked.

"It's still too damaged to traverse—this new information doesn't change that," Toran explained. "Think of it like paralyses due to scar tissue—the limb is still there, but it doesn't have feeling any longer, so it can't be used."

That analogy hit a little too close to home for me, and my right hand instinctively went to my left shoulder, remembering the injury that had shaped much of my outlook on life, before we were transformed.

"Meaning, we're still protected from an attack at that location," the commander determined.

"Yes, but that may now be one of the *only* places," Toran continued. "Our glimpse of the hyperdimensional plane on which the Saps reside showed that they have a densely populated world and a substantial fleet. I think the only reason they haven't sent more ships to our planets already is because there are only a few 'access points' for transitioning from 6D to our spacetime reality.

"Based on what we've observed, and learned—" he omitted Hoofy's presence, "—there are specific places that allow interaction across the different planes. The viewing crystals are one such trans-dimensional access point, in addition to their other functions. The local-reset crystals offer more limited points of access, and it seems like there's at least one main control crystal on each planet, which provides an intermediate degree of functionality; I think that's how the Darkness first spread, entering the main crystal and then spreading through the rest of the planet's network. But, there aren't many of these points in open space, which makes it difficult to move a fleet. Either the Saps will find another location to use as a jump point to bring their fleet into our spacetime, or they'll take a land-based approach through the crystals on each planet they want to conquer."

I thought back to the infection of my own world and how I'd seen the Darkness in the canyon's crystal but not in my town square. The planet's control crystal must have been in another city—maybe the planet's capital—and that's what prompted the order for a planetary reset.

"To determine which option they'll pursue—continue trying to find a solution for their fleet, or revert to a land-based assault—we need to know what their goal is," Colren mused. "As insightful as this information is, it doesn't actually help us."

I hated to admit it, but he was right. We'd learned more about the nature of our enemy, yet we still had no large-scale way to effectively fight back or even know where to head them off, since we had no idea where they were going. I couldn't keep a frustrating groan from slipping out. "You'd think learning the secret nature of the universe would answer a lot more questions."

"Yeah, if only we knew more about the dimensional planes above the Saps, maybe there's something that could help us there," Kaiden mused.

"There is someone who might," Toran said.

For a moment, I thought he was about to reveal Hoofy. However, Colren nodded. "Bounce some ideas off her. Something may stick."

"Excuse me." Toran rushed out of the conference room through the bridge.

"Sorry, did I miss something?" I asked.

"One of the Hegemony scientists Toran has been working with," Colren explained. "She has the kind of brilliance you can't train—incredible at making connections and bringing grounding to the extraordinary."

"In other words, exactly what's needed right now," Kaiden said.

The commander smiled. "I think we could all use some answers."

"Definitely." I recalled Toran mentioning a scientist acquaintance the other day, and I was happy to get a trusted outside perspective on our recent experience.

"Well, while Toran gets more into the science and engineering, can you offer any more insights into the tech you observed during your vision of the Saps' society?" Colren asked.

"*Something isn't right,*" Hoofy said suddenly in my mind. Based on how Kaiden and Maris tensed, I suspected he'd spoken to them, too.

"It was a lot to take in," I said, hoping the commander might reveal more of his intentions before I said anything too specific.

"Do you get any sense of their manufacturing capabilities, or their power source?" Colren pressed.

"He is asking on behalf of his superiors," Hoofy said. *"They want the core."*

I swallowed, not sure if I should listen to the commander or our new hyperdimensional companion. Though Colren had once left me to die, it was under unavoidable understandable circumstances; Hoofy, on the other hand, I didn't know at all. Yes, he'd led us through the 8D maze to the exit point, but could we trust him implicitly?

While I was still trying to figure out what to tell Colren, Kaiden brushed his foot against mine under the table, a signal I'd noticed him use over the past week when he saw me struggling to answer a relationship question and he was about to jump in to field it.

"Their structures all look organically grown," Kaiden said. "Couldn't say any more at this point with certainty."

The commander nodded. "Very well. I know that wasn't the focus of your investigation."

"Maybe we can take some time to sort through what we saw and talk more tomorrow," Kaiden suggested.

"Yes, of course, you must be exhausted." Colren rose, and we followed his example. "Thank you, as always, for your efforts."

I forced a smile. "Here to help."

Colren adjourned the meeting, and I led Maris and Kaiden to a private section of corridor outside Central Command.

"What was that about? Do you think the Hegemony is after the alien tech?" I asked after checking that no one was around.

Kaiden shook his head. "Why *wouldn't* they be? I can't believe I didn't think about that before."

"What do you mean?" questioned Maris.

"We've come across a race that's potentially figured out how to tap into the crystal control interface and use the crystalline network's innate properties to rearrange matter. Think about how valuable that kind of control would be to the Hegemony—you could remake an entire planet in a very short time, or maybe even scale the tech down to manufacture anything you could imagine."

I gaped at him. "Stars, you're right."

"The Hegemony is fairly stable and united at the moment," Kaiden continued. "But what if knowledge about this tech got out? Use it for the military, and private industry would get upset. Give everyone access and risk it falling into the hands of someone who'd use it to hurt others… It's a total gamechanger. Introducing this kind of tech is what sparks civil wars."

"Makes you wonder what really happened on Crystallis," I murmured.

Kaiden scoffed. "It wouldn't surprise me in the least if the civilization took out itself and the Saps had little to do with it."

Maris crossed her arms. "That's a disturbing concept."

I lowered my voice to a whisper. "Look, I think I trust Colren, but the people he reports to have shown some *really* bad judgment. We should be careful what we say."

"Agreed," Kaiden whispered back, and Maris nodded.

"Should we go see what Toran is up to?" I asked, returning to a normal volume.

"May as well. I'm curious what an outsider has to say about all this," Kaiden said.

We took the lift to the level that house our lounge and living quarters.

As we neared the door, Kaiden gently tugged my arm, holding me back. "Go ahead, we'll be right there," he said to Maris.

She raised an eyebrow and pursed her lips then sauntered into the lounge. The door closed behind her.

I gave Kaiden a questioning look. "Why did—" I'd barely gotten the words out before he leaned me against the wall, kissing me deeply. I happily relaxed into his arms, releasing my tension from our crazy day.

"I've been wanting to do that for hours," he murmured as we eventually parted.

"Same." I smiled up at him, still wanting more.

The doors to the lounge hissed open down the hall, and Kaiden hastily took a step back from me.

"Cool it, lovebirds," Maris said with a smirk as she poked her head out of the room. "The biology lesson can wait—Toran is all amped up to give us some schooling in quantum physics." She disappeared back inside.

Kaiden shook his head, holding in a snicker. "Wow, how long do you think she's been waiting to use that line?"

"Probably days," I replied.

Still chuckling, he gave me another kiss. "To be continued."

We followed Maris inside to find Toran leaning over the touch-surface table. A holoconference was in progress with a woman who appeared to be in her late-forties, graying hair pulled into a messy bun.

"Elle, Kaiden, this is Lisa Manswell," Toran introduced. "She'll be modest about it, but she's the Hegemony's top scientific mind when it comes to theoretical physics."

Lisa brushed off the compliment with a wave of her hand. "I muddle through. I must admit, Toran's account of your recent experience has introduced some interesting notions."

"Yes, I believe you were just about to offer an explanation for what we've been experiencing," Toran said. "I figured you'd all want to be here for that."

"Absolutely. So, what are we dealing with?" I asked.

"Dimensionally ubiquitous, zepto-elemental singularities," Lisa replied.

Kaiden raised an eyebrow. "Come again?"

"There was never any direct evidence of these singularities, but your observations are in line with what had been considered hypothetical models on the scientific fringe," the scientist explained. "They appear to be some kind of sub-fermion singularity with a quantum entanglement link spanning the dimensional planes."

I blinked at her. "Zepto-what?"

"Dimensionally ubiquitous, zepto-elemental singularities," the scientist repeated.

"Nope, that name is never going to work," I stated. "D-U-Z-E-S… How about we call them 'Duzies'?"

Toran sighed. "Elle—"

Lisa's brow knit. "That's so…"

I smiled. "A little ridiculous, I know, but it's short and memorable."

After a moment, Lisa smiled back. "You know, I actually kind of like it."

Toran flushed, casting the scientist a pleading look she seemed keen to ignore.

Kaiden smirked. "So, Toran, what were you saying about the Duzies?"

"I'm not going to call them…" Toran took a deep breath. "Anyway, these elemental singularities can explain everything we've experienced with our abilities. Theoretically, they are the building blocks of everything in our physical reality, extending into the hyperdimensional planes we recently visited. If we've been granted some sort of control-level access to those singularities, that might explain how we can now redirect the matter and energy around us into what appear to be magical effects."

"Did that happen when we were re-formed with the bioprinter?" I asked.

"Duzies almost certainly have something to do with the process, but I expect there's more at play than that alone," Lisa replied.

"Maybe something to do with our artifacts?" Kaiden suggested.

"Perhaps. The artifacts seem to be linked with the Duzies, maybe are even saturated by them," Lisa continued. "I couldn't tell you for sure without getting them into my lab, but I get the impression you won't be heading back to the Capital anytime soon."

"No, we won't, but we *can* say for certain that the artifacts exhibit strange properties," Toran said.

The scientist nodded. "I have no doubt about that. In lieu of the artifacts being in my lab for detailed analysis, I'll review the scans of them taken during the decontamination procedure and also look over your medical records with the biologists on our team. We may yet be able to get you more detailed answers about the mechanism behind your abilities."

"I really don't care so long as they work," I said.

For practical purposes, yes," Kaiden said, "but understanding *how* our abilities function might yield more information about the crystalline network itself—or what the aliens seek to control."

"We don't yet know what is above the eighth-dimensional plane we experienced," Toran said.

"Well, there are three options that we know about," Lisa replied.

I came to attention. "You know what's there?"

"In theoretical models, anyway. Before today, we never had any firsthand accounts of anything beyond 6D," she said. "The science suggests that 9D, which the sword seems to be linked to, is the crystalline network itself, 10D is consciousness—the part of ourselves that resyncs after a reset— and the eleventh dimension is the domain of the barely-understood dimensionally ubiquitous, zepto-elemental singularities. Duzies really are a *doozy*." She grinned.

I laughed. "I was waiting for someone to do it. Well done."

She bowed her head. "Delivering bad science puns is my second job."

While we were joking, Maris stood with her eyes wide. "Consciousness is *above* the crystalline network storage?"

Lisa composed herself. "It's important to distinguish between 'thought' and 'memory'," she explained. "Our memories are the organic constructs, which are recreated through neural pathways during the reset process. It's our consciousness—our internal self-awareness and volition—which utilizes our memories and creates our thoughts, bringing in the near-term feelings and recollections from the time after a reset point is established. Memories, consciousness, thoughts—all of those components make us ourselves."

"What about the universal resets?" Kaiden asked.

Toran nodded. "I'd pieced together some of it before, but I didn't have the dimensional map to complete the picture until now. See, all of our physical traits and memories are stored in 9D via the crystalline network backups. Restoring that much information during a universal-scale reset must eat up almost all of the available 'bandwidth' in the crystals—so there's only enough data for our 10D consciousness to recall memories for various past moments in time. Therefore, memories of previous-futures, which could be innumerable and incredibly complex, are lost or lose focus. Localized resets, by contrast, don't put nearly the same amount of strain on the crystalline network, so we are able to get an accurate 'download' of our memories from previous-futures, as well. That's why, after the universal reset, we could sense something was missing but couldn't grasp it. I think it was only due to our proximity to the locus of the reset event that our team was able to remember; the network dedicated a little extra bandwidth to enable a partial download of our previous-future memories since we initiated the reset."

"This reset thing is a whole lot more complicated than I realized," I said.

"Makes you appreciate what a thin line we walk to keep society from falling apart, huh?" Kaiden replied.

I shook my head. "Yeah, no wonder they minimize resets on the Capital."

"Oh, stars, yes!" Lisa said. "It's a wonder there aren't more mishaps. I mean, I have no recollection whatsoever about the universal reset. I wouldn't even believe it, except the rest of data Toran has presented lines up."

"Not to mention the potential for tampering," Toran said.

Lisa nodded gravely. "That's true. We've already seen what happens when the reset interface is highjacked. The aliens essentially hacked the crystalline network to modify planets however they saw fit. At least, that's our working hypothesis."

"Speaking of them," I began, leaning forward, "if the matter-rearranging is done through these 11D Duzies—which I'm guessing are completely invisible, then how can we see the dark cloud coming from the alien ships that dissolves anything in its path?"

Lisa nodded. "That's not the same. My guess is that the

dark cloud might be some sort of 6D nanotech."

"And how are we supposed to disable it so we don't instantly die?" Kaiden asked.

"Easiest thing would be to work from a higher dimensional plane. Couldn't touch you that way," she stated.

"Ah, yes, of course." I caught myself and I sighed. "And there it is. My judgment for what constitutes a reasonable answer is officially broken."

14

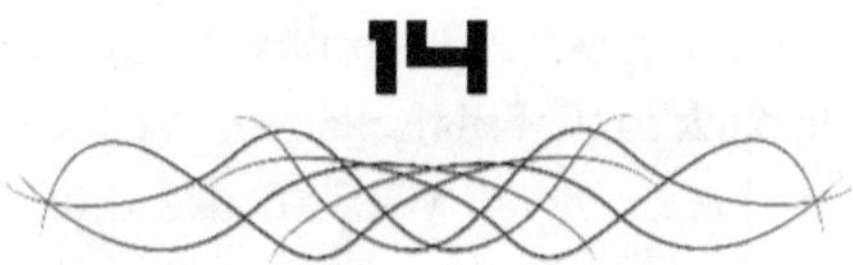

"I HAVE NO idea what to do," I admitted to my friends as soon as we ended the holoconference with Lisa.

"The problem is we don't have enough information." Toran propped his elbows on the tabletop and leaned forward.

"How are we supposed to *get* information?" Kaiden asked. "We can't even see the Saps from our normal reality."

"Like Lisa said, we just need to be on a higher plane," Maris replied. "Don't you see? We can travel through 7D and pop in at the correct corresponding places in 6D. Aaand, we happen to have a guide who's native to 7D and can show us the ropes."

As much as I appreciated Hoofy's willingness to help, I wasn't confident we should place so much faith in our new friend. Aside from the fact that he was, well, a unicorn—a creature I'd been taught growing up wasn't real—Hoofy had gotten himself lost and trapped. I figured it warranted a bit of skepticism when it came to following a guide with that kind of track record.

Unfortunately, Hoofy's telepathy was a step faster than my brain's connection to my mouth. *"I would gladly guide you."*

"That's a generous offer, but is it smart for us to go back to that place, knowing what we know now?" Kaiden asked, to my relief.

"Yeah, we were lucky to get out of there the first time," I said. "The moment the Saps start looking for us, we'll be at a huge disadvantage."

Kaiden nodded. "Lots of exposure, both while we're landing and wandering around."

Maris rolled her eyes. "No, don't you see? We don't have to take a shuttle back to that planet at all. We have the viewing-sphere here on the *Evangiel.* We can use that as our access point."

Toran's eyebrows drew together in thought. "That *would* be an interesting approach. Since distance and time don't follow the same rules we're used to in this plane, I suppose it might actually be feasible for us to get there from here."

I eyed him skeptically. "Are you talking about *walking* back to that planet?"

"In 7D," Maris interjected.

"Yeah, but we're more than a four-hour ship ride from there in normal space," I objected. "Even with the differences in transit, is that reasonable?"

"Not to mention, I thought when we perceived the higher planes, we were also *here*—we don't actually 'go' anywhere," Kaiden said.

"That's not exactly true," Toran replied. "When we access the higher dimensions, we also theoretically gain the ability to act upon and take shortcuts across the lower planes. As such, I believe we can alter the degree to which we are seen in the lower planes, in the same manner we can't see Hoofy in our spacetime unless he wants to be seen."

Maris grinned. "I knew you'd come around to the nickname."

"I am simply using it as a matter of convenience," Toran replied. "That's hardly the issue at present."

I raised an eyebrow. "Yeah, more importantly, you're still glossing over the part where we walk across the star system in 7D."

Maris sighed. "That's *not* what I said."

Kaiden pursed his lips. "Now that I think about it, if we did a fly-by…"

I didn't like the sound of that. "Please tell me you don't mean what I think you mean."

"If you think I meant have the *Evangiel* swing by the planet at near orbit distance to drop us off, then yes."

"That's a terrible idea," I said. "We'll be stranded until they can loop around to grab us."

"No, remember, the time passage isn't the same in higher dimensions," Maris said. "When we transitioned before, it was like no time had passed at all in this plane."

"So, you're saying the *Evangiel* will fly in close, we use the viewing-sphere to transition to 7D, do our thing, get back to the viewing-sphere, all before the *Evangiel* leaves range?" I asked.

Maris nodded. "Easy."

"No, *not* easy. It's nuts." That was without even taking into consideration the part of Hoofy needing to successfully navigate for us.

"It actually might work," Toran said.

I stared at him. "You *can't* be serious." I was used to being the one to come up with crazy ideas. What did it mean that I was now the most rational person sitting in the room? Either I was missing something, or fear and desperation had caused my teammates to lose their minds.

"We do have unique skills, Elle," Kaiden said. "Shouldn't we use those to our advantage?"

"Yes, but..." I trailed off, not knowing what I could say that would make a compelling argument against the insane plan they were hatching. Truth be told, the more I thought about it, the more brilliant it was starting to sound.

We knew our fleet was no match for the Saps, and the four of us couldn't take on an entire civilization using our weapons. To win the fight, we needed to think outside the box—and operating from a different dimensional plane was *definitely* unconventional. If we could learn about the right weakness and make a targeted strike from a higher plane, no Hegemony ships or soldiers would come to harm and we'd be relatively safe ourselves.

"All right," I continued after a pause. "Maybe you *are* on to something."

Maris smirked. "Told you."

I took a deep breath. "One big concern does come to mind—"

"Only one?" Kaiden interjected with a smile.

I smiled back. "Just trying to keep things reasonable. But, Toran, didn't you say we can *theoretically* alter our presence? I mean, the Saps are native to 6D. Even if we can access 8D or above, does that really give us the ability to make it so they don't know we're there?"

"You have done this before, when you were in the dimension where we met," Hoofy said in our minds. *"I believe this strategy is your best chance."*

"That's all the confirmation I need," Maris said.

I took a slow breath. "I think we should take some time to process all of this and get some rest. I don't trust myself to make smart decisions right now."

"Yeah, I know what you mean," Kaiden agreed. "Why don't we meet up in... six hours?"

"Very well." Toran inclined his head.

Maris tossed her hands in the air. "Fine. But I think we should do something before the Saps decide to send another ship in our direction."

"I'm certain they would have done that already if they had a means of engaging us at this location on our plane," Kaiden said.

"Still, I'll advise Colren to keep the ship in motion," Toran murmured. "Anything we can do to make ourselves a more difficult target."

"No argument here." I headed for the door.

"See you in a few," Kaiden said to the others, following me.

I took a brisk pace down the corridor to my quarters with Kaiden close behind. I palmed open the door, and he slipped inside behind me before the others had emerged from the lounge.

"Inviting yourself over, I see." I smiled up at him.

"I believe it was an unspoken invitation."

"Perhaps." I placed a hand on his chest. "All sense of logic and reason has gone out the window, hasn't it?"

He laughed. "Yeah, I can't believe that plan is actually sounding like a good idea."

"I know, right? I thought all of you had lost it, but then…"

Kaiden placed his hands gently on my upper arms. "This is way too much for any one of us to comprehend on our own. I don't think we have a choice other than to trust our instincts."

"And your gut says we should follow a unicorn through a higher dimensional plane to somehow trap some hyperdimensional baddies bent on galactic domination?"

"I was actually thinking about how we skipped dinner, but maybe I was misinterpreting the sensation."

I rolled my eyes and shuffled toward the bed, drawing him with me. "You're impossible."

"You love my humor. I can tell."

That wasn't the only thing I liked about him. The more time we spent together and more we experienced, I found myself increasingly drawn to him. More than lust and attraction, there was a level of familiar comfort, similar to what I'd shared with my longtime friends. I felt safe with him, like the dangers in rest of the universe didn't matter so long as he was nearby.

As he traced his fingers down the side of my arm, I wanted to tell him those things. Except, I couldn't form the words. I wanted to show him.

"Now, where were we before?" I cupped the side of his face in my hand and kissed him.

He eagerly kissed me back.

We lay back on my bed, and I allowed myself to forget about our mission. Our higher dimensional selves may have no use for our corporeal bodies, but I certainly liked how he made mine feel.

There was no denying the ache of desire, yet I held back. Knowing a universal reset was coming, I hated to think that I might forget our time together. We'd already shared so many firsts, but such a big one for my lifetime… I wasn't ready. Not yet.

I inched back from him, not wanting to be too much of a tease.

Kaiden sighed when he sensed me pulled away. "Yeah, I know."

"I'm sorry, I—"

"Elle," he brushed my hair from my eyes, "there's nothing to apologize for."

Stars, he was so understanding it made me want him even more. "It's not that I don't want to."

"We agreed to wait, so we'll wait."

"And you're okay with that?"

He chuckled. "I think you're trying to entrap me."

"No."

"Come on, you know there's no good answer to that question."

I propped an arm under my head as I pivoted to face him. "I warned you I'm terrible at this relationship stuff."

He placed a hand on my thigh, biting his lower lip as he avoided my direct gaze. "This is always the tricky part, when the emotional and physical aren't quite in sync." He finally looked me in the eyes. "I like you a lot, Elle—from your personality and wit…" his gaze drifted downward, "…to you being absolutely stunning. And, frankly, I'd say we shouldn't be contemplating a relationship if there wasn't mutual desire—which is obviously not an issue. But the difference between straight-up lust and the makings of a proper partnership is that I know being fully with you will be worth the wait, however long that is."

My shipsuit seemed impossibly tight and warm. "I think I need a cold shower."

Kaiden laughed. "I really didn't mean that as a turn-on."

"Respecting boundaries is sexy. Don't you ever forget it."

He smiled. "I'll always strive to respect you."

I shook my head, grinned. "Now I think you're using my words against me to get yourself laid right now."

"Hey, you opened the door." He smirked, but then promptly sat up. "Seriously, though, we don't need to rush into anything. We'll know when the time is right."

I nodded and sat up next to him. "Like when the fate of the universe isn't hanging over our heads."

"I dunno… that seems like exactly the *right* time."

"Fair point."

"But not tonight." He patted my knee. "I can't make a speech about self-control and then cave."

"You're so principled."

"Well, stubborn, at least."

I smiled. "I appreciate your dedication to proving a point."

"The pleasure of your company does make it worthwhile."

"Such a charmer when you want to be." I shook my head.

"Only for you." His hand found mine.

I swirled my fingertips around his open palm. "I can't help but wonder what things are going to be like when this is over."

"What part?"

"What our lives will look like afterward, once we've won."

Kaiden didn't reply at first.

"What are you thinking about?" I prompted.

"I..." He sighed. "All right, I'll just come out and say it. I know we've been focusing on the Saps and this seemingly impossible task that was placed before us, but I never thought this experience would also mean meeting you. And even when the battles are over, I don't want that to mean I never see you again."

I scooted closer to him. "I don't, either."

"But with a universal reset as part of the endgame..."

"We remembered the other previous-futures eventually. I have to believe we will again."

He didn't seem entirely assured, but he nodded. "Once we do, I have no idea how it'll work—literally living on different planets."

"Yeah." I hadn't wanted to confront that reality, but it had crept into the back of my mind in the quiet moments over the past several days. I knew that us being together meant that one of us would need to give up our home. Since Kaiden was only on an internship, my initial reaction had been that he should come to me. However, thinking through it, I realized that I no longer felt the ties to Erusan I did before this experience. The time away had changed me, and I wasn't sure I *wanted* to go back.

"I guess that's jumping ahead a bit much, isn't it?"

I laced my fingers through his. "To the contrary, it's nice to know we're on the same page."

He brightened. "Okay, good."

I leaned over and kissed him, slow and deep. "We should probably get some sleep."

Kaiden stood up. "As much as I'd like to stay, I don't think sharing a bed would be particularly restful for either of us at the moment."

"On this occasion, I have to agree." I rose to see him out.

"I'll see you soon." He gave me a light parting kiss.

My heart fluttered as I showed him out the door. Despite the war, something good had come out of the recent drama, and I intended to hold onto my new future.

15

FIVE HOURS IN bed never felt like a proper night's rest. As I entered the lounge, I tried to shake off the remaining grogginess that my shower hadn't cured.

I hadn't been able to get to sleep straight away after my conversation with Kaiden. My mind had kept drifting back to Erusan and my uncertain life path—knowing that I wanted Kaiden to be a part of it but being overwhelmed by thoughts of the logistics. I'd reprimanded myself for losing focus on the mission, in the way I'd promised myself I wouldn't, which had then only stressed me out more. Ultimately, I'd thought through the key events that had happened since I'd been extracted from my world, and I reminded myself that there didn't need to be a clear distinction between my life before and my present. Everything we were doing was to fight for our *future*, and I shouldn't feel guilty about looking forward to what was to come after the final battles. If anything, that made me more committed.

"Good morning!" Maris greeted in far too cheery a voice for the hour.

I massaged my temples. "I don't suppose I could get one of those pick-me-ups of yours?"

"Of course." She smiled.

A shimmering, green wave washed over me, as I felt instantly energized as it passed. Unfortunately, the effects of the spells didn't last for as long as real rest, but it was marvelous at first. By the time it started to fade, I hoped I wouldn't remember I'd been so tired in the first place.

"You're getting good at these spells," I told her.

She beamed. "Not all that different from bartending in some ways—just tonics of a more magical variety."

"I can tell you must have been great at your job. How did you get into that line of work, anyway?"

Her smile faded. "Fairly easy money for someone with not a lot of other prospects."

I tilted my head. "What do you mean?"

She hesitated. "I was on my own since I was pretty young. My mom remarried this asshole when I was fourteen, and after three years I was sick of wondering if that would be the day he'd do more than just look at me." She took an unsteady breath. "So, I left at seventeen. I had to get used to taking care of myself fast. Realized I was good at putting on a smile, and looks helped. I'm not proud of using those assets, but I did what I needed to, you know? At least waitressing and bartending were on my terms, not *him* undressing me with his eyes every time I walked in the room."

My chest constricted. "Sorry, Maris. That sounds awful."

She shrugged it off, but I could see the distress was still deep inside. Living in that kind of environment changed a person in an enduring way. "A lot of people deal with much worse. I was able to get out before it got bad, and many aren't that fortunate."

I looked down. "Guess I had it pretty easy."

"You were hurt when you were young, right? Something with your shoulder?"

"Yeah, but that's not remotely the same thing," I replied, feeling a little ashamed that she'd draw any parallel between our experiences. "That was me making my own dumb decisions and paying the price. In retrospect, I'm glad it happened because it forced me to confront the reality that everything can change in an instant and we don't always get our own personal 'do-overs' when we mess up. I treated resets like a game. That round, I lost."

Maris nodded. "In many ways, it's the mistakes and hardships that shape us more than the victories."

"For sure. I can't imagine how insufferable I would have been if I hadn't learned some humility through that experience."

"That's what's important right? The person we grow into in the end. The path along the way is always rocky and unexpected."

"Some rockier and more treacherous than others."

She smiled. "The test of character is how we deal with those challenges."

"I'm impressed with your positive outlook, Maris. I honestly had no idea you had it so rough."

"Nah, could have been a lot worse."

I raised an eyebrow and leaned forward. "You were supporting yourself at seventeen. That's not insignificant. By comparison, I'm embarrassed by how spoiled I was."

"Having a good home life isn't something to be embarrassed by," she replied. "You clearly appreciate what you had and didn't turn out all stuck-up and self-centered."

"I'm sure it helped having a therapist as a mom. Hearing

stories about what some of her patients were going through—anonymously, of course—did help keep things in perspective."

Maris looked me over. "It's more than that. You have the sort of innate confidence I admire, Elle."

I shook my head.

"No, really," she insisted. "You're the kind of person who's a natural leader—you have vision and focus, but you still think of the team and greater good. There was a time I would have said I was envious of those qualities, but considering that we were transformed into our 'ideal selves' or whatever, I know I must not need that in myself to be happy. But, it's… inspiring to have you on the team."

I smiled. "Thanks. For what it's worth, I can't imagine the Dark Sentinels without you." I paused. "I know we didn't get off to the best start."

She waved her hand dismissively. "I'm well aware I didn't make a great first impression."

"Those initial shoes you picked…"

Maris laughed. "I'll never admit there isn't always room for being fashionable, but okay… those were not a good choice. More than that, though, I didn't act like a member of the team. You tried to include me, and I resisted at every turn."

"It was a tough situation to be thrown into."

"That's no excuse. All of you faced the same thing." She took a deep breath. "I think I was just used to having to take care of myself and needing to have my guard up."

"I don't blame you."

She was silent for several seconds. "That's why I was so excited to get that shield. It's beautiful, but also powerful—a tool I could use to keep away anything that might hurt me."

I nodded with understanding. "It's not *just* a shield or an artifact. Something symbolic."

"Yeah."

I took a moment to reflect on everything she'd told me. I'd gotten the wrong impression about her. "I'm glad you opened up, Maris. I know some of that must be difficult to talk about."

She smiled weakly. "Thanks for listening."

"Always! I'm sorry for not making a better effort to be friendly earlier."

"Don't worry—that was on both sides." Maris got a wistful look in her eyes. "It's interesting which abilities we each manifested, even beyond our alignment with the disciplines. I always wished I could have a protective wall around me and to grow up faster so I could get away, and I ended up being able to cast magical shells and change time perception."

"Stars, I hadn't thought about it that way." I reflected on my own abilities in that context and realized that many of my abilities were centered around things I couldn't do because of my injury; I even wielded my sword lefthanded.

Maris held up her hands and studied them. "Maybe my desire to protect myself is what's driven me to help others. I hope I can find a way to use this healing magic."

I didn't have the heart to remind her that we would likely lose our abilities after the universal reset. "I know you will."

The lounge door hissed open and Kaiden entered, flashing a warm smile.

"Morning jolt?" Maris offered him.

He shrugged. "Sure, may as well." A green wave washed over him, and he noticeably perked up. "I don't know why we don't do this all the time."

"Because it's only special when it's a treat," Maris replied matter-of-factly.

"Yeah, I guess." Kaiden looked around. "Hey, where's Toran?"

"I was wondering the same thing," I said.

"He dropped by a few minutes ago and muttered something about 'contingency plans', then headed to Central Command," Maris replied.

I exchanged glances with Kaiden. "Should we follow him?"

Maris shook her head. "He said he'd be right back."

"All right." I plopped down at the table. "Any more thoughts on what we discussed last night?"

"I really think we should go," Maris responded, sitting down across from me. "I had a long talk with Hoofy."

"About what?" I asked.

"It started out as a discussion about our mission, but he ended up telling me more about his experience with the other planes, and about the Saps."

I raised an eyebrow. "If he knows so much, then why didn't he say anything sooner?"

Maris pursed her lips. "He wanted to make sure we wouldn't use the information for our own gain."

"How?"

She dropped her voice to a whisper, beckoning us closer. "Apparently, the Saps have some pretty interesting tech that's powerful enough the beings on higher dimensions have taken notice."

I cocked my head. "What does higher-dimensional tech look like?"

"I'm guessing it's more complicated than a toaster," Kaiden replied.

Maris groaned. "This isn't a joke. It's not just the tech itself but how they use it. It sounds like there's some kind of energy grid."

"Like, the crystalline network?" I asked.

"No, Hoofy said that's in a higher plane. This is something

in 6D where they reside, but it does offer a link to the higher dimensions. The Saps themselves can't access the higher planes, but the energy grid is tied to them, and it will be a threat if it's left unchecked."

My brow knit. "How would that even—"

"Our sense of place and time is different," Hoofy interjected in my mind. *"Paths and doorways aren't the same to us."*

"Neither are thoughts, apparently," I muttered.

"I am not reading your mind, Elle. That would be a violation."

I wasn't sure I believed him, but I didn't want to belabor the matter. "Okay, so there's this 6D tech. What does that have to do with us and our mission?"

"Because I know where you can access the core of their energy grid," Hoofy replied.

Kaiden's eye widened. "All right, I'm intrigued."

"Okay, yes, that sounds like a genuine lead," I admitted.

Maris nodded emphatically. "Last night, he walked me through how we get there. We can do it."

"Did you tell Toran about it already?" Kaiden asked.

"Yeah, we both got here early this morning," she said.

I looked to Kaiden. "I'm guessing he jumped the gun and messaged something to Colren, and now the Hegemony is making plans without us."

Kaiden nodded. "Remember when Colren was asking about tech before? Any hint of a real lead and I bet they'll get all starry-eyed."

"Is Toran trying to get them to back off or collaborate?" I wondered aloud.

"He cares about his family more than anything. He wouldn't make a deal that undermined our ability to get back to our loved ones—I'm sure of that," Maris said.

I crossed my arms. "Well, he better not promise *anything* without running it by us first. When we're inevitably running for our lives after doing whatever it is we end up doing, I don't want him to say, 'Wait, we need to do this thing I said we'd do'."

"Like they can actually hold us to anything," Kaiden pointed out. "Our best-case scenario is performing a universal reset. No one is going to remember what we did or didn't do, anyway."

"I will remember," Hoofy said.

"Unless you plan to file a full report with the Hegemony about whatever we do, the unicorns remembering the fine deeds of the Dark Sentinels doesn't change much for us," I shot back with more bite than I'd intended.

"Elle…" Kaiden began soothingly.

I took a deep breath. "Sorry, I just really don't like the idea of us trying to get weapons or tech from the bad guys. We all saw what they're capable of."

"The Black Cloud of Death is awful any way you look," Kaiden agreed.

The door hissed open, and I snapped my head around to see Toran taking up the doorway.

"Sorry I'm late." He entered.

"Please tell me you didn't sell our souls to the Hegemony," I said.

Toran's brow knit. "I think I missed something."

"Your impromptu meeting in Central Command," Maris supplied. "Elle and Kaiden got it in their heads that you were striking a deal with the leadership about stealing alien tech."

He leaned on the table next to me. "I've been gone for, what, fifteen minutes? That didn't take long for you to jump to some strange conclusions."

"Not *conclusions*," I backpedaled. "Just, uh… notions."

Toran looked me over. "Right. Well, I wasn't making clandestine deals, sorry to disappoint. I actually went to talk with Colren about the comm issues we've been having on many of these worlds with alien activity."

"That makes a lot more sense," I murmured.

"Any remedies?" Kaiden asked.

"I couldn't sleep last night, so I was thinking about the interface for your pendant," Toran explained. "Before, we were only looking at the connection between the crystals in terms of frequencies and signals, but now that we know the network is hyperdimensional, I started wondering if we could augment the standard hyperdimensional comms using a crystalline connection."

Kaiden came to attention. "As in, use my pendant as a booster for the comm signal?"

"Yes, that's the gist of it," Toran replied. "And the viewing-sphere is already on board, so it could be tied into the ship's long-range communication suite."

"I have to say, I'd feel a lot better about our seventh-dimensional plan if we had a way to talk to the *Evangiel*," I said.

"Yeah, absolutely," Kaiden agreed.

"Okay. Then, I guess we're proceeding with the plan to do the flyby and trek through 7D," Toran said.

I suppressed the urge to second-guess our decision. "How long will it take to get everything set up?"

"Should have it ready by the time the *Evangiel* reaches the planet," he replied.

I nodded. "Okay, let's get ready to go."

Kaiden, Maris, and I spent the next hour chatting with Hoofy about his knowledge of the Saps and what we could expect to encounter in the seventh dimension along our route.

Whenever he started discussing his home plane, I couldn't help imagining a fairytale land filled with unicorns and dragons and rainbows. I got the impression the last one was a reach, but the other two... Well, it started to get pretty clear where the ancient lore came from—maybe some travelers had somehow ascended to a higher plane or of the supposedly mythical beings had once dwelled in normal spacetime. I was looking forward to witnessing the ancient majesty firsthand.

As the time for our transition through the viewing-sphere neared, we met up with Toran in the secret chamber near Central Command. He was in the process of testing the new connection when we arrived.

"I think this will actually work," he said, admiring the product of his labors.

"Won't know for sure until we're wandering around 7D." I placed my hands on my hips.

"We'll be at the drop point in two minutes," a familiar voice said behind me from the doorway. I turned to see Colren watching us.

"If this goes as planned, it won't seem like we've gone anywhere," I said to him.

"Then it feels a little silly for me to say I'll see you soon." He cracked a smile.

"I'll never turn down well-wishes." I flashed a smile back, then approached the sphere.

"Good luck to all of you," Colren said, passing his gaze to each of us in turn. "May you find your way safely back to us."

We'd made a calculated decision to keep Hoofy's existence to ourselves, and this wasn't the moment to reveal that we'd have a hyperdimensional guide. "We'll do our best," I told him.

Maris got in position near the viewing-sphere. "It feels weird to be leaving without our gear packs."

"I dunno, this will force us to up our magic game," I said.

"That it will." Kaiden stepped up next to me. "So, how do we do this?"

"Same as last time, I suppose." I drew my sword, knowing now that it was a key aspect of making the transition to the higher planes. "Imagine what we want to happen, and hopefully it will."

"Here's hoping," Kaiden murmured.

"I'm all set with the comms," Toran announced. "We can transition whenever we come into optimal range."

Colren studied the info panel on the side wall. "Just over a minute to go."

"Okay, you know our target," I said to the rest of my team.

"I will guide you," Hoofy said in our minds, unbeknownst to Colren.

"Ready whenever you are," Maris replied aloud to both of us.

We stood poised around the viewing-sphere, waiting for Colren's acknowledgement that we were in position.

At last, he nodded to us. "It's time."

Gripping my sword, I reached out to the sphere with my free hand in unison with my teammates. "Here we go."

16

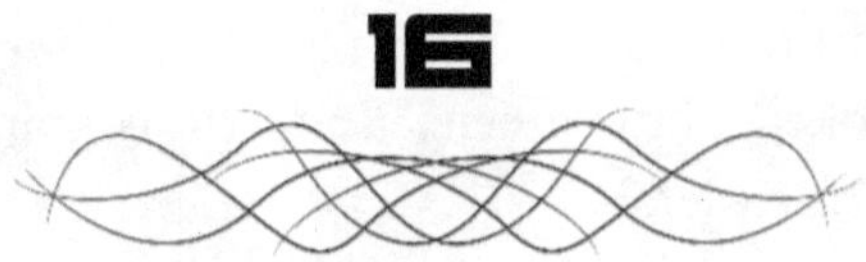

AS MY HAND made contact with the smooth crystal, a tingle ran up my arm then spread through my body. My vision fractured and unfolded into different facets. On one of the distorted planes, the majestic form of a unicorn came into focus.

"This is the path to the plane you seek," Hoofy instructed.

I willed myself toward the facet where he stood waiting for us.

Though I imagined myself passing through the facet like a doorway, I instead sensed my awareness expanding until I unfolded out into the seventh-dimensional plane. The sensation disoriented me, unhinging my sense of self. I fought to imagine a physical form—something familiar for me to latch onto. Slowly, a new perception of reality unfolded.

A bridge stretched out in front of me, seemingly suspended in midair. Soft, diffused light came from every direction, casting no shadows. The bridge itself was barely perceptible, a mesh of translucent filaments that reminded me of spider silk. Based on appearance alone, it looked like the bridge would bend underfoot, but it felt as strong as if I was standing on stone.

Toran, Kaiden, and Maris appeared around me in the same configuration in which we had been standing on the *Evangiel*, with the viewing-sphere suspended at the center of the bridge between us. Hoofy was standing in full view several meters away.

Kaiden immediately rested the end of his staff on the bridge and placed his free hand on his stomach. "That was way worse than last time."

Maris looked a little green. "You'd think going to a lower plane would be easier."

I took a steadying breath and sheathed my sword, seeing no immediate threat. "We still have a lot to learn about how these transitions work, but that can wait."

"Yes, clock's ticking." Kaiden caught himself. "Or, maybe not. I suppose we're outside the normal flow of time in our plane, aren't we?"

Maris shook her head. "I don't want to think about it. Hoofy?"

The unicorn tossed his head and snuffled. *"The energies of this plane are difficult for your kind to focus on. Now that you are here, the discomfort will dissipate."*

"Well, that's a relief," I said.

"And while, yes, we are above the flow of time here, it is not prudent to delay. Follow me." Hoofy loped across the bridge away from us.

I broke into a run, finding my movements easy and natural, just like they had in the eighth-dimensional window maze. If we found ourselves in an engagement, at least I'd know how to handle myself.

Just as I'd experienced on the hyperdimensional planes before, distance was distorted and difficult to judge. For that matter, my sensation of time passing was also impaired—like my internal clock was off. Were it not for my rhythmic strides as we ran across the ethereal bridge, I'd have had no confirmation that I'd traveled anywhere or that any time had passed.

"What is this place?" I asked to break the silence.

"This is a thoroughfare connecting the worlds," Hoofy replied. *"The closer to an inhabited place, the more possible branches and drop-out points."*

"So, we really *could* walk between planets," Kaiden murmured.

"Yes, though even here, I do not know if your kind would have the patience for the journey. To walk a path of that length leaves one alone with their thoughts, and not everyone would welcome that kind of prolonged introspection."

"Do you feel time passage?" I asked him.

"I sense time in the way you might dip your hand into the current of a stream. I can direct it and pause its progression for a time, but it will ultimately continue its advance the moment my intervention fails. Therefore, my kind focused on specific moments and experiences. If we wish to capture a moment, we make a dam in the stream. When we are ready to move on, we allow the current to take over once more."

Maris smiled. "That's really beautiful."

"A wonder to you and a simple matter of existence for my kind."

"I don't know that I'll ever get used to this perspective," Kaiden said.

"Me either." I shook my head.

"Some matters are beyond our understanding," Toran murmured in the tone he used when discussing philosophical matters. "And it's okay for us to accept them as they are."

"Works for me." I picked up my pace, realizing that we'd started to lag behind Hoofy.

Eventually, the bridge widened and then split into a multitude of pathways, each branching into new bridges. The forms had an organic quality to them, curving gently around an unseen sphere.

"Are these bending around the planet?" I asked.

"In a sense, but it is not a direct parallel to your physical reality. Think of it as being structured around the natural energies of this world."

"Where do the rest of your kind live?" I was willing to suspend my disbelief, but I was getting unnerved by everything we'd seen so far. Though the lack of distinct 'place' was disconcerting, my more pressing concern was that we hadn't seen any other creatures since we arrived. Considering that this plane was supposedly Hoofy's home, I'd expected to see other unicorns by now.

"Yeah, it does feel a little… empty around here," Kaiden agreed.

"Oh, we are far from alone," Hoofy replied. He slowed his pace and veered to the right side of the bridge. He extended his horn beyond the boundary of the pathway, and a bright point originating at its tip burned through the diffused light, parting clouds I hadn't realized were there.

The fog dispersed, revealing a breathtaking pastoral landscape framed by towering, distant peaks and a forest with trees unlike anything I'd ever seen. Their overall forms were similar to trunks and branches as I'd expect, but their makeup and material, rather than being wood and leaves, appeared to be pure energy—white-blue trunks sprouted directly from the ground and morphed into branches, which eventually discharged into the air to create an electrical canopy. The 'ground' itself was a welcoming shade of green, though like the filament bridge, it was an apparently solid material floating in near-nothingness. Short, reed-like grasses covered the field, and their bases simply merged into the ambient light.

Three figures in the distant reaches of the field raised their heads while we observed—the unmistakable silhouette of unicorns.

Hoofy stepped back. The opening remained, though the edges began slowly closing in.

"Do you know them?" Maris asked.

"All of our kind are known to each other."

"Then why aren't you going to see them? Why can't you go home after being trapped?" I pressed. Hoofy's behavior didn't make any sense, and it was unnerving me even more now that we were relying on him to guide us.

The unicorn bowed his head, taking several moments to reply. *"I was not entirely truthful before. When you freed me, I could have gone home, but my choices have made me an outsider."*

Maris' brow knit. "What do you mean?"

The opening to the serene pasture closed.

"By aligning myself with you, I am no longer welcome among my kind."

My heart dropped. "Huefneril, I'm so sorry. I had no idea." Using his full name seemed more appropriate in the moment. My gut twisted at the thought of having doubted his intentions when he'd given up his home to help us.

Maris paled. "But why? What does helping us have to do with anything?"

"The truths I led you to are revered and guarded. You are young and untested; others of my kind would deem you unworthy. But I knew from my experience of being trapped,

unable to do anything but observe, that you hold rare power and must continue in your quest at any cost. I have no shame in doing what I know to be right, even if the others do not see it that way."

"Sounds like good riddance to me," Kaiden muttered.

I shot him a warning glare.

"But being excommunicated sucks any way you look at it," he hastily added. "And we really owe you for helping us out."

"Yes, we do," I agreed. That was assuming Hoofy was telling the truth. The explanation still seemed too simple and didn't quite add up.

"*Come, we are almost to the destination.*" Hoofy resumed loping down the bridge.

I took a deep breath. "Lead the way."

We followed the filament bridge to the left, taking an offshoot which twisted the path so we wound up walking upside down from our original orientation.

"That was a first," I quipped as soon as we'd completed the transition.

"A scientist could have a field day in here studying the physical laws of this place," Kaiden said.

"More like multiple lifetimes," Toran replied.

Maris grinned. "See? Aren't you glad we came? We're getting to see something no one else in our lifetime ever may."

"That is pretty special," I had to admit.

"Wish the circumstances were a little different," Kaiden said. "You know, not a desperate attempt to avert certain doom."

"I think we've been able to upgrade from 'certain' doom to 'possible', given that we now sorta have a plan." I flashed a playful smile.

"Oh, yeah, we've totally got this."

I brushed my fingertips along his as we walked, happy to steal a moment of clandestine contact while we had the chance. Though we were in extensions of our familiar bodies, I somehow felt even more connected to him through the gentle touch.

Hoofy stopped. *"This is the place."*

"Where is it, exactly?" Kaiden asked.

"This corresponds to a central location in the Overlord's domain," Hoofy explained, reverting to his term for them, I noted. *"Transitioning here will place you at the entry—the properties of the place make it too risky to go directly inside."*

I sighed. "Sounds like we'll be walking right into the middle of a nightmare."

"The Overlords will not expect you, and that will make you difficult to see. More importantly, you have something they do not—the ability to transition out of their plane at will."

"We were wondering about that!" I said. "One of them attacked us before we met you, and we couldn't figure out why more of them didn't come to help."

"They must use these trans-dimensional gateways to make the transition, such as the viewing-spheres," Hoofy explained. *"Even then, they must be charged to make the transition and maintain their abilities. They have been seeking a more efficient way to remain on your plane."*

"Okay, that explains why we weren't overrun," Kaiden said.

"What is this 'charging'?" Toran asked.

"You will see," Hoofy assured us. *"If you run into difficulty, I will direct you back to here as I did before."*

Maris bit her lip. "If you're staying here, how do we get… down there?" She gestured vaguely at the ground.

"More of an 'over there', I think?" I made an equally vague

swirling motion with my hard around me.

"Whatever, you know what I mean." She cast an imploring gaze toward Hoofy.

"I will guide you, but I can only stay a moment. They must not know any of my kind are aiding you."

"Why not?" I asked.

"It would upset the balance."

I wanted to question the cryptic response, but Hoofy had started to fade from my vision. *"Do not use your artifacts. They will sense them."*

"Don't we need them to change planes?" I asked.

"Your higher-dimensional constructs are restricted to one plane at a time. You are now saturated with enough Duzies to transition to adjacent planes without your artifacts, but larger transitions will still require the use of your artifacts," Hoofy replied. His presence filled my mind even as he continued to fade from my vision. *"Trust, Elle. This is not a time for doubt."* I could tell the words were meant for me alone.

"I'll try," I replied telepathically, doing my best to embrace the words as truth. Reservations or not, I needed to do whatever was necessary to make it to the next phase of our mission.

Holding Hoofy's presence in my mind, I followed him as he reached toward the lower plane. The bridge and light faded around me, replaced by blackness.

Subtle shapes came into focus—a black wall rising eight meters, several three-meter-tall columns, distant towers. I could barely distinguish the shapes from the surrounding darkness. After a moment, I realized the only source of light was Hoofy's soft glow.

"You are here. I will be watching and waiting to guide you back when your task is complete." The unicorn disappeared.

"Why is it so dark?" I whispered.

Percussive clicks sounded in the darkness from a dozen meters away, and one of the forms I'd taken to be a column moved. Eyes wide, I realized that it was actually a sentry.

"Shit," Kaiden swore under his breath, backing away next to me.

I kept my voice at a low whisper, "So much for a stealth approach." I reached for my sword.

"Wait." Toran held us his hand, stilling us.

The clicks ceased and the sentry shifted its position. Then, they returned to stoic stillness.

Toran pressed behind his ear, and I hear a chirp in my own ear as the comms activated. "I don't think they can see us," he said at the barely audible level the devices were designed to facilitate. "We need to find a secure vantage point." He pointed backward away from the sentries.

I turned my attention to the matter at hand. "They can't 'see us'—meaning they can't visually see, or they haven't spotted us?"

"We'll need to test that," Toran replied. "I don't want to do that here."

"He's right. Come on." Kaiden formed a dim orb in his palm to provide just enough light for us to find a path leading away from the guards.

The ground was covered in the same fibrous, mossy substance we'd encountered on the alien ship, and I noticed several vines snaking across the dark landscape. I could just make out the path of some of the vines leading into nearby structures, which I'd first mistaken for natural hills.

"Over here." Maris motioned us toward an alcove between two of the structures. Protected on three sides, we could get our bearings without having to watch our backs too closely.

"Okay, this is *exactly* what I should have expected, but it still seems strange," I said once we were in the relative safety of the alcove.

"It really does bear a striking resemblance to the infected worlds," Toran agreed.

Kaiden nodded. "Definitely supports our original hypothesis about the Darkness being for bio-optimization."

"Guess they wanted to spread the love and share all this… greatness." I looked around with distaste at the bleak surroundings.

"Regarding the light," Kaiden went on, "I seem to recall that the creatures on the Valor world didn't have eyes—or that the eyes were black."

"Yeah, that's right," I confirmed. "The thing I saw on the ship had red eyes, though, and it *definitely* saw us."

He pursed his lips pensively. "That may have been modified. For that matter, the thing we encountered on this planet in the chamber after the labyrinth had eyes, too."

"It would make sense that they'd be blind, being in an environment like this," I said.

Toran sighed. "But not having sight, their other senses are no doubt enhanced—possibly even senses we can't fathom."

"Well, they haven't been able to track us well in the past," I pointed out. "So, at least there's that."

"But we've also never been on their home turf," Kaiden countered.

"We came here to learn about them, so we should do that rather than speculate," Maris urged.

I peeked out the alcove, finding no visible creatures nearby. "You're right. Staying in a hidey-hole won't get us anywhere. I say we try to test out our detection theories first, but not on those sentries. Let's see if we can find somewhere a little less prominent."

"Hoofy, can you hear us?" Maris asked at a slightly higher volume. "Do you know where we can find one of the Overlords on their own?" Several anxious seconds passed with no reply. "Hoofy'?" she repeated.

"I am searching," the unicorn said at last. *"There are not as many inside this facility as in the rest of the city."*

"What is this place?" I asked. "Saying 'facility' makes it sound like some sort of industrial complex."

"Yes, think of it as the outer yard of a power station. I will return."

While we waited for Hoofy's report, I took another peek outside the alcove to further orient myself. My vision had acclimated somewhat to the dark, so objects were easier to make out. It wasn't pitch black, as originally had seemed the case, but rather there were tiny pinpoints of light throughout each of the vines; they had probably been there all along on the other planets, but the brighter surroundings had hidden the detail. The pinpoints of light pulsed gently in a rippling wave.

"They're alive," I whispered to Kaiden, directing his attention toward one of the vines near us, a larger one nearly a meter in diameter.

His brow drew together. "You know, if this place is a power station, then these are likely power conduits."

"I have found what you requested," Hoofy cut in. *"Leave this hiding place, and I will lead you to an Overlord that you can study."*

Maris frowned. "I suddenly don't like this plan."

"We either proceed or go back to the *Evangiel* with nothing," I replied. "Gotta push forward."

She took a steadying breath. "I know."

17

WE CREPT FROM our hiding place and picked our way through the vines to the right, following Hoofy's telepathic directions. After what felt like several minutes, Hoofy's instructions abruptly stopped.

"I cannot follow along with you further. Any closer and they may detect our communications."

I started. "They can sense telepathy?"

"They can do much more than that."

Toran's eye widened. "Why didn't you tell us this sooner?"

"I have already interfered more than I intended. Some things you must discover on your own as part of your path. I am only here to point you in the right direction." Leave it to a unicorn to make a declarative stance on what extent it's okay to meddle with the future.

"Where do we go from here?" I asked.

"Continue in this direction. You're almost there." He paused. *"I have already spent too much time here—they can sense me. I will be waiting for you when you complete your mission."*

"Wait!" Maris cried, but I could detect that Hoofy was no longer linked with our minds.

"Come on, nothing we can do about it now." I forged ahead.

We soon encountered what Hoofy had undoubtedly intended for us to find.

"Stars…" Kaiden gulped.

This creature almost fit the embodiment of the 'Overlord' moniker. Standing three meters tall, it sat atop a bench made of dark vines. The ends of the vines were embedded in its flesh, with pulsing light emanating from each of the connection points. The resulting effect was both regal and terrifying. It had the same flexible body and smooth skin that we'd seen on others of its kind, with tendrils parted and draped along its torso where the vine-like cables connected.

"What's it doing?" Maris whispered through our comms, terror evident in her tone.

"It's almost like it's… charging," Kaiden said, his face twisted with disgusted awe. "Is that what Hoofy meant before when he was talking about them needing to 'charge' in order to transition between dimensional planes?"

Maris scrunched her nose. "But what's the power source?"

"Very curious," Toran murmured.

I evaluated the scene. "So, I'm guessing these vines are for more than decoration."

"Their purpose as some sort of energy transmission medium is different than I imagined," Toran replied. "I wouldn't have expected the creatures themselves to draw directly from it."

"Might not be *just* energy," Kaiden pointed out. "Could have an information component, or something else."

I considered the suggestion. "Maybe not all of them

interface like this. I mean, that doesn't seem very practical. What if this one is… special?"

"You think that's why Hoofy took so long to locate it?" Maris questioned.

"I'd be nice if he'd stuck around for us to *ask him*," I muttered.

"Hey, he's putting himself at risk to help us," she shot back.

"Hardly as much as the risk we're taking, ourselves." I took a deep breath. "It doesn't matter. We need to make the most of the situation."

"Right, checking their perception of us," Kaiden said.

Toran pensively examined the alien being. "Despite Hoofy's intentions, this might not be a good subject. Though it's alone, since it seems to be connected to a network, disturbing it may immediately trigger an alarm if it spots us."

"Should we wait for it to disconnect?" I asked.

"If they're telepathic, do hardwire connections even matter?" Kaiden countered.

Toran frowned. "I don't like the idea of waiting here for an indeterminate amount of time, but I also don't like the idea of sneaking into their fortress without having a sense of what we can get away with."

"Agreed," Kaiden said. "Let's give it a little bit. If it doesn't make any sign of moving, we can reevaluate."

"I can live with that," I replied. Really, I hated the idea of staying in the creepy dark place a moment longer, but I liked the notion of getting into an unwinnable engagement with the hyperdimensional aliens even less.

We settled into a fairly protected nook between some of the larger vines where we had a decent vantage on our alien subject while still retaining multiple escape paths if we got unexpected company. The strange time passage in the plane made the waiting especially bizarre, and I soon had no sense for how long we may have been there. However, I felt none of the anxiousness I normally would have under such circumstances. I was so in the moment that I was surprised when the alien being roused on its bench.

"Here we go," Kaiden whispered.

I re-centered myself. "That didn't take long."

"Honestly not sure about that," Toran replied as he shifted his position to get a better view.

"What's the plan?" Maris asked.

I looked around to be sure there were no other creatures nearby. "I think we should start out with a basic visual test," I said.

Kaiden frowned. "Meaning?"

"Walk out in the open and see if it responds. Well, creep out quietly," I replied.

"There's no doubt these beings can detect our presence," Toran stated. "Even if it can't 'see' you in a traditional sense, heat, electrical impulses, magical energy signature, or any other factors will almost certainly bring you to their attention."

"But that's kind of beside the point, isn't it?" Kaiden asked. "What we *really* need to test isn't that they notice we're here, but if they view us as a threat—or if there's a way to behave that makes them ignore us."

I nodded. "Yeah, exactly. I don't mean to literally test if it can see me, but rather if we can walk by one of these things without getting into a fight."

"And if it instantly attacks you?" Toran questioned.

"Well, then there's a whole team here to jump in." I shrugged. "I know, not ideal. But we don't have a lot to go on here."

"True. And like Hoofy said, we can return to the higher

plane if things get too intense," Maris said.

"Exactly." I took a deep breath. "My crazy idea, so I'll play bait."

"Of course you will." Kaiden sighed.

While I appreciated his desire to protect me, I wasn't about to let it distract me from learning what we needed to beat the Saps. "I'll see how close I can get without raising suspicion."

"Have fun being bait!" Kaiden's tone was playful, but I could see the worry in his eyes.

"I'll just obliterate it with my 9D sword if it gets too ornery." I smiled at him.

"Speaking of which, you might want to heed Hoofy's advice to keep it sheathed until you need it," Toran advised. "Activating our artifacts may bring… unwanted attention."

"Yes, thanks for the reminder." An item powerful enough to help us transition between planes *had* to stand out. But, we hadn't been swarmed—or even acknowledged—yet, so it would seem that the items must be in some sort of dormant state while not in active use.

Keeping the blade sheathed, I slowly stepped from our hiding place, approaching the alien creature as it slid from its perch atop the bench. Its sleek form fluidly shifted from two limbs to four as it touched down on the mossy ground. Blue sparks appeared underfoot with each step for the first dozen paces, then it was almost invisible again in the dim ambient light.

It went against my instincts to approach the enemy with no weapon drawn. I walked as slowly and silently as possible, hoping to minimize the variables in our test. There was no indication that it had noticed me during the initial approach, but when I was ten meters away, the creature suddenly halted and looked directly at me with its eyeless head.

I froze. "I think it sees me," I whispered just loud enough for my comm to pick up.

"There's no doubt it can sense your presence in one way or another," Toran replied in a calm tone. "Just try to be… nonthreatening."

"Gee, thanks." I tried to steady my racing heart. Maybe I'd watched too many monster movies as a kid, but I couldn't help thinking that the creature could sense my fear.

It glided forward, the tentacles along its torso lifting up to point toward me.

Doing my best to project an aura of calmness, I stepped to the side to avoid the creature's approach path. Its tentacles rustled, but it made no further motion toward me. I continued my slow semicircle around it, glancing occasionally to see if it was still watching me.

"You're doing great," Toran said over the comm. "Try to get near that bench where it was connected."

If anything was likely to upset the Sap, messing with the bench probably would. I tiptoed forward to get a closer look.

The structure was covered in the same strange, dark vines that were ubiquitous in the plane, but the ones on the bench had a higher concentration of the glowing dots. When I was within three meters of the bench, some of the tendrils unfurled and reached out toward me.

The Sap snapped its head around and fixed me in an eyeless glare, its tentacles shuddering. It stepped toward me, vocalizing a series of rapid clicks.

I reached for my sword. "Time for Plan B."

"Wait!" Toran commanded over the comm. "See what it does."

I remained still, my hand hovering centimeters from the hilt of my sword. The Sap slinked toward me with its tentacles fanning out to view me from multiple angles. Even on all fours, the creature was taller than me, blocking my escape path. Its jaws parted.

"Wait, Elle," Toran said again.

I took a slow breath, fighting every instinct to grip my sword.

The creature leaned forward, less than a meter from my face. Its tentacles swept around me, some nearly brushing my clothes and hair.

Then, the tentacles suddenly folded back against the creature's body and it turned to depart, loping into the darkness in the opposite direction from which we'd come.

"Stars! What the…" I placed a hand above my heart pounding in my chest.

"I have to say, I wasn't sure that would work," Toran admitted.

Kaiden nodded. "Yeah, I thought you were going to be lunch in a matter of seconds."

I glared at them. "All right, that's the last time I volunteer as bait."

"But why *didn't* it see you as a threat?" Maris asked. "I'd think they'd be all over anything unusual around here."

Toran took on a pensive expression. "Unless there's some aspect of us that *does* belong in this place."

I raised an eyebrow. "So we… blend in?"

"Perhaps." He shrugged. "Really, there's only one way to find out."

18

THOUGH A SINGLE encounter wasn't enough experience from which to draw definitive conclusions, even hours of testing might still lead to the wrong conclusion about what we could get away with near the Saps. So, we decided to go directly for the big prize: whatever was beyond the guarded wall.

"All right, slow and steady," I instructed while creeping from the hiding place near where we had first arrived. "Watch your footing."

The spongy ground made it easy to move quietly, but the tendrils snaking through the landscape introduced numerous tripping hazards. We'd elected to avoid showing unnecessary light that would draw attention to us, so our approach to the guarded facility was mostly on feel.

Having successfully made it past our test subject earlier, I took the lead. We didn't have much of a plan beyond watching each other's backs and trying to minimize noise, but there were too many unknowns for a more specific plan.

"Don't look directly at the guards," I whispered as we approached the wall.

The two sentries sat on their rear haunches, looking more like stone statues than living beings in the dim light. Half of their torso tentacles were raised in the position I'd come to associate with 'sensing mode', and their barbed tails were wrapped around on top of their front feet. Like the other Sap I'd just approached, they had no visible eyes in their skulls.

I kept my gaze on the path in front of me as I walked toward the facility wall. Our staging location was approximately thirty meters from the wall, and the ground in between was mostly open with nowhere to hide. Thin tendrils shifted underfoot as I walked, though none tried to climb my legs and tether me. Thanks to the soft ground, our movements were all but silent.

When we were ten meters from the nearest sentry, the creature's tentacles stirred and its head pivoted to face us while it make a series of low, percussive clicking sounds.

"Stay calm," I whispered, not breaking stride.

"I can feel it," Maris whispered back. "It's trying to get into my mind."

"We're just part of the landscape. Nothing special to see," I replied, hoping she could convert that sentiment into a convincing mental image. When the creature made no further movement and its vocalization subsided, I assumed she had been successful.

We came abreast of the sentries, passing between them while their tentacles swiveled to track us.

"Where's the door?" Kaiden questioned.

"Dunno. We'll have to inspect the wall," I whispered back. Part of me hadn't expected we'd get this far, so I hadn't planned what to do next.

Up close, I discovered the wall was a tight mesh of vines, and the blue pinpoints of light along their lengths pulsed in unison. The wall extended at least three hundred meters—the strange distance perspective of the plane notwithstanding—and there didn't appear to be any breaks that we could use to get through.

"We'll have to go over it," I realized.

Kaiden evaluated the wall from next to me. "It has to be eight meters tall. How do we get up there?"

"Climb." I pointed to the grooves made by the interwoven vines; they'd provide perfect hand and footholds.

"We'll be completely exposed," Maris objected.

"Not to mention, touching it may set off an alarm," Toran pointed out.

"Maybe. I mean, the security seems pretty lax, doesn't it? There're only a handful of guards," Kaiden commented.

I shrugged. "No natural enemies?"

"Yes, this is what I would expect to see from a society that is maintaining internal order rather than protecting against an outside threat," Toran said.

"Well, our options are to give up or press forward, and I know we're not turning around," I said.

Kaiden faced the sentries. "All right, start climbing. I'll keep watch."

I carefully reached out to grip the vines, bracing for an alarm or attack. Nothing happened.

"So far, so good," I told my friends. The vines wriggled under my fingertips, but I was able to get a firm grip. I hoisted myself up with my arms and found a toehold for my boot.

"Scout ahead for what's over the top," Toran advised.

"I'm on it." I easily scaled the wall, finding the woven texture quite suitable for the task.

I slowed as I neared the upper ledge, listening for any sign of more creatures. My fingers found the top of the wall, and I pulled myself up just enough to peek over the top. Unfortunately, there was nothing to see aside from a flat vine-mesh rooftop and a single, thick column rising into the blackness one hundred fifty meters away.

"I'm not sure we can get in this way," I told my friends over the comm, then described the view.

"There *has* to be a way inside," Toran insisted.

I pulled myself the rest of the way onto the roof, testing my weight on it; the mesh flexed but held. "I'll scope it out."

I jogged across the rooftop toward the vertical column in the distance. I'd gone no more than thirty meters when I noticed a dark area in the surface to my right. I changed course to get a better look and saw that it was a hole open to inside, only covered by a thin mesh of fibers. "Hey, I think I've found a skylight!"

"Can you see anything inside?" Kaiden asked.

"No, pitch black in there." I tugged at the fibers across the skylight, and they ripped away in my hand. "Not sure how we're going to get down there without rope, but it's a way in."

"Should we go for it?" Kaiden questioned.

"It's that or walk around the perimeter of the structure," Toran replied.

"I vote for skylight," Maris said.

"All right, we'll be right there," Kaiden told me.

I set about clearing the remaining mesh from the opening while waiting for them to arrive. By the time I saw Toran cresting the lip of the building, I'd opened a two-meter-by-two-meter hole. My three friends jogged over.

"We're about to go against everything I was taught as a kid about not crawling into creepy, dark places," Kaiden said.

"Pretty sure we've been ignoring that kind of advice for weeks now." I smiled.

"We need to know what's down there. Might be time for some light," Toran advised.

I sighed. "I *really* wish we could have brought our gear packs."

Kaiden shook his head. "I can do a light orb, but that'll mean using magical energy."

"Have to risk it," I told him.

Kaiden conjured a small orb in his palm—faint compared to his usual spells, but blinding after my eyes had become so used to the dark. He dropped the orb through the hole, directing it to drop slowly so we could see what was beneath us. No objects or architectural features were visible at first, but four meters down I spotted the outline of charging benches similar to what the lone Sap had been seated on earlier.

"Make it brighter," I urged.

He fed a little more energy into the sphere, giving us a better view of the room below. Based on what was visible from our limited vantage, multiple benches were arranged around a central, unseen structure. None of the seats were presently occupied.

"I hate the idea of dropping down there, but we'll never get a proper look around from up here," Kaiden said. He left the orb resting on the floor eight meters down.

"But *how* do we get inside?" Maris asked. "That's way too far to jump."

Toran sized it up. "I may be able to make it."

I shook my head. "Too risky if you get hurt. And that doesn't help the rest of us."

Kaiden rested his staff on the rooftop and leaned on it. "Options?"

I looked over at the pile of fibers I'd pulled from the opening. "I wonder if we could make a rope out of that stuff."

The others assessed the pile. “Where’d that come from?” Kaiden asked me.

“It’s what was covering this skylight.”

Toran picked up several strands, pulling on either end of the strands; they stretched but didn’t break. “This could work.”

I grabbed a bundle for myself and began braiding them together to reduce the flex and increase the strength. With my friends following my example, we soon had a healthy pile of two-meter-long segments, which we knotted together to form a single length long enough to reach the floor.

“I’ll go first this time,” Kaiden volunteered. “Second heaviest, so it should hold Elle and Maris if it’ll support me.”

“I’ll anchor it,” Toran agreed.

The two men got into position, and Kaiden tucked his staff into his back waistband so both hands would be free for climbing. He dropped through the hole and began lowering himself down.

“This is just one chamber—maybe twenty meters square,” he said into his comm.

“Any doors?” I asked.

“Yeah, a couple of archways.”

“Okay, I’ll come down next.” I looked at Toran. “We’ll need to figure out where to tie off the rope when you come down last.”

“I’ll figure something out, don’t worry,” he assured me.

I climbed down, followed by Maris. The chamber contained six benches arranged around a bundle of vines in the center of the room. It seemed odd that the room was empty, but there was no way to know how frequently the creatures ‘charged’, if that’s what was really going on. In line with the center of the room, archways opened to the right and left.

Toran began tying the rope to the mesh rooftop material.

"Stand back in case this doesn't hold," he advised. He swung through the hole and put his full weight on the rope.

For the first three meters, everything was fine. Then, he suddenly dropped down a half meter before the rope went taut again. "It's slipping!" He picked up his pace. A moment later, the rope came free.

He plummeted the final four meters, rolling as he hit the ground.

Maris ran over to him. "Are you okay?"

"Yeah." He rose, rubbing his side. "Ooph. Now I wish I'd just jumped."

I looked up at the skylight in the ceiling, now completely inaccessible without the rope. "I guess we aren't getting back out that way."

"Might not need an exit, anyway," Kaiden pointed out. "Just because we couldn't plane-transition *into* this place doesn't necessarily mean we can't get out by that method."

"True. I guess we'll need to wait for Hoofy to show himself to find out for sure," I said.

"He'll come through for us," Maris reiterated.

I still didn't share her certainty, but now knowing what he'd given up to help us, I had more faith in him than when we'd set out on the mission. "Let's find their weak point and get out of here."

"Isn't it a little overly optimistic to think there's *one* weak point for their entire civilization?" Kaiden questioned.

"Hoofy said that was the case," Maris replied.

I had to agree with Kaiden's skepticism on that point. "But isn't that a really, really terrible design?"

"From our perspective, yes," Toran replied. "However, if they have no natural enemies—as we hypothesized earlier—then there's no reason to not have centralized systems. After all, that's most efficient."

"Okay, so if we can destroy something critical at the core, that might cripple them?" I asked.

"Or at least be a major setback," he said. "The trickier thing will be to make sure they can't easily rebuild."

I nodded. "Trapping them on this plane would be ideal, if we can."

"Definitely easier said than done. But, I'd like to learn more about this energy grid of theirs," Toran went on. "Perhaps that will help us formulate a plan."

"For starters, what's the deal with these benches and the 'charging'?" Kaiden said. "Sounds kind of robot-like."

"I'd liken it more to photosynthesis, how plants get energy from the sun," Toran posited.

I thought about it. "If this place is indeed the central generator, I can see how taking it out would be pretty damaging."

"Temporarily," Kaiden cut in. "This civilization didn't come from nothing. They could rebuild."

"Hence the need to isolate them," I said, heading toward the archway to the left. "But, I'll settle for neutralizing the threat right now."

Kaiden sent a light orb hovering in front of us, illuminating a vine-lined corridor that led deeper inside the facility. The interior reminded me of the ship we'd boarded at the anomaly site, only the proportions of this space were at least twice the size. I sensed a hum of energy in the air originating from the depths of the place.

"Did you notice those columns rising from the rooftop?" I asked.

"Kinda difficult to miss," Kaiden replied.

"I bet those are above the energy core," I continued. "This

corridor is heading in that direction."

"A reasonable assumption," Toran agreed.

"How can we destroy a place like this?" Maris asked. "We don't have anything aside from our artifacts and magic."

"Maybe that would be enough," I replied. "We've never tried to go all-out on an inanimate object before."

"We shouldn't attempt anything until we have a better sense for how this civilization operates," Toran cautioned.

I nodded. "That's why we're heading to the core."

Kaiden flitted his gaze around the hallway. "I still say something is wrong about all of this. There aren't enough Saps here… and there's so little security. Either the place isn't as important as we've been led to believe, or this is a trap."

The same feeling had been nagging at the back of my mind, too. It had all been far too easy. It didn't make sense that they'd just ignore us. "I don't know what we're missing."

"We'll find out soon. We're getting close," Kaiden said.

The hum of energy intensified. Eventually, the corridor terminated in what appeared to be a solid wall of vines.

I frowned at the wall. "This can't be right."

Maris tilted her head. "Hidden door?"

"Must be something like that." I approached the wall. "Remember how the tunnel started closing in on us when we were leaving the ship?"

"Yeah. Meaning, these walls might be 'alive', for lack of another term," Kaiden replied.

"How do we get them to move?" Maris brushed her right hand along the vines.

"There must be some sort of trigger… like a certain type of energy associated with the Saps," I mused. "It seems like right now we're registering as 'background', but if we could figure out a way to make ourselves seem like *them*…"

"I have no idea how to run that kind of analysis without equipment I don't have," Toran said.

Kaiden brightened. "We might not need it. Elle, you have telekinesis."

"You want me to rip the wall apart?"

"It's a lot more precise than a fireball. Just break apart enough vines to make an opening."

"I dunno..." Using any form of magic would certainly draw attention to us as being something other than ambient background blips, and that kind of attention seemed like a bad idea.

"Think about it," Kaiden insisted. "The Saps 'charge' using those bench things—concentrated energy. If you direct concentrated energy at the wall, it might spoof it into thinking that one of the aliens is trying to get through."

"Or, some as yet unseen security force will descend upon us in an instant," I countered.

"Either way, we're presently trapped at a dead end. Might as well attempt to move forward."

I couldn't object to that argument. "Fine, I'll try."

My friends turned around to watch the corridor behind me while I prepared my telekinetic attack. I extended my right hand with the special focusing glove, a white orb forming in the palm. I released the ball of energy, and it struck the center of the back wall. Radiating from the point of impact, the interwoven vines began to unfurl and move apart to form an arched doorway.

"That was too easy," I said, my concern growing that we were being directed exactly where they wanted us to go. It was impossible that somewhere so important had next to no security, whether the civilization had known enemies or not.

"This place doesn't make any sense," Kaiden said.

"Doesn't matter. What's *that*?" Maris pointed through the archway toward a massive chamber filled with thick, pulsing vines that shined with the brightest light of any we'd seen so far in the plane.

The chamber's roof was six meters above, covered in vines that met to form a thick column in the center. The arched entryway where we stood was two-thirds of the way up the side wall, with the rest of the chamber dropping away below into a massive nest of vines. The vines spread from a single, small device at the bottom of the pit, pulsing with a bright blue light.

"Stars! What the…?" I gasped.

"That must be the core," Toran said.

Kaiden shook his head. "There's no one here. This is so weird."

"Agreed." I checked along the walls for a pathway to the bottom of the pit. There was no obvious staircase or ladder, so we'd have to climb along the vines. "Let's get a closer look."

Maris gulped. "I was afraid you'd say that."

I took the lead climbing down the curved wall. It was easy-going with so many vines to grab, though the way they squirmed under my grasp was disconcerting.

We reached the bottom of the pit and climbed over the large vines toward the center. I'd thought perhaps that warped perspective had made the core of the device appear to be only a meter across, but I found that was accurate as I approached. A blue orb hovered at the center of the thick vines, simultaneously the origin point of them and also nestled inside them. Normally I'd consider it a trick of the light for the orb to appear both in front of and behind the same vines, but I suspected that there was actually a hyperdimensional component to what I was seeing.

Maris squinted. "Huh. I expected it to be bigger."

Kaiden frowned at the device. "That doesn't look like a normal power generator. What's the fuel source?"

"Nothing in this plane," Toran replied cryptically, squatting down to get a better look at the vines. "After everything we've seen, I believe the only answer is that this device draws power from a higher dimension, and the Saps feed on that energy."

"I came in here thinking we might get answers, but now I just have more questions," I admitted.

Kaiden shook his head. "An alien race with a hyperdimensional energy source… Why are they bothering to mess with us and the crystals?"

"Stars…" Toran murmured, his eyes widening.

I crouched down next to him. "What?"

"I think I just figured out what the Saps are doing," Toran said, then fell silent.

"Okay, you can't say something like that and not follow it up with an explanation!" Kaiden hissed, dropping down next to me.

Maris knelt beside us.

Toran pointed at the device. "If I'm right, back in our plane, we'd consider this to be a zero-point energy device. Based on what we've observed here, this energy source is integral to the Saps' existence—it's what makes their ships work, feeds them, and powers the mechanisms of their civilization. It's connected to *everything*. But they can't access the higher planes, where they want to go. The best connection to the higher dimensions is—"

"The crystalline network," I completed for him.

"And our spacetime has an interface system." Kaiden sat back on his heels. "Stars! Why didn't we see it before?"

"If that's what they're after, there are terrible implications,"

Toran continued. "The crystalline network controls and utilizes the infinite power of the eleventh-dimensional Duzies, the very building blocks of the entire cosmos! So, if the Saps found a way to tie their energy grid—the thing everything in their society is connected to— into the interface system for the crystalline network, that could theoretically give them full control of the Duzies *without* needing a separate interface console."

"Shit!" Kaiden gasped. "They'd be like… gods."

"Full control… rearranging matter and directing energy at will." I shook my head. "Nope, these guys are way too unstable for that kind of power."

"If that's what they're after, then why start with the Darkness and invasion fleet?" Maris asked.

"I don't know. That part still doesn't—" Toran cut off, snapping his attention upward.

The doorway we had entered through was now filled with half a dozen figures, and they were staring directly at us.

19

"STARS! WE'RE CORNERED down here." My heart leaped in my chest.

"Time to get away!" Maris said. "Hoofy?"

There was no reply.

"How are we supposed to transition to the higher plane without him?" Kaiden questioned, a panicked pitch to his voice.

"Stars if I know." I drew my sword. "Time to fight." The blue flames ignited as soon as the weapon was out of its scabbard.

The moment my weapon was exposed, the six Saps dropped down into the pit, gliding toward us on all fours.

I raised my sword into a defensive pose. "I told you this was a trap!" A purple protective shell courtesy of Maris appeared around me.

"Like we wouldn't have come anyway," Kaiden replied.

"Irrelevant." I charged for the two Saps barreling toward me.

My instincts took over as I swung my sword, faking out the first Sap so I could redirect a jab at the second. A moment before my blade was set to pierce the torso of my target, its barbed tail whipped around to strike me in the back of the knees. It was stopped by the protective shell around me but then unexpectedly broke through, knocking me to the ground.

The first Sap took the opportunity to pounce. I rolled to the side just in time to avoid it pinning me, one of its clawed feet landing a mere two centimeters from my right shoulder. I angled my blade upward to strike its belly. It let out a cry as the blade entered, and then it disintegrated into black ash.

Having seen its comrade fall, the second Sap edged away from me toward the four others, which were presently engaged with my friends.

"One down!" I said, chasing my second attacker.

The other Saps were alternating attacks on my friends, sometimes breaking through the protective shells and other times stopped. Only the forcefield cast from Maris' shield seemed to reliably deflect the assaults. Kaiden's lightning attacks appeared to be wounding the creatures, but Toran's punches only seemed to annoy them. My sword was by far the most effective weapon.

I extended my right hand and lobbed an energy ball toward the Sap running from me. It lurched to the side to avoid the blast, then it rounded on me.

Its eyeless gaze bore into me. "*Stop.*" The command filled my mind.

Against every intention, I halted. I tried to will myself forward, but I was completely frozen, my arms dropping to my sides and legs unwilling to move. I'd never felt so utterly trapped, let alone without anything physically holding me in place.

Nearby, my friends had likewise ceased their fighting. Each was transfixed by one of the Saps, and the fifth creature sauntered between us, its attention lingering on each of our artifacts as it passed by. The protective shells, aside from the forcefield extending beyond Maris' shield, had collapsed.

"*It is ours,*" a voice hissed in my mind. I sensed that it was coming from the Sap that was walking around rather than the one focused on me.

"*What is?*" I tried to mentally form the words.

The Sap didn't reply, but it tightened the telepathic vise locking me in place. It extended its tentacles toward my sword arm, poised to pry the weapon from my grasp.

Next to me, Toran kicked his captor, followed by a rapid series of punches to the creature's neck and chest.

The others started with surprise, their concentration broken.

I thrust my sword forward, piercing the chest of the Sap in front of me. Dark blood spilled down its front, and then it dissolved into black ash.

Kaiden cast a shower of lightning over the two Saps nearest him, while Toran continued to pummel the creature in front of him. I dashed to the creature clawing at Maris' shield, swinging my sword around to slash its side as soon as I was within range. My blade connected, and the Sap turned to ash.

"Elle, over here!" Kaiden called.

I ran toward him and vaulted over one of the vines, using the extra height to sail over the first of the attacking Saps. I plunged my blade into its back and ripped downward, and it disintegrated before I landed. As soon as I touched down, I jabbed my sword behind me into the rear haunches of the second creature engaged with Kaiden. Only Toran's opponent remained.

The final Sap let out an aggravated series of clicks as it charged for Kaiden. I sprinted forward to broadside it—not enough to knock it off its feet, but it halted when I raised my blade to its throat.

"What do you want from us?" I asked aloud.

The creature stared back at me with its invisible eyes.

"Tell us what you—"

I choked on the words as the creature snapped its neck forward to be sliced on my blade. It spasmed briefly before turning to ash in my hands.

"Stars..." Kaiden murmured.

Maris swallowed. "Guess they really didn't want to tell us."

I took several panting breaths, willing my heart rate to slow. "I really hate these guys."

"They're the worst," Kaiden agreed.

I glanced at the power core. "Others will probably come soon. Let's destroy this thing while we have the chance."

"Wait," Hoofy said in our minds. *"Not like this."*

"Oh, *now* you show up!" Kaiden exclaimed.

"It was important for this scenario to play out to its end. I see that my faith in you was not misplaced."

"That's—" Before I could finish, the chamber unfolded, replaced with white light. A segment of filament bridge appeared beneath my feet, at the core of a complex intersection with innumerable branches extending into the mist in either direction.

"Why did you do that?!" I glared at Hoofy. "We were about to take these guys out."

"Destroying the core in the way you intended would not stop them. There is still much for you to learn."

"It would really help if you told us what you know... or anything at all," Kaiden replied.

The unicorn bowed his head. *"I know my actions do not make sense now, but soon you will understand."*

"I understand plenty. You let us walk right into a trap!" I shouted at the unicorn.

"Elle—" Maris tried to soothe.

"Don't defend him," I cut her off. "He's been playing games with us."

"No, I did what was necessary for you to come into your true power."

I worked my mouth; that wasn't the response I'd anticipated. "What do you mean?"

"Your transformations were not complete the moment you were reborn," Hoofy replied. *"You have been growing and evolving. After your transformation had completed, your strength needed to be tested."*

"Normally that's done in training, or whatever. You sent us into the heart of their operations!" I spat back.

Hoofy tilted his head. *"You learned what you needed to, did you not?"*

"Yeah, we did," Maris replied. "And we all made it out okay."

"Barely," I muttered.

"We were at the core. We could have ended the fight right then and there," Kaiden said.

"It is more complicated than that," Hoofy replied. *"Now that I know you are ready, I can explain."*

I crossed my arms. "Okay, so talk."

"Not yet. I will tell you after you are back on your ship and can gather the tools you need."

I couldn't help rolling my eyes. The unicorn had done nothing but talk in circles. I wasn't sure we were ever going to get anywhere.

He fixed me in a level gaze. *"I sense your exasperation, but everything will fall into place soon."*

"It better." The reply came out as more of a threat than I'd intended, but my patience had worn thin. If Hoofy didn't offer a detailed explanation within the next several hours, I wouldn't listen to anything else he had to say.

Seemingly unfazed by my hostility, Hoofy trotted toward the left along the bridge. *"Come, the exit is this way."*

We followed him through a complex intersection of multiple bridge segments and continued along a path toward the left. Eventually, we reached a single long expanse—presumably the path by which we'd entered—and jogged for what seemed like an eternity in my antsy state.

"We're here," Hoofy said.

Maris stopped in front of me. "I don't see the sphere."

"What, it's not there?" I passed by her to search for any sign of the viewing-sphere that had been visible when we arrived, but I couldn't see it either. "This is the right place, isn't it, Hoofy?" I asked.

"Yes," the unicorn acknowledged. *"The ship must have moved."*

I tried to hold back the panic threatening to take hold. "Well, where is it?"

That wasn't part of the plan at all. We should have only been gone a few moments in relative time in the lower planes. It was next to impossible that the *Evangiel* could move on so quickly.

"Uh oh," Toran murmured.

"No, Toran, 'uh oh' is *not* an okay thing to say in this situation." I peered further along the bridge, hoping that maybe we hadn't gone far enough.

"Well, last time we were in 8D and no apparent times passed in our normal reality," Toran said. "This time, though, we were in 6D and 7D. They're still above spacetime, but maybe it's… different."

Kaiden wiped a hand down his face. "Why didn't that occur to us earlier?"

"Because this idea seemed straightforward and easy at the time." Maris winced. "Sorry."

"That should have been our clue." I took a deep breath, committed to not lose my cool. "How can we tell when or where we are?"

"From here? I have no idea," Toran admitted.

"But we *do* know that the *Evangiel* should be here, and they know it," Kaiden said. "I'm certain they'd loop around for another pass as soon as they realized we weren't on board."

"Regardless, how do we get back?" I questioned.

"Can you help us find the ship?" Maris asked Hoofy.

"I'm already trying. However, we will not be able to remain on this bridge. The ship is no longer in proximity to any of these hyperdimensional paths."

I didn't like the sound of that. "Okay, so where do we go?"

"We will have to cut through another part of the plane," Hoofy replied.

"Can we do that? Is there anything there?" I asked. After all, we were technically in a place that corresponded to open space relative to our home plane of reality.

Hoofy trotted to the edge of the bridge and touched his horn to the mist. An opening formed in the clouds, revealing an open plane that seemed desert-like compared to the pastoral scene we'd witnessed earlier. *"Nothing is completely empty."*

Maris hesitated. "You said before that you were not welcome to enter that place anymore."

The unicorn shifted on his feet. *"Getting you back to your ship is more important. Come."* He leaped through the opening onto the scrubby grass.

"No argument here." Kaiden jumped through after him, and the rest of us followed suit.

As I passed through the opening, the light level flickered and I sensed a change in the ambient energy. Everything around me felt charged and vibrant, though there were no discernible landscape features or signs of life.

We raced forward in the general direction we'd been following on the bridge but angling away from it. Hoofy loped ahead with the rest of us running to keep up. It was easy to keep pace in the strange gravity of the place, but I found it disorienting to not have any landmarks by which to gauge our progress.

Hoofy stopped short. *"No, they are not supposed to be here."*

I leaned back on my heels. "Who? What?"

In answer to my question, ten heads with distinctive crystal horns appeared in front of us, and with a ripple through the air, the rest of their equine bodies came into view. I wasn't sure if they'd just entered through a transition point or had been cloaked in some manner, but these were clearly members of Hoofy's former herd based on how they were glaring at him.

"You were not supposed to interfere," the lead unicorn said, stomping forward.

Hoofy stood his ground. *"This was too important for us to stand back and do nothing."*

"It is not our place," the other insisted.

"So was declared last time, and look where it got us." Hoofy tossed his golden mane. *"I will not make the same mistakes you did."*

The other unicorn turned her attention from Hoofy to us. *"You do not understand the forces at work."*

I chuckled. "Yeah, you can say that again! No frickin' clue."

She squinted at us, to the extent her unicorn features allowed. *"You think this funny?"*

"No, not at all!" Maris hastily cut in. "We've had a really weird week. Well, several weeks. We're kind of at the point where we don't know what to believe or who to trust anymore."

"Yet, you have aligned yourselves with this traitor." The elder unicorn glared at Hoofy.

"Traitor?" So, Hoofy hadn't told us the whole story, after all.

"It is true, I was not forthcoming with you," Hoofy revealed.

"What do you mean?" Maris asked, her tone pained.

"Fanciful notions and rash actions," the elder replied. *"Stars know why you freed him."*

I held up my hand. "Whoa, wait. *You* trapped him on the other plane?"

The elder unicorn huffed. *"Nonsense. The fool got himself trapped by going where he did not belong."*

"Enough dancing around it. What happened?" Kaiden interjected.

Hoofy hung his head. *"For generations, the Overlords have been building their energy grid. We knew your kind were at risk, but the others insisted it was not our place to intervene. But during our migrations, I watched the echoes of ancient times, when we used to roam your forests and share our knowledge with your kind. I could not bear the thought of your falling victim to their evil—not after the friendship our people had shared.*

"I saw a chance to thwart the Overlords, by means of an anomaly that crosses the planes. I believe it has been expanding since they brought their power core online, and all it needs is the right nudge to wall them off. Unfortunately, I did not have the correct tools, and I found myself trapped."

The elder snuffled. *"That is what happens when you wander from the herd."*

Hoofy met her gaze. *"You would not take action."*

"Right or wrong, that's in the past now," I said. "Now, we're already a part of this. Sorry if a collaboration wasn't on your wish list, but we're invested now. And, we have a ship to get back to."

"They have overcome their influence. They are integrated now," Hoofy told the elder.

She evaluated us. *"Is that so?"*

"They have mastered the artifacts," Hoofy continued. *"They are the best chance to see this through."*

"We swore to not involve ourselves. You broke that code, and nothing can undo that. However, that also means we cannot stand in your way now." The elder took a step back.

Hoofy bowed his head. *"I hope eventually you will see that this was the best way forward."*

"If you are successful, then perhaps we will. What has already happened is not always destined to remain." The elder and rest of the herd faded from view as suddenly as they had appeared.

Kaiden scratched his head. "I have to say, that was one of the stranger encounters we've had."

"Agreed," Toran said. "I was worried that we might get stampeded."

"They would never behave in such a fashion," Hoofy said.

"Fine, then shoot us down with rainbows," I offered as an alternative.

Kaiden smiled. "Or choke us with magical dust."

"Do unicorns do magic dust? I always thought of that as more of a faerie thing," I said.

"Definitely pixies," Maris cut in.

Toran cleared his throat. "The ship is getting farther away with every moment."

"Stars! Unicorns are very distracting." I resumed running in the direction we'd been heading, with Hoofy once again taking the lead.

"I sense it is close," he said, followed by an image projected in our minds. An echo of the *Evangiel* was overlaid on the landscape in front of us, with a more distinct bright point where the sphere resided in the viewing room. The ship was pulling away from us ever so slightly.

"Faster!" I urged my friends. I could see the sphere now in my normal vision.

We picked up our pace and began gaining on the sphere. It was so close…

"Get your artifacts ready," Kaiden said. "We need to do this at the same time."

I drew my sword in preparation. Just half of the ship's length to go.

We sprinted the final distance, dropping our pace just enough to match the travel of the ship.

"On three," I said, extending my hand. I counted down, and we simultaneously touched the sphere.

Reality folded, going black for an instant before there was a bright flash. The viewing room resolved around me, with the solid sphere between me and my friends. My stomach flipped as I was struck by the sensations of being in my normal physical self.

"What happened? You disappeared," Colren asked from where he was still standing near the doorway. "It's been nearly two minutes."

"That's going to take some explaining," Toran replied.

"All right, so I guess we really do 'go somewhere' after all."

I took a shaky breath, overcome with a wave of nausea. "I never want to go there again."

Kaiden gave me an apologetic smile. "Well, you're going to have to. Like, soon."

"At least we'll get the bad guys," Maris offered.

There was that. And I was definitely ready for it to be over.

20

IN HIS USUAL fashion, Colren listened patiently while we gave an account of our experience as the five of us stood in the viewing room. The explanation was fairly straightforward until we got to the part about the fight near the energy core.

"But then Hoofy wasn't there to help us transition," Maris said.

I winced. It was only a matter of time before one of us slipped.

Colren's brow drew together. "Hoofy?"

"Erm," Kaiden hesitated.

I took a deep breath. "So, we didn't tell you *everything* before."

The commander crossed his arms. "What did you leave out?"

"On our earlier venture into 8D, we came across a sentient being," Toran explained. "His name is Huefneril, but we've been calling him 'Hoofy'."

"You say that like you're still in contact," Colren stated.

"Because we are," I revealed. "He's been helping us

negotiate the transition between the planes."

"And what kind of being is this Hoofy?"

I bit my lower lip. "A unicorn."

His eyes widened. "A…?"

"Turns out they're real and actually hyperdimensional beings," Kaiden said.

Colren worked his mouth. "Why didn't you say anything about this sooner?"

"Because we were worried it would sound like we'd lost our minds," I replied. "And we weren't sure it would be important, but it turns out that the information he's led us to is actually pretty critical to bringing down the Saps."

"And I'm supposed to trust you after you withheld details?" he eyed us.

"Well, we're telling you now," I pointed out. "We have every intention to do what's necessary to take out the Saps and restore our worlds. Do the details really matter so long as we're working toward that common goal?"

He paused in thought. "And you can trust… Hoofy?"

I nodded slowly. "His motivations were unclear at first, but now I believe we can trust him, yes. His heart is in the right place, though we need to keep his zeal in check."

Colren let out a long breath. "I suppose I'm in no position to pass judgement on this matter. You were given autonomy."

"It's been a crazy few days," Kaiden said.

"That it has," the commander agreed. "Now, tell me more about the energy core." There was a hunger in his eyes I hadn't seen before.

I exchanged worried glances with Kaiden. "It's at the center of everything for them," I replied. "Destroy that, and it will cripple them."

"Everything, even their ships?" Colren pressed.

"It appears to be hyperdimensional in nature," Toran explained. "We've witnessed the strange vine-like structures everywhere we've encountered the aliens. I believe the vines are networked conduits, which simultaneously draw on and transmit the energy. Since the network is hyperdimensional, that direct connection is not necessarily apparent as a physical tether in spacetime."

The commander nodded thoughtfully. "How do you know that core is the only one?"

"We have only the word of our guide," I said. "But, he took great risk to help us, so I believe he's telling the truth. As a hyperdimensional being from a higher plane than the Saps, he knows more about the Saps' civilization than we ever could."

"That kind of technology would be lifechanging for the Hegemony," Colren stated.

There it was. I knew the pronouncement had been coming, and now we were officially in a bind. While I agreed that an infinite power source would be revolutionary, I was also too acquainted with the Saps to want anything to do with their technology. For all we knew, it was constant contact with the power source that had twisted them into the evil creatures they were. Hegemony's wishes or not, I had no interest in helping them get hold of that device or get plans for how to make their own.

My friends seemed to have similar misgivings, based on their expressions.

"The energy technology and the Saps can't be separated from one another," Toran replied on our behalf. "If we make any attempt to preserve the core, we risk our worlds and future."

"That isn't a decision for us to make," Colren said.

Toran's face darkened. "You haven't seen what we have."

The commander shook his head. "And you have no idea what kind of threats the Hegemony has faced in our history. We go to great lengths to protect our citizens from the evils of this universe, but one of these days we won't be able to stop them. If we have a chance now to get something that will give us an upper hand in an inevitable future engagement, that's an opportunity we need to seize."

"I don't disagree with that sentiment, but this tech is not the answer," I insisted. "The Darkness, the beings, the vines, the energy core—it's all part of the same hyperdimensional organism. If we try to adapt that, we'll just infect our worlds all over again."

"You can't know that for sure," Colren responded.

"No, and you can't be sure that it won't. It's not a risk I'm willing to take." I wasn't sure what would come from standing up to the commander, but I figured we had little to lose. It's not like anyone else could actually go after the energy core if we refused.

Colren paced in a circle. "Leadership won't be happy about your lack of cooperation."

"The goal has always been to get our worlds back. Why the sudden interest in the alien tech?" Kaiden asked.

"We've always been a curious race, and greedy," Colren mused. "No one can remember where we came from or how we came to be—we're always focused on the future and the next phase of our development." He chuckled. "It's kind of funny, when you think about it, considering how much we rely on resets to fix our mistakes."

"And once we reset, no one is going to remember what we did or didn't do in this moment," Kaiden pointed out. "But our decisions now will affect what happens to our people in the future. Do we want to leave them—and ourselves—open to future danger, or do we want to end this once and for all while we have the chance?"

"There will always be danger," Colren murmured.

"And fighting one evil with another isn't the answer," I said. "If we really want to reach that 'next phase' for our society, we can't go stealing tech we don't understand. We need to make those discoveries for ourselves."

The commander glanced at the viewing-sphere. "I'm in an impossible position. I can't officially order you to do anything, and I also can't ignore my own orders."

"In that case," I said slowly, "we understand our instructions, and we'll do what we can to fulfill your request while completing the mission to the best of our abilities."

He cracked a slight smile. "Thank you. I trust you'll do what needs to be done."

My friends nodded.

"We will," Kaiden said.

"Now that that's settled," Colren continued, "I believe you were just about to explain this alien attack?"

I nodded. "Right, when they used their telepathy."

Toran gave an account of his experience with the rest of us interjecting anecdotes. Hearing the encounter from other perspectives, it was quite clear that Toran had had a very different experience than the rest of us.

"Why do you think you were able to resist them?" Colren asked.

Toran shook his head. "I have no idea. I could feel the creature trying to control me, but it just didn't… take."

The commander tilted his head. "Could this have anything to do with your abilities?"

"I honestly can't say," Toran admitted. "We didn't exactly get a User Manual to go along with our transformations."

"Fair enough." Colren chuckled. "Well, it might be worth another chat with the science team to see if they have an explanation. That seems like a crucial ability worth investigating."

"We'll do that," Toran agreed.

We finished recounting the end of the fight and our return to the *Evangiel.* Since Hoofy was a sore topic, we glossed over the exchange with his herd, only noting a few highlights which supported our argument that the unicorn was on our side. My advocacy would have been halfhearted a day earlier, but after seeing how he stood up for his actions to help us, my perspective had changed. In many ways, I now saw him as an idealistic teenager like me—making rash decisions without thinking through every aspect of the plan, but those actions coming from a place of good intentions. Regardless of age, we were all entitled to mistakes. What mattered in the end was making it right, and that's exactly what he was trying to do with us.

When we had completed our account, Colren studied us. "While that was a rousing mission brief, you've made no indication of how you intend to destroy this energy core and then trap the aliens in their plane."

"Yeah, we're still working out the details on that," I hedged.

"I'll need more to go on than that," Colren replied. "I can't have the ship circle this system indefinitely, and the Hegemon himself is asking questions."

"We will discuss as soon as you are finished here," Hoofy said in our minds.

"Give us a few hours and you'll have your answer," Toran said.

Whatever solution we devised, I was certain it would require going back into the heart of the alien civilization.

Except, this next time, they'd know not to underestimate us. It was a very real possibility that we wouldn't make it out of the next engagement alive.

"Very well." Colren agreed, then he dismissed us so he could give his superiors an interim update—no doubt including our intention to retrieve the energy core. There had been too much interest in his gaze for me to believe he had given up hope for us to follow through, but I think he at least understood the reasons for our resistance and wouldn't hold it against us personally.

We left the viewing room and returned to our lounge to strategize.

"We're in it deep now," I said as soon as the door was closed.

"I think that happened some time ago," Kaiden replied, taking his usual seat at the table. He propped up his legs on an adjacent chair.

Toran remained standing, arms crossed. "We're agreed that no alien tech makes it out, right?"

"Absolutely." I sat down next to Kaiden.

"Yeah, I want this *over*," Maris agreed.

"Okay, so we can blow shit up without worrying about finesse," Toran concluded.

I laughed. "Well, that's one way to look at it."

"Hoofy, do you want to fill us in on your plan now?" Maris asked, sitting down across the table from me.

A ghostly image of the unicorn appeared to my left next to the table. "*Thank you for trusting me. You are still missing one piece. Speak with your scientist friend again and explain what happened when the Overlord tried to control you. Once you understand, then we will talk.*" He disappeared.

I groaned. "I've had it with cryptic non-answers."

Kaiden massaged the bridge of his nose with one hand. “Another chat with Lisa it is.”

“Maris, you’d better make Hoofy come through for us after this,” Toran said.

“He will,” she assured us. “I know he’s been a little cagey, but he’s trying to walk the line between his vow to not interfere and his desire to help us.”

“Sides always need to be taken in the end.” Toran leaned over to activate the desktop so he could initiate a holoconference with Lisa in the Capital.

It took thirty seconds for the hyperspace relays to connect, and then a holographic image of the scientist appeared above the desktop. She smoothed back the stray strands of hair from around her face. “Hello, again. What can I do for you?” she asked.

Toran smiled. “We just completed another hyperdimensional expedition.”

Her expression brightened. “Tell me everything.”

We repeated the tale we’d told Colren, tailoring it to the most relevant details about the structures of the hyperdimensional planes we’d observed. The envy was clear in Lisa’s eyes as she vicariously lived the experience.

“Amazing,” she murmured when we finished.

“Can you think of an explanation for the telepathic resistance?” Toran questioned her.

“Well, it’s all connected,” she began. “Since our previous conversation, I’ve been doing a lot of thinking. It all comes back to the Duzies. They’re not just the building blocks of, well, *everything*, they’re also pure energy—they’re everything that *could be*.”

I blinked. “You lost me.”

“It’s not like one of our cells that has a unique function,” she explained. "Instead, they can be in a certain state, but also any number of other states at the same time. It's what allows you to redirect energy and 'cast magic', though really you're just ordering the Duzies to suddenly perform a different function."

Kaiden pursed his lips. "Okay…"

Lisa smiled. "But it gets more interesting. It's not just that you have been granted access to these Duzies, I believe you've also become super-saturated with them—like giant batteries. That's how you were able to cast magic in the vacuum of space without having much direct matter to draw on. And, I think that anything that's remained in your possession for some time also starts to get super-saturated."

"Like our clothes and stuff?" Maris asked.

The scientist nodded.

"Hmm. I guess that might explain why I felt so attached to my outfit," I realized. "A few times it would be easier to print a new one, but this one always felt… special."

"And our backpacks!" Maris exclaimed. "Those didn't come with us when we transitioned before, even though the other items did."

"We must not have spent enough time with them for those accessory items to have become saturated," Toran speculated.

"Exactly," Lisa confirmed. "Subconsciously, you've been aware of the Duzies for far longer than we've had a label to place on them."

"And what about the telepathic resistance?" asked Toran.

"Again, the Duzie super-saturation," Lisa replied. "The more your bodies get saturated with the Duzies, the stronger your abilities become. Your brains were the last part of you to become saturated. And, since Toran's abilities are about strength and resistance, I suspect that extends to his mind."

I stared at her image. "Wow." I supposed that also explained how I was still able to maintain some of my own thoughts, since I had the 'Protector Lite' treatment with my own abilities; Kaiden and Maris had indicated that they had almost no memory of the encounter, only a sense of being suffocated.

"Maybe the extra distance from the 5D thought-plane wasn't all of it!" Toran exclaimed. "The Duzie saturation may have been a part of why the Saps' telepathic influence broke so suddenly when we transitioned to 8D. It seems like that action of transitioning to a higher plane is what fully activated the Duzies that had been slowly saturating us. It must have flushed out the lingering telepathic link, so afterward we only remained susceptible to their control when in their presence—when their influence was stronger and faster than the natural 'repair' functions in our minds."

"Of course, I can't say with absolute certainty that this is what's going on with you," Lisa said, "but I can say that the evidence from your individual reports supports these conclusions. And, that means you should now be reaching your maximum potential."

"Yes. Now do you understand?" Hoofy interjected.

I took a deep breath. "I think that's the answer, Doctor."

The scientist smiled. "Call me 'Lisa', please. I'm happy I can help give you some clarity, if that's what this is."

Maris slumped in her seat. "Mind-melting stuff, but yes."

"Thank you, Lisa," Toran said. "We'll be in touch once we wrap our heads around this."

"Of course. I'll be here." The holoconference ended.

I massaged my eyes with my fingertips. "I have no words."

Kaiden shook his head. "I'm not sure what I find more disturbing—that this is the reality we're facing, or that it makes sense and I'm not all that surprised."

"You're not?" I snorted. "Stars, I don't know. Maybe I'm not actually as shocked as I should be."

"I appreciate that we now have an explanation of our abilities," Toran said. "This knowledge doesn't change our circumstances, but perhaps it will give us more control."

"Knowledge is power," Kaiden said.

"Yeah, something like that." I almost wished I didn't know what I did now. My abilities had seemed like simple augmentations at first, but realizing that I was saturated with these Duzies—that they were in my *brain*—was a lot to process.

Toran moved to sit down. "So, I was thinking—"

"I'm going to be honest," I cut in, "I can't talk about this anymore right now."

Maris nodded. "Me either. Just thinking about those Duzie things being in us…" She shivered.

"Let's take a break to digest this new info," Kaiden suggested. "After that, we'll work on our plan."

"I'll work on getting Hoofy to open up," Maris said.

Toran huffed. "Very well."

I rose from the table. "See you in a bit."

21

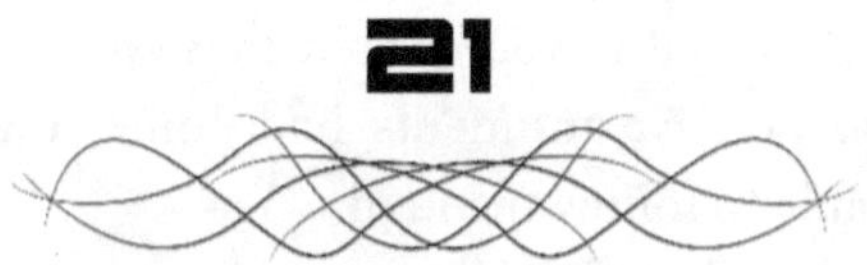

AFTER LEAVING THE lounge, I hung back in the hallway with Kaiden while Toran and Maris went ahead to their cabins.

"Mind if I invite myself over?" I asked.

He smiled. "I was hoping you would."

"That was a day," I said while we stepped into his cabin. "I don't think I've ever been so mentally exhausted."

"You haven't been through a college finals week."

I chuckled. "Yeah, that's true."

"This is different, though." He turned somber.

"I know… I want to say that I still know myself, that we haven't changed, but those things are in us. How different are we because of it?"

"That's bodies. What makes us who we are—our minds—that's above physical transformation."

"Is it, though? Can you really separate the two?" I sat on the bed.

Kaiden eased down next to me, placing a comforting arm around my back. "Whatever may have changed, we've gone through that transformation together."

"Yeah, there is that."

He took my hand. "We're in the final stretch, Elle. We'll get through this."

I shifted to lay my head on his shoulder. He tightened his arm around me—the kind of physical grounding I needed in that moment. Having seen the other planes, I realized just how small and insignificant our individual existences were. Yet, we'd been handed the power the change the direction of an entire civilization. I'd never wanted that kind of power, and now that the decisive moments had come, I was scared I wouldn't be able to follow through.

"I spent my whole life worrying about things that aren't actually important," I murmured.

"Importance is relative."

"Yeah, well, the color of my hair doesn't rank very high compared to the fate of the universe."

Kaiden laughed. "Okay, that would be silly to argue. But I do like this shade, for the record."

"Past me would have been thrilled about it. Now, I'd gladly give up my looks if it meant I could skip this fight."

"A few hours ago, you couldn't wait to get your hand on the Saps and put them in their place."

"That was before one of them bored into my mind. Don't get me wrong—I still want to whip their asses—but I don't take pleasure in this."

"Me either."

"This'll change us," I went on. "Even if we don't remember the details after the reset, this seems like the kind of experience that would imprint on our high-dimensional consciousness."

He reclined on the bed, and I lay back with him. "The universe will be better off without them."

"All the same, I hope we can trap them rather than have to

do a full-on extermination."

"Yeah, I don't want that on my conscience." He paused. "I'm glad we're going through this together. If we remember anything after the universal reset, it'll mean a lot to have a friend who understands what happened."

I scooched closer to him. "I think we're more than friends at this point."

He turned so he could look me in the eyes. "I wish we hadn't met like this. I can't stomach the idea that I may never see you again after this is over."

"We'll find each other."

"I want to believe that, but…"

"I know." My throat tightened with the notion that our time together could be cut short at any moment. In just a few weeks, I'd grown closer to him than I'd ever anticipated. He'd given me a glimpse of a different side of myself and the kind of connection that was possible with another person. I realized how alone I'd felt for years, and I didn't want to give up the possibility of a future together.

I stroked the side of his face, and he drew me to him. Our lips met and I kissed him back, gently at first, then with the hunger of wanting to be as close to him as possible. My hands slid downward, working under his outer layer of clothes as he caressed me in turn. The more he touched me, the more I wanted.

This is when I'd always put on the brakes before, citing one excuse or another. But this time, I didn't want to stop. "I know I said before that I wanted to wait until there won't be any more universal resets, but what if we don't make it through this?"

"Elle—"

"We can't ignore that possibility. I…" I looked into his eyes. "I don't want to have any regrets."

Kaiden leaned in and kissed me deeply. "I don't, either." He pulled back just enough to make eye contact. "So I want to say now, while I can… I love you, Elle."

My heart jumped and my breath caught in my throat. A contented tingle spread through me.

"Maybe that's too soon to say, but—" he hastily added when I didn't reply.

"No, we threw conventional timelines out the window a long time ago," I said, smiling. "I love you, too."

Joy washed over me having finally been able to vocalize what I'd been feeling. I knew it was still early in the relationship and I was still *falling* in love rather than being all the way there, but that distinction didn't matter on the eve of our potential deaths. What I knew for sure was that I didn't want to spend my final moments—if this was the end—wondering what could have been.

I pulled him to me, and our lips met again. The threats and worries of the outside world didn't matter. We had each other, and nothing that happened in the future could take that away.

I savored every moment as we made love, knowing I'd only have one first time, and not sure if it would also be my last. I was thankful I waited for someone I truly cared about and who loved me in return. The connection came through in every kiss and caress. No matter what the future held, I'd be able to look back and know I had true happiness in that moment.

We lay together afterward, his arms around me and my head on his bare chest. I felt different—maybe not in a way anyone else would notice, but I sensed it in myself.

"You okay?" Kaiden asked.

I smiled up at him. "Yeah, I'm great. Just… reflecting."

"I have to say, I wasn't expecting this now."

"Me either, but that's probably how it should be."

He kissed the top of my head. “The eve of saving the universe *does* seem like a pretty appropriate time.”

“That does have the makings of an epic love story.” I snuggled closer to him. Being in his arms, I felt safe from the dangers awaiting us. “Hey, random question: why fire?”

He gave me a quizzical look. “What are you talking about?”

“Your magic. You were first drawn to fire. I jokingly said you must have been a pyromaniac as a kid, but is there any other story there?”

“Oh.” He lay his head back. “Where is this coming from?”

“Just something I talked about with Maris earlier. We were reflecting on our abilities and why we were drawn to certain things with our disciplines.”

“Hmm, well, I’m not sure there’s a profound deeper meaning to my interest. Growing up on a ship, a runaway fire was always a worst-case scenario—we took every precaution to avoid accidentally burning ourselves up. Maybe I had some lingering desire to have control over it.”

I slid my hand along his chest. “Maybe.”

“What about you?”

“Oh, I just wanted to be a showoff.” I laughed.

“Shocker, Miss All-Three-Disciplines.”

“So high-maintenance, I know.”

Kaiden chuckled. “I think I’m starting to figure you out.” He traced a finger down my back and bent his head to kiss me. “You know… we don’t have to go anywhere yet.”

I kissed him back. “Is that so?”

He moved his hips toward me. “Uh huh.”

The ache of desire rose in me again as his warm breath brushed against my neck. “In that case—”

“Come on!” Maris exclaimed in our comms.

“Gah!” I winced, wishing I could rip it out of my ear. “Of

all the…"

Kaiden drew back from me, then tapped behind his ear to open the channel. "Maris, this isn't a good time."

"Stop napping. We have strategizing to do," she replied. "And if you're not napping, I don't want to know."

"Give us a few minutes. We'll meet you in the lounge," I grudgingly responded and then severed the commlink. "Seriously, they couldn't give us even an hour to ourselves?"

"Hey, at least she didn't interrupt in the middle of things."

"Yes, very true."

Making the mental shift from lover back to teammate, I suddenly felt exposed lying naked in his bed. I reached for my clothes. "We should get going."

Kaiden gently extended his hand to stop me from getting up. "Elle, I meant every word I said. I think you're incredible, and I can't wait to get to know you more."

I gave him a light kiss. "Me too." I paused. "I'm glad this happened."

"Same. Honestly, I'm surprised we were able to hold out for this long. Two super-hot young people with magical abilities? I mean, come on." He grinned.

"It was definitely worth the wait."

We dressed and tried to quickly re-style our hair so we weren't a giant, flashing beacon for 'Just Hooked Up'. It went without saying that it was a special experience between us, and we didn't need to broadcast it to anyone else.

Once presentable, we returned hand-in-hand to the lounge to find an impatient Maris and Toran waiting for us.

Maris looked us over. "Finally! About time you jumped each other. Okay, we have strategizing to do, so sit down."

"Happy for you two," Toran added.

My jaw dropped. I guess that happy glow I was feeling

wasn't as subtle as I thought.

"Uh…" Kaiden hesitantly approached his usual seat.

I slowly sat down next to him, certain my face was bright red. "So, the plan…"

"Not to a plan yet," Maris continued like everything was normal. "We're still at the information consolidation stage."

"All right." I tried to melt into my chair, wishing we could have stayed in bed awhile longer.

"We've been discussing the relationship between the elements in play here," Toran began. "Specifically, the Saps are on the 6D plane, seeking to ascend to higher planes. The crystalline network is at 9D with close ties to consciousness at 10D. And we have access terminals in our spacetime, which provide a direct link to the hyperdimensional crystalline network. Now, the 9D crystalline network has a special relationship with the 11D Duzies, storing information about the configuration of our spacetime reality, which can then be rearranged according to instructions from the 'reset terminals' or by direct instruction from 10D consciousness."

"Right, but…" I faded out. "Stars, I don't even know if I should ask, but why are there only access terminals down on our plane?"

"That's the question we kept coming back to," Toran replied.

"The only place those links could be formed?" Kaiden speculated.

"But why are they needed at all?" I insisted. "Or resets, for that matter."

Toran cracked a smile. "All the right questions. After talking it through, and getting some hints from Hoofy, the only reasonable conclusion is that life wasn't always as it is now. Remember, there were Ancients… and they ascended."

I thought about it. "Colren did indicate that the crystalline network was *made*, not a natural formation."

"Exactly." Toran nodded. "I'd bet that way back when, the Ancients found a way to step outside of time, away from their bodies. Physical reality was no longer a constraining factor, but they wanted a record of what they once had been. They devised a means to preserve those states through a civilization-wide network, stored indefinitely in the highest dimensions possible, to allow for effectively infinite capacity. Their descendants forgot that anyone had ever come before, and eventually they stumbled across the crystal interface and devised their own use for it—the ability to get a second chance whenever it was needed. And so, the quest to ascend began again with no memory that others had already walked that path."

Kaiden let out a long breath. "You know, it wouldn't surprise me in the least if that's *exactly* what happened."

"So, the Saps," Toran continued, "maybe they're an offshoot of the Ancients who were never able to ascend completely, or perhaps they're something else entirely. But they clearly understand the power of the crystalline network, and they're sick of it being under our control."

"Whoever they are, they're hungry for power," Kaiden agreed.

Toran looked around the room at us. "Agreed. And now that we have an inkling about what they're trying to accomplish, what are we going to do about it?"

22

"It's time for answers," I said. "Hoofy, it's now or never." I agreed with Toran's assessment about the Saps potentially being a rogue branch of the Ancients, but I wanted more than just hints to go on. The unicorn had been giving bits and pieces of some grand master plan to take down the Saps for hours, and I wasn't interested in planning *anything* without getting a straight answer.

"Can we talk now?" Maris asked more gently.

"Yes, the context has been established. We may speak freely," Hoofy replied, appearing once again as a ghostly image in the room.

"All right, so what's this plan of yours?" I asked, folding my hands on the tabletop. "How do we trap the Saps?"

"In the same way I was trapped," he replied. *"You must create a dimensional anomaly and then seal the entry."*

Kaiden frowned. "You say that like it's an easy thing to do."

"It will not be, but it can be done."

"Then explain," I prompted.

"The pathways to enter 8D, which my kind use for

migrations, are a natural form of these anomalies. In the anomaly, the division between the planes is… less distinct. In the locations where one of these anomalies exists, the affected planes behave as one."

"And which planes are those?" Toran asked.

"*Everything up through 6D, as you would distinguish them, become unified, but only a few access points from 6D through 7D to 8D would appear in specific locations. However, such shortcuts are only fleeting.*"

Toran leaned back in his chair, pensive. "If that's the case, would a spatial disruptor blast affect the higher planes?"

"*It would, precisely. And, the energy grid linking the Overlords would carry that blast through everything under the influence of that central core.*"

My stomach knotted. "That would *kill* them, not trap them."

Hoofy shook his head. "*No, you are thinking in terms of your physical forms. This would only be a setback, not death.*"

I raised an eyebrow. "I don't see how a 'setback' accomplishes our goal. We need to permanently disable them."

"*It would. Think about the anomaly.*"

Kaiden held up his hands. "*What* anomaly? There isn't some dimensional pocket thing that spans all of the territory the Saps now control."

"*Isn't there? Have you forgotten about the Darkness?*"

I did a doubletake. "Wait, what?"

"*The Darkness is evidence of the collapsed dimensional barriers. Only you four can set foot there, because only you are infused with the Duzies—as you call them— which enable you to be present in any plane. The Overlords were using the crystalline network to enable the merging of their reality with yours, granting them easier access to the terminals that would give them a connection to their ultimate goal.*"

"The Duzies themselves—to control everything." My jaw went slack.

"*Yes.*"

Kaiden swore under his breath. "I thought the worlds themselves were transformed."

"They were… just not in the way we thought." My head swam. Had we really been looking at everything incorrectly the whole time?

Maris' eyebrows drew together. "Does that mean we were wrong before?"

Toran was silent, thinking through the new information from Hoofy. "The Saps *did* gain partial control of the crystalline network—we detected the signals through the crystals and on their ship. But, it would seem that the spread of the Darkness was actually the expansion of the anomaly—*not* the result of reprogramming the crystalline network's reset mechanism."

"Except, we saw hybrid creatures," I pointed out. "We've been to those worlds—it wasn't just some blurred line with 6D!"

"Yeah, a lot of other things were different," Kaiden agreed.

Toran nodded. "Knowing what we do now, though, I think our assumptions about the *mode* of transformation were incorrect. Perhaps the alien hybrids were the result of each planet's native life being exposed to the Sap's energy grid."

"Huh." Kaiden absorbed the words. "That makes sense. Some things were able to meld with the grid, and they morphed to survive in the dimensional anomaly. Anything that didn't adapt… I bet the vegetation and everything falling apart when we touched it—and the corrosion of ships—was just the physical bonds breaking down from the forced transition to a higher plane."

"Yeah." I felt like my entire sense of reality had been pulled out from under me. "Stars! Somehow, this is so much worse."

Maris looked ill. "What about the black particles we all saw in the crystals?"

"They must have been the leading edge of the anomaly," Toran replied. "Most of the alien energy grid didn't appear to be quite solid when we saw it in our plane. Think about the conduits we saw radiating from the crystal in the town square on Windau."

"That's true. Some things *were* solid—the transformed stuff, I guess—but all of those 'energy conduits' did have a distinct not-quite-there-ness. One, giant spatial anomaly," I murmured.

"That would explain why our comms didn't work right on the Darkness-infected worlds," Toran said. "Spacetime was… different."

Wonder spread across Kaiden's face. "Only your modification to the comms to use the crystalline network itself could bypass that."

"And Crystallis… it has some sort of dimensional-alternateness of its own," I realized.

Kaiden sat up straighter. "Hold on, the Archive wouldn't be hurt by the disruptor wave, right?"

"No, it is not connected to the Overlord's network. Not yet, anyway. They are headed for it. It is a place of great power, which they have sought to control for a long time," Hoofy replied.

"Okay, so every place that we've seen the Darkness is connected to the energy core on the planet, and all of those places are within a broad-reaching spatial anomaly with blurry dimensional plane lines, right?" I summarized. "But on the

Saps' home planet itself—there's only limited evidence of the Darkness around the viewing-sphere. Is there an anomaly, or…?"

"No, that is the issue," Hoofy said. *"They have been careful to prevent the anomaly from breaking down the dimensional membrane around their home planet, to protect the core of their civilization and energy grid which empowers them. A disruptor would need to be placed in their native plane, but then the echo would carry to the other worlds."*

Kaiden placed a hand on his chin. "Problem: how do we do that?"

"Yes, a serious concern, indeed," Toran concurred. "Analysis of the detonation at the anomaly site revealed that the spatial disruptor functions up to 5D on its own. So, the device would need to be deployed on a higher plane in order to affect the Saps in 6D. However, the disruptor would need to be Duzie super-saturated in order for us to bring it with us through the dimensional transition."

"I am aware of that, and I do have a potential solution," Hoofy said. *"I have spent my time with you on this ship studying your technology and capabilities. I believe I have devised a way to supercharge your disruptor by creating an anomalous cross-universe dimensional rift at the epicenter, which can then expand to take out everything within the rest of the network. This transitory bridge would essentially suck out everything linked to the Overlord's energy grid and force it into a pocket universe that is confined to the 6D plane. The Overlords could never return to our universe."*

Maris blinked. "How could we make this anomaly-universe-bridge thing?"

"By using the properties of your artifacts and the viewing-sphere from your ship."

I winced. “Oh, Colren would not be happy about that.”

“That sphere is our only means to initiate a universal reset after the battle has been won,” Toran said.

“Short of going to the Archive,” Kaiden pointed out.

“No, there’s still the other sphere on the planet,” Maris interjected. “Couldn’t we use that one instead?”

“That would require going back to that place,” I replied. “And, they’d certainly be waiting for us.”

Kaiden brightened. “Unless we took 7D pathways to get there, the same way as when we went to the core earlier today. We could use the *Evangiel*’s sphere to enter 7D, then travel to the sphere on the planet, pick it up, bring it to the core’s spacetime location along with a spatial disruptor—”

“Nope,” I cut him off. “Can’t travel through 7D with the disruptor, remember? Not unless you want to hug it for a few days to get it all Duzie-saturated.”

“Hard pass,” he replied. “If we can’t bring the disruptor with us, then instead we need a shortcut. We could still enter the chamber containing the viewing-sphere on the planet through 7D, but not exit that way.”

“What’s the alternative?” Maris asked.

“We pop in, plant a locator to pinpoint the chamber’s location on the planet, blast a tunnel to the surface, then pick up the sphere with a shuttle,” he stated.

I laughed. “Yeah. Right.”

“I’m serious. It could work,” he insisted.

“But, the energy core location,” I continued. “We’d still have to get there to plant the disruptor, and how would we know where that is?”

He shrugged. “Same strategy.”

Sex really *did* make people lose their minds. “It would never work,” I said.

"Not in that order, but if we located the spacetime location of the core first, *then* go after the viewing-sphere and are able to take a direct path back to the core's position, maybe," Toran stated.

I stared agape at him. "You've both gone insane."

Maris shimmied her shoulders. "I dunno, sounds kind of daring and exciting."

"Hey, *I'm* supposed to be the one with the crazy ideas." I sighed.

Kaiden nudged me. "You know you love it."

"I think we're doomed."

He smiled. "But you kinda want to try it now, don't you?"

I rolled my eyes. He already knew me too well "Okay, yes, it's so crazy, I *do* want it to work." I paused. "How would we blast those holes, though? A shuttle doesn't have that kind of firepower."

"The *Sanctum* does though, right?" Maris suggested. "Richards and Kess were all about seeing us in action."

"They'd be even crazier than us to agree to this plan," Toran said.

Kaiden nodded. "Which is exactly why they will."

"But, will Colren authorize the use of a disruptor?" I pointed out. "I mean, he wants us to extract the core intact. The disruptor is, well, destructive in that 'obliterate everything' kind of way."

"That part we won't know without asking," Kaiden replied. "But, I think this plan is just unconventional enough that the Saps won't see it coming and we have a genuine chance of pulling it off."

"We'll only get one shot," I said.

Kaiden grinned. "The Dark Sentinels only need one."

Maris chuckled. "This is either going to be amazing or fail

spectacularly."

"Come on, have a little faith!" Kaiden urged. "We've tackled way worse."

I cast him a skeptical glance. "Oh, really?"

He faltered. "Okay, so maybe this is the most 'out there' thing we've attempted. But, I believe in us."

"This is what we were called to do." Toran nodded solemnly.

I clapped my hands together. "All right, let's get the pieces moving."

We found Colren in his usual place on the bridge and pulled him aside into Central Command's conference room. After a brief summary of the information we'd pieced together regarding the true nature of the Darkness and the alien invasion, we laid out our plan. Not surprisingly, he didn't seem overjoyed.

"That's, um…" I hadn't often seen Colren at a loss for words, but I couldn't blame his reaction in this instance.

"I know it's crazy," I said. "I thought the same thing."

"But, I really think this has merit," Kaiden insisted.

"Frankly, I'm in no position to question it," the commander replied after a long pause. "I haven't seen what you've seen, and I simply must trust that your recommendations are informed and in the Hegemony's best interests. I've conveyed to you the wishes of my superiors, which is all my position allows for me to do with non-military citizens."

It didn't take much to read between the lines. "A disruptor is essential to our plan. Will we be able to have access to another one?" I asked.

He inclined his head. "I'll put in the request immediately."

"And the *Sanctum*?" Kaiden questioned.

"You'll have what you need for your mission," Colren assured us. "This is a time for decisive action. We can't hold back."

I nodded. "We're ready."

"I'll make the necessary preparations. Stand by." He dismissed us, and we returned to our lounge to wait for the go-ahead.

"This is it, team," Kaiden said as we settled around the table. "The final battle is nigh."

"Dramatic much?" I raised an eyebrow.

"I *hope* this is really the end. I want to get back home," Maris said.

"If all goes well, we'll never know we were gone," Toran replied. "Now that we're almost to the end, I'm saddened to think I may not remember this time we've spent together."

Another pang struck my heart as I was once again reminded of that reality. "We'll figure out a way to find each other."

"What an unusual sight that would be, seeing the four of us meet up in a bar." Maris laughed.

I smiled at the mental image. "A Dark Sentinels reunion."

"It'll happen," Kaiden said with assurance. He took my hand under the table and gave it a loving squeeze.

I hoped more than anything he was right.

"Aside from the disruptor, do we need anything else?" Maris asked.

"Not that I can think of," Toran replied.

"You know, by the time we got to this point, I figured we'd be getting all sorts of new, fancy equipment," I mused.

Kaiden smiled. "Yeah, like that powered armor we saw!"

"Exactly. But," I looked down at my clothes, "now I can't imagine replacing this Duzie-saturated set."

"I never thought I'd utter these words," Maris took a deep breath, "but I'm actually satisfied only having one outfit. I mean, I even had this one patched when it was ripped rather than getting a new shirt." She bit her lip. "Stars, I don't know what's happened to me!"

I laughed. "I think all of us have changed our thinking about what's really important."

Kaiden placed his hand on his abdomen. "With that said, we should probably eat before venturing out the save the universe."

"Very true," Maris agreed. "A hero shouldn't try to save the universe on an empty stomach."

I smiled. "Glad our priorities are in order."

23

"OKAY, ARE WE ready to do this?" Fed and with my sword in hand, I looked around at the members of my team gathered around the *Evangiel*'s viewing-sphere.

Kaiden nodded. "We should probably go before we realize this is insane."

"For the record, I am *well* aware how crazy it is," Maris said. "But Hoofy agrees this will work, so I'm in."

"Whatever will get me back to my family," Toran stated.

"All right," I said. "On three."

At the end of the countdown, we simultaneously placed our hands on the viewing-sphere.

The plan was far from straightforward, but it was clear. We'd scout ahead via the 7D pathways to get back to the energy core chamber. Knowing now that the chamber was directly below the column we'd seen rising from the facility's roof, we could guesstimate the core's placement within a reasonable measure without having to return to the chamber itself. With any luck, Hoofy could help us drop in from 7D close enough to our destination that we wouldn't need to remain in 6D for long. As soon as we'd established that location in our relative spacetime, we could begin the next phase.

Reality unfolded around us, and the ethereal filament bridge resolved underfoot with the viewing-sphere floating between us.

Hoofy was waiting nearby. *"Come, we must move quickly."*

I sheathed my sword, and we raced after him as he loped along the bridge toward our destination. The pathway branched and turned several times along the route. A few of the intersections seemed familiar, but it was clear to me that we'd be lost without Hoofy as a guide. As skeptical as I'd been about the unicorn at times, he was now an integral member of our team.

Eventually, we neared the intersection of bridges I remembered from our previous extraction from the 6D plane. Seeing it now from a distance, the complex junctures reminded me somewhat of a tree.

"This is as close as you can get from here," Hoofy said.

"Is the center of that intersection the energy core?" I asked. Something about the formation drew me in—a sense of great power within it.

Hoofy shifted on his feet. *"The core's position is not a coincidence. Hurry, we don't have long before your ship moves out from alignment."*

Reality folded around us again, replaced by darkness. Slowly, my eyes began to adjust to our new surroundings. We were standing near the base of the power station wall in 6D, only four meters from one of the sentries.

"Quiet," I mouthed to my friends, hoping they could make out the instruction in the low light. I pointed upward toward the vine-cover wall.

No sooner had I moved than a series of alien vocal clicks

broke through the darkness.

"Go!" I dashed to the wall with my friends, jumping as high as I could to get a head-start on the climb. A protective shell cast by Maris appeared around me, but I didn't trust it to hold back the attacker.

The Sap snapped at our heels as it started to climb the wall after us, far faster and nimbler than we were. All the same, I was happy we were in its plane so it couldn't jump ahead of us like we experienced in the engagement back in our spacetime.

I drew my sword and tried to swing at it, but it was too far away. Rather than waiting for it to catch up, I figured I should keep climbing and confront it on the level surface of the rooftop instead.

Kaiden shot a crackling lightning beam downward to buy us extra time. As thankful as I was for the help, the use of magic in combination with my sword being drawn would likely draw every Sap in the vicinity to our location. So much for a stealthy entrance and exit.

I reached the top of the wall and pulled myself over the lip. Leaping to my feet, I turned back to face the pursuing beast.

Rather than one head, ten cleared the ledge.

"Run!" I shouted to my friends. Toran's telepathic resistance wouldn't be enough to give us an edge against that many at once.

"Where did they come from?" Maris yelped while heading for the facility's central column up ahead.

"No clue," Kaiden replied while sprinting next to her. "Whose crazy plan was this?"

I groaned. "Yours!"

Toran jagged to the side two paces ahead of me. "Watch the hole."

We sidestepped the opening we'd ripped in the skylight on

our last visit. I risked a glance over my shoulder and saw the ten Saps we fanning out into a semicircle to trap us. Their attention was fixed on us, and two were headed directly for the hole.

A surprised yelp sounded a moment later as one dropped inside. The second jumped at the last second to avoid falling, leaving us with nine pursuers. To get an accurate location for the core chamber, we'd need time to get situated near the column, and that would be impossible with the Saps after us. We needed to fight.

I came to an abrupt halt and dove sideways, positioning myself between the path of two Saps at the center of the pack. I angled the blade toward the creature on my right, the tip just grazing its chest as it reached me. The creature instantly began to dissolve, and I swung the sword to my left a moment before the other Sap could snap at me. The second creature turned to ash as my blade connected. Seven remained.

My friends had stopped running and were positioning themselves back-to-back five meters from me. Five of the remaining Saps ran to surround them and two headed for me.

"It will be ours," a voice hissed in my mind.

"You said that already." I swung at the one closest to me, but it leaped back. *"Not going so well for you."*

"Submit."

"Nope." I kept my gaze averted, lest they try a telepathic assault. I wasn't sure eye contact was necessary, but it certainly seemed to make it easier for them to get control.

The other Sap made a strike toward my legs, whipping its barbed tail up to slash my face.

I leaned back to avoid the sharp point, and it missed me by mere centimeters. Recovering my balance from the sudden shift, I blindly thrust my sword toward where the creature's torso should be. The blade met resistance, and a moment later the tail turned to ash as it flitted by.

Letting out a growl, the remaining Sap backed out of my reach. *"You are nothing without your blade."*

"I'm not giving it up, so we won't have to find out either way," I replied in my mind.

My limbs started to feel heavy, making it difficult to move. I sensed the creature's control closing in around me. I tried to resist the telepathic influence as it beckoned me to turn my head and look at it. My sword was too heavy. I dropped my arm to my side, my grip loosening.

"Elle, fight back!" Toran called in the distance. He seemed so far away.

"This can all be over. Give in," the voice urged me.

It would be so easy to let go. I wouldn't have to fight anymore. I wouldn't have to be a hero. I was so tired from the stress and responsibility that had been weighing on me for weeks.

For a moment, I was tempted. But the Saps didn't understand that 'easy' wasn't our way. We were driven by a deeper commitment, and I wouldn't give up.

I shook off the attempted telepathic seduction, charging the Sap. I swung for its neck, slicing off its head at the base of its skull before rounding on the others that were going after my friends.

Kaiden and Maris were frozen in place while Toran desperately tried to protect them. I rushed to his aid.

The five remaining Saps jumped backward as soon as they saw me, but I gave them no opportunity to retreat. I slashed at them, leaping and spinning to avoid their counterattacks. Each disintegrated in turn as my blade made contact.

Moments later, it was over. Only small piles of black dust

offered any indication there had been a fight.

"Wow," Kaiden murmured. "Remind me to never upset you."

I smiled sweetly. "I'm unlikely to go into a murderous rage if you don't pick up your laundry. Probably."

"No time for chit-chat!" Maris resumed running toward the central column.

I took off full speed after her. More of the Saps would no doubt be after us any moment. We needed to get in position before they arrived.

We ran the remaining distance to the column base, glancing over our shoulders occasionally to see if we were being pursued. By the time we reached the column base, a second wave of Saps was coming for us—at least three times the previous force.

"Shit, we have to do this now!" Kaiden said.

"Okay, let me make some estimates, hold on." Toran assessed the column, looking around its side to gauge thickness and checking our rise relative to the roofline.

The swarm of Saps was halfway across the open span. We had seconds before they'd be on us.

"We have to go!" I urged.

"This way." Hoofy's voice called to me, and reality folded into nothingness.

With a flash, the view of a sandy plane resolved around me. I took an unsteady breath as I adjusted to being in my physical form again. The nausea was even more intense this time—possibly due to having a different exit point than where we transitioned into the higher plane—and I had to resist the urge to double over.

My friends were looking rather green themselves.

"Everyone okay?" I managed to ask.

"Yeah," Maris replied weakly. "That was too close."

Toran's brow was furrowed. "I wish I'd had time to take proper measurements."

"It will be close enough," Hoofy assured in our minds.

"Yeah, based on that last disruptor explosion, this entire place will be ancient history," I said. "Let's just signal the *Evangiel* and get out of here."

"All right." Toran beckoned us to him. "I believe the power core location would be approximately twenty meters below us relative to this plane."

"Okay." Kaiden pressed behind his ear to open a shared comm channel. "We're in position," he said as soon as the connection chirped.

No reply came at first.

"We see you, Dark Sentinel team," the *Evangiel*'s communications tech acknowledged. "Position marked. Shuttle is on its way."

This was the part of the plan that left us the most exposed. We had no way to transition back to the higher plane from here, so we had to wait for a shuttle to bring us back to the *Evangiel.* At that point, we could re-enter 7D through the ship's viewing-sphere and then use those pathways to navigate to the location of the other sphere on the planet.

I kept my sword drawn as a precaution. "Strange that the location is underground here."

"Not really. We can walk through walls as easily as stepping over a chalk line when we're on the higher planes," Kaiden said. "A lot more than that, actually."

"Still, knowing there are such different landscapes out of sight..." I wouldn't have believed it if I hadn't witnessed those other planes myself. To have my awareness opened to such a broader perspective, this plane and everything I'd taken for granted in life seemed so restrictive now.

"It's incredible." Maris traced the toe of her boot through the sand. She stopped and bent down. "Hey, this is more of that crushed crystal. A *lot* of it."

Now that she mentioned it, I realized the walls sloped upward slightly and we were actually at the bottom of a massive, shallow dish. Normal sand had blown in, but the presence of crystal was unmistakable upon closer inspection.

"What was this place?" I wondered aloud.

"A location of great influence," Hoofy said, still nowhere to be seen. *"When the Ancients still ruled this world, it was their holiest of sites—the nexus of their power. Those pure of spirit could use places like this to ascend to the higher planes, to become beings of pure consciousness. But, the Overlords tried to force their ascension through twisted means. They destroyed the crystals in the process, and these ruins are all that remain."*

"Must have been beautiful to see so many crystals here," Maris said.

"I never saw it for myself, but the elders always spoke of the magnificent crystal tree that once stood here. Its branches still live on in the network of bridges. It is said that all planes could be accessed from this place."

My heart dropped. "Wait, *all* the planes?"

"So it was said."

I shook my head. "No, no, no! If that's true, then the spatial disruptor might not behave how we planned—5D on its own, boosted to 6D from the anomaly. But, if this epicenter has different properties, is it possible that it would take out the higher planes, too?"

Toran paled. "I can't say with any certainly that it wouldn't."

"We have to call off this plan!" I cried. "The Saps aren't the only hyperdimensional beings here. The bridges, the unicorns, the window maze…" My stomach turned over. How could we have overlooked that possibility before?

"Eliminating this threat is more important than the preservation of one location. The hyperdimensional pathways can be rebuilt. Trapping the Overlords, however, is not an opportunity likely to come again."

I couldn't believe how dismissive Hoofy was being. No wonder the other unicorns were furious with him.

"Why didn't you tell us this place was special?" Maris asked, distraught.

"The others are content to turn a blind eye, but while I was trapped, I did nothing except watch the Overlords plot their dark designs. I have seen their evil spirits and know they will not stop until they achieve their goal. Temporarily relocating from our lands is a small price to pay, to make sure no other races suffer at the Overlords' hands."

"Stars, this isn't what I thought we were signing up for," I murmured.

"I did not mean to mislead you," Hoofy said. *"The sacredness of this place was spoiled long ago. Our actions now can finally begin to heal those past wrongs."*

I wasn't entirely convinced by his logic, but I did recognize the truth in the words. We held the power right now, and we'd vowed to do anything to save our worlds. Displacing the hyperdimensional beings on this planet wasn't right, but allowing billions of others to die was a greater injustice.

The roar of an approaching engine broke the silence, and I looked up to see our shuttle approaching on autopilot.

"We have to move forward," I said.

My teammates gave grim nods of agreement. We were in the fight to the end.

24

"ALL RIGHT, PHASE One: complete." I settled into my usual seat on the shuttle.

I still had misgivings about using the spatial disruptor in a place where it might result in collateral damage, but the more I thought about it, the more I found myself agreeing with Hoofy's viewpoint.

"Okay, so now we do it all over again?" Maris questioned.

"More or less," Kaiden replied.

The most difficult parts of our mission were still to come. As soon as we were back on the *Evangiel*, we needed to reenter 7D and make our way to the location of the viewing-sphere on the planet. We would then transition back to our normal spacetime so we could send the pickup signal to the *Sanctum*, which would blast a hole to the chamber to serve as an egress point for us to take the planet's viewing-sphere with us. At least, that was the plan. Given how not-swimmingly our first phase had gone with the unexpected attack, I had no illusions that accomplishing the next tasks would be any easier.

Our shuttle flew on autopilot to the *Evangiel*'s main hangar. After completing the decontamination protocol, we quickly made our way to Central Command.

Colren met us in the corridor outside the lift. "Well done," he said as soon as he saw us. "We've run a geological survey of the site you identified, and we found a dense mass near the specified depth. We'll use that as the target for the spatial disruptor when the time comes."

"Just have to get the viewing-sphere," I said.

He nodded. "The *Sanctum* is standing by to meet you. The *Evangiel* will be waiting at the pickup point."

"All right, we'll see you again soon," Kaiden said while we headed for the viewing chamber. He paused, giving us the look of someone potentially saying goodbye for the last time. "Thank you," he murmured.

"Just doing what's needed." I turned my attention to the task at hand.

It felt like we were running in circles, but the viewing-spheres were the only way we could transition into the higher planes from our normal spacetime. Movement between the higher hyperdimensional planes after that initial transition seemed easy enough—at least with Hoofy's guidance—but we had to work within the constraints of the system.

Knowing the Saps would be going on the offensive and practically had eternity at their disposal compared to our present time passage, we hurriedly gathered around the viewing-sphere.

"Ready?" I drew my sword, and my friends nodded. "Okay, on three…"

As soon as I completed the countdown, we initiated the transition. The world unfolded around us and we returned to the filament bridge in 7D.

"Welcome back," Hoofy greeted us, trotting forward. *"This way."*

We ran down the bridge after him. I found my stomach settled faster this time, presumably because my body was getting used to the bizarre transitions. I still couldn't believe what I was doing, let alone that I'd done it enough to be getting accustomed to it.

Our path along the bridges took us further toward the right than our previous route. Based on how long we'd been running, I knew we must be getting close to our destination. I was just about to ask Hoofy how much longer it would be when the unicorn unexpectedly slowed his pace. Up ahead, a herd of two dozen unicorns blocked our path.

At the front of the herd, I recognized the female elder we'd met earlier. *"Do not do this, Huefneril,"* she cautioned telepathically.

Hoofy continued forward slowly, meeting her gaze. *"This is the only way, Maricaela. Leave now and let this play out as it may."*

She turned her attention to the rest of us. *"It is just like your kind to think only of yourselves."*

I stepped forward to stand abreast to Hoofy. "The future of the Hegemony is at stake. We're doing this for all of those worlds."

"Bringing your problems to us," Maricaela replied.

I didn't care that I was talking to an ancient, powerful being; I wouldn't stand by while I was belittled because I was trying to save my civilization. "No, *this* place is the origin, and those problems came to find *us*. I won't make excuses for my commitment to protecting my home and my people."

She tossed her mane. *"Such a young race. You believe your lives and homes are the only ones which matter."*

"Not at all," I softened my tone. "I'm sorry if it seems that way, but that isn't the case. In fact, I suggested that we call off our plan because I found out what damage it may cause to your realm. I feel awful about it, truly. If you know of another way for us to stop the Overlords, then please, tell us. But right now, this is the only way I know. I understand that the structures on this plane can be repaired, but our worlds can't. This is our chance to eliminate an evil that will keep coming back over and over again if we let them go now, and I can't allow that threat to be a shadow on my people's future. We want to seal the Overlords away and then reset our worlds back to how they were—to give people back their lives and futures. Maybe that's selfish, but we wouldn't be worthy of survival if we didn't fight for it."

Maricaela evaluated me in silence. *"I sense purity of intent in your heart. However, actions must be judged on the result, not the motivation."*

"Then let's look at the results," I said. "If you allow us to proceed, you'll need to leave this place and go somewhere safe. I don't know how long it will take, but the hyperdimensional bridges will mend, and eventually you can return here. The Hegemony and all of its worlds will be saved. However, if you insist on stopping us, all of the Hegemony will eventually fall to the Overlords, and stars know how many other civilizations. They will figure out how to ascend, and you won't be safe, either. When you look at it like that, I'm not sure you can call *us* the selfish ones."

Hoofy bowed his head. *"This is why I have aligned myself with them,"* he stated. *"I would gladly accept banishment for helping to save this young, promising race on the cusp of coming into their own."*

Maricaela looked to the other members of her herd,

possibly in a private telepathic discussion. *"We will leave this place, as you ask, and make sure others follow. Sacrifice is needed for the greater good."*

Maris clasped her hands. "Thank you."

Kaiden and Toran murmured their thanks, as well, and I smiled. "If we meet again, I hope it will be to begin rebuilding the past friendship between our races."

"Yes. Perhaps when the Overlords are no longer a threat, we will one day walk among you again." She turned away from us. *"We will alert the others about the need to evacuate. May you succeed in your mission."* The herd bounded into the mist alongside the bridge and disappeared.

Kaiden placed a hand on the small of my back. "Amazing job, Elle. Well said."

"I wasn't sure they'd listen," I admitted.

"They were never truly against us," Hoofy said. *"Their desire to avoid interference can blind them, but they would never condemn billions to death."*

"It certainly *seemed* like they were ready to let that happen," Kaiden said.

"A test of your resolve, more than anything," Hoofy replied. *"To ensure the destruction of their home would not be in vain."*

I nodded. "Can't blame them for checking. I'd want to vet us, too, were the roles reversed."

"And now we must deliver," Toran said. "The others are waiting on us." He motioned down the bridge in the direction we'd been going.

"Let's go get that sphere." I resumed running after Hoofy.

Several bridges and intersections later, I spotted our target at the center of a six-way intersection: a translucent sphere identical to the one on the *Evangiel*. We'd reached the location of the underground chamber.

"Time to summon our ride," Kaiden said.

I drew my sword. "The Saps are going to be waiting for us—I know it."

He gave me an encouraging smile. "Then you'll slash them into oblivion like always."

"Standing by with a shield for as soon as we transition," Maris said.

"I will be watching," Hoofy said. *"Stars be with you."*

"Thanks, see you soon." In unison with my team, I reached out to touch the sphere.

Reality folded inward and new surroundings resolved with a flash. A protective shell appeared around me, and I raised my sword in anticipation of an attack, but the underground chamber was empty.

I lowered my weapon. "That's strange. I really thought they'd be waiting for us."

"Yeah, I did, too," Kaiden agreed. "Well, no complaints."

"We should summon the *Sanctum* before the Saps change their minds about an attack," Toran advised.

"On it." I tapped behind my ear to open a commlink. "*Sanctum*, this is the Dark Sentinel team. We're in position." Only static sounded. "Stars! Are the comm's working?"

Toran frowned. "Should be. They were working before."

"Could the rock be interfering?" Kaiden asked.

"Possibly, but—"

"We read you," Richards replied over the comm, cutting Toran off. "Sorry about that. We needed to clean up the signal."

"Great to hear your voice!" I breathed a sigh of relief. "We're in position in the cavern."

"We see you," Kess acknowledged. "Geological survey has us cutting through clay and then several meters of rock. The beam weapons on this ship weren't designed for precise excavation, so I suggest you clear the area."

"There's an adjacent chamber where we can go to," I told her.

"Perfect. Keep an eye on our progress and let us know when it's about to punch through," Richard stated. "We won't be able to see where we're going once everything starts to melt."

"Good thing we have shields," Maris said.

"Yours will be more reliable than the ones you cast for us. Mind being on watch duty?" I asked her.

She smiled. "Happy to."

"All right, give us a minute or two to get situated," I said while motioning Kaiden and Toran to deal with the sphere. We'd agreed during our planning session that it would be best to move it away from the drilling site so it didn't get coated in molten rock. While the crystals were supposed to be near-indestructible by most physical means, it wouldn't be easy for us to move if it was glued to the floor by a blob of rock.

Kaiden bent down to nudge the base supporting the crystal wrapped in the dark, alien tendrils, but it gave no sign of movement. "Argh, this thing is on here good."

Toran joined him, grimacing as he reached through the mass of vines to grip the inner support structure with both hands. It wouldn't budge. "I did not anticipate this problem."

"Hold off on the drilling," I instructed. "We haven't been able to clear the area."

"ETA?" Kess asked.

"Not sure. Hang on." I motioned for Kaiden and Toran to back away. "Let me try levitating it off."

I focused on the base, imagining the bonds within the stone and breaking them down. I held out my right hand, palm open, and shot a dark orb toward the center of the column. The vines recoiled, and the rock underneath condensed and crumbled at the impact site. When the structure began to tip over, I redirected my energy to catch the sphere and lift it up, then set it gently on the ground atop the bed of vines.

"You should really do that kind of stuff more often," Kaiden said.

I shrugged. "Too difficult to do in battle. I need a ton of concentration."

Toran jogged to where I'd set the sphere down. "We need to get it to the other chamber. Kaiden, your cloak."

Hesitantly, Kaiden removed the outer garment and handed it to the other man.

Toran draped the cloth over the crystal so he could grip it without touching it with his skin or gauntlets. He easily lifted the meter-wide sphere in his arms and strode toward the doorway to the adjacent chamber. "A little light?"

"Of course." Kaiden conjured a light orb in his palm and sent it floating ahead of Toran.

"Stars, no!" Toran almost dropped the sphere.

Red eyes reflected the light from the orb. Dozens of eyes.

Toran quickly stepped back. "Maris, shield. Now!"

Maris cast a shield over the passageway a moment before half a dozen of the Sap fighters lunged toward us.

"What are they doing in there?" Kaiden took a step back.

Maris cautiously approached the passageway so the silvery magical forcefield from her artifact sealed most of the opening, in case the cast one failed. "We might have to get cozy."

I looked between the Saps and the chamber that was about to turn into a lava tube. "They set us up."

Kaiden's face dropped. "Must have known we could use the sphere to go to back to 7D and get away from them. So, they tried to ambush us where we'd have nowhere to run."

I groaned. "And we *could* use the sphere to escape now, but there'd be no way to take it with us. Except, stars! The sphere is how they transition. We need to… block it somehow before more come through."

"Maybe, like, one hand on it?" Kaiden speculated.

"I dunno, worth a shot," I agreed. "Not sure if it's a one-activity-at-a-time thing, or it doesn't matter."

"I'll try," he said.

"Hey, what's going on down there?" Richards asked over the comm.

"Unexpected company," I replied.

"If we huddle together, maybe…" Maris sounded unsure.

"No choice," I said. "Come on."

Maris regulated her forcefield to allow us to pass inside while keeping the enemies at bay. The three of us had to crouch near the ground where the bubble was widest, but we managed to get within its boundaries along with the viewing-sphere, still wrapped in Kaiden's cloak except for the one bit he was touching.

"Okay, we're ready," I told Kess and Richards.

"All right, activating the beam," Kess stated.

The ground trembled and loose bits of rock and dust rained from the ceiling. On our other side, the Saps redoubled their efforts to break through Maris' special forcefield, though their clawing and biting bore no results.

I inched closer to Kaiden as the shaking intensified. "We were never supposed to be in the same room as this."

"Improvisation," Maris said.

"Three meters down so far," Richards informed us.

"Long way to go," Toran responded.

The Saps shifted in and out of our perception, but each time they tried to dimensional-jump to the other side of the bubble they immediate retreated because of the heat from the drilling.

Kaiden closed his eyes as one of the Saps snapped at him ten centimeters away on the other side of the forcefield. "These guys are getting antsy."

The mass of Saps pressed against the shield, unable to push through, but a force nonetheless. Maris slipped backward, unable to stand up to their combined strength. Snouts and limbs of some of the creatures began slipping through new gaps between the forcefield's dome and the passageway walls.

"Gah! I can't hold them." Maris leaned into her shield artifact, which formed the front of our defensive wall.

Toran braced himself behind her. "We're in this together."

As much as I loved the sentiment, that desire didn't change the physical realties of the situation. We needed to force the enemy back. I concentrated on my sword, trying to put myself in the mindset that had enabled me to augment our shield on the shuttle to stave off destruction from the spatial disruptor before. Energy surged through me, and I directed it toward the shell already around us.

"Kaiden, try to charge the shell," I instructed.

Confusion flitted across this face, then he nodded his understanding. A moment later, an electrical charge shot from his staff to the dome, which transitioned to the outer barrier.

The Saps cried out as electrical bolts shot toward them when they tried to touch the forcefield. The pressure sliding us backward began to dissipate enough that we could seal the gaps around its edges by pressing further into the passageway.

"How's it coming, Kess?" I asked over the comm.

"Getting close," she said. "You see anything yet?"

I checked the caver's roof but there were no signs of the drilling beam aside from the continued tremble and loose rocks falling. "Not yet."

The seconds dragged on as the Saps continued to snap at us. The electrical charge began to wear off.

"Recharging," Kaiden said, holding up his staff to pass the electrical current. However, with the sparks dancing on his staff, he suddenly froze.

"Hey, what are you—" It took me a moment to realize what had happened, but then I saw one of the Saps staring at him with its glowing, red eyes. Somehow, it had managed to ensnare him through the shield. "No, Kaiden, snap out of it!" I shook his shoulder.

The electrical charge arced inside the forcefield, unable to pass through without his coordinated direction with Maris. I bobbed to avoid being struck.

"This is going to fry us!" Maris cried. I saw her attempt to create smaller shields around each of us inside the dome, but her attention was already too directed on maintaining the larger protective dome for them to take hold.

I passed my hand in front of Kaiden's face with no response. The lightning continued to dance along his staff. If it kept up, we might fare better with the beam drill in the cavern.

"Stars, the rock on the roof is starting to glow!" Maris noticed.

Okay, so our chances in that chamber had just dropped significantly. I didn't think our odds against that many Saps was much better. We needed to do something. "Kaiden…" I pleaded.

"Let him go," Toran's voice boomed to my right. He was staring directly at the Sap who had telepathically linked with Kaiden.

The creature faltered.

"Let him go," Toran repeated even more forcefully.

To my surprise, the Sap ducked its head and turned to walk away.

"What the..." I faded out as Kaiden took a gasping breath.

"What happened?" he asked, his tone one of confusion and distress.

"One of the Saps got you," I replied. "But Toran here... he just gave it a treatment of its own."

"Do more of that!" Maris urged. "These guys are still pushing."

Toran locked in a staring contest with the Saps. "Leave us," he commanded. A couple of the Sap fighters hesitated, but there were too many of them for that to make a difference. It would seem one-on-one was the only effective strategy—at least where his abilities were now—and that would take more time than we had to address each of the creatures in turn.

"We're going to have to make a run for it," I realized. "As soon as the platform drops—" I cut off, noticing the roof of the cavern. "Stars, that's glowing a lot!"

"Dialing it back," Kess stated over the comm. "Almost through. We'll drop the charge." The bright point faded the slightest measure. "Detonating in three... two... one!"

I instinctively covered my head with my free arm as an explosive charge broke through the final section of the ceiling so the beam didn't cook us. Chunks of rock flew throughout the chamber, leaving a pile of super-heated rubble at the center, on top of the alien vines. As the dust cleared, I could see our three-meter-wide access shaft to safety now dominating the center of the ceiling.

"Get ready to run," I told my team.

"Lowering the evac platform," Richards said.

The deployment took nearly a minute, requiring Richards to hold the ship steady so the platform didn't touch the near-molten rock walls, which had yet to cool. It would be impossible for us to exit through the chamber if it wasn't for Maris' protective shields.

Finally, the platform came into view—a simple rectangle two meters by one with a railing around three sides.

"Okay, Maris, wall off this opening as best you can," I instructed. "Toran, get the sphere. It'll be a mad dash to get out of here."

"Ready," all members of the team confirmed.

I planned my running path to avoid the patches of hot rock. "Okay… go!"

We sprinted across the sweltering chamber and made a running leap for the platform hovering a meter above the ground. I landed first, lending my hand to Maris to help her aboard. Kaiden and Toran easily made the jump. To my relief, Maris' shield had managed to hold back the Saps.

"Get us out of here!" I shouted into my comm.

The *Sanctum* began to rise while the winch on the lift simultaneously engaged, pulling us toward the belly of the ship. Maris encased the platform in a new shield, diffusing the heat. The glow had faded from the rocks lining the shaft, but I could still see distortions in the air from the heat.

After a slow initial ascent, the platform finally cleared the shaft. A gust of wind rocked the platform, knocking me off-balance. I held onto the railing as the platform swung dangerously far to the side, pitching us toward the open side of the platform.

"The sphere," Kaiden warned, hugging the sphere still wrapped in his cloak.

Toran steadied it on the other side. "We won't let it go anywhere."

I looked between the sphere and my friends once we had

safely entered the *Sanctum*'s cargo hold. "Let's go put those hyperdimensional bastards in their place."

25

THE PIECES WERE in place. All that we needed to do was detonate the spatial disruptor alongside the crystal sphere… and then somehow escape with our lives. True to form, the part of the plan where we didn't all die had been the most glossed over.

"Okay, how does this go, again?" I asked.

"We ride the detonation wave to 8D and seal the Saps inside," Toran replied.

"Right." I paused. "No, I still don't get it."

"It'll make sense in the moment," Maris said. "Hoofy will be there with us as a guide."

I took a deep breath. "All right."

The *Sanctum* was speeding toward the location we'd identified during the first phase of our plan, corresponding to the location of the energy core in the Saps' native 6D plane. If our assessments were correct, we'd be able to survive the detonation and then return through 8D to the *Evangiel*, which would be waiting for us, safely out of the blast range. And if we were wrong… well, we wouldn't be around to feel bad about it.

Theoretically, it wouldn't matter, since anyone could subsequently initiate a universal reset to before the Darkness ever appeared. Still, I hoped I'd get to be a part of that special moment.

"ETA two minutes," Richards informed us over the ship's comm.

"All right, standing by," Kaiden confirmed.

One of his hands still rested on the sphere; thus far, no creatures had transitioned through it, so we didn't want to press our luck. It was only in retrospect we realized how lucky we'd been for no invasion force to enter through the sphere on the *Evangiel*; keeping the ship moving whenever it was within the Saps' territory had likely saved us from an unexpected attack.

Toran stood next to Kaiden with the spatial disruptor at his feet. "One more task."

"It's gonna be a wild ride," I said.

Kaiden nodded. "I have no doubt."

The *Sanctum* closed the remaining distance to our destination and dropped in altitude.

"You sure about this?" Richards asked over the comm.

"Not at all," I responded, "but we're doing it anyway."

"I like your attitude," the captain replied. "Blasting now."

A low rumble reverberated through the cargo hold as the *Sanctum*'s beam weapon charged. Through the viewport in lower deck hatch, I watched the beam lance toward the sand and crystal pit we'd identified during the first phase of the mission. The beam easily melted through the ground, too bright to look at, even with the auto-tint shading on the viewport. After seven seconds, the beam shut off.

"One entry shaft, made to order!" Kess declared.

I smiled. "Thanks."

The cargo hold hatch opened. We gripped the railing of the rescue platform as it began to lower toward the twenty-meter-deep pit. At the base, a dense boulder of dark rock now exposed, had survived the beam blast.

"That must be the manifestation of the energy core on this plane," Kaiden said.

"Then that's where we'll set the disruptor." Toran patted the device.

Kaiden continued to keep one hand on the viewing-sphere as we were lowered, knowing that the risk of Saps trying to transition through it increased as we got closer to the site.

A meter from the bottom of the blasted-out shaft, the platform stopped. I motioned my friends to jump off of it.

"All set," I told Richards as soon as we were clear. "Now, get back to the *Evangiel* and jump out of here."

"Don't worry about us," Richards replied. "It's been an honor."

"Happy hunting," Kess added.

The platform began retracting into the belly of the ship.

"Okay, Toran, get the sphere in place—remember to keep a hand on it. Kaiden, get the spatial disruptor set."

They got to work.

I turned to Maris. "We're going to have a major blast coming our way. The shield needs to hold. That'll be the only thing between us and…" I didn't want to complete the thought.

She nodded, determination in her eyes. "Everything up until now has been practice. We're ready."

"That's right." I drew my sword, savoring the power of it in my hand. Much of the plan would come down to me and my timing.

Above us, the *Sanctum* blasted away the moment its cargo hatch was closed.

Kaiden took a deep breath. "All right, we're committed now!"

I watched the ship disappear into the sky. "Ten minutes to go." The default timing had been set with Colren in advance, which should provide adequate time for the *Sanctum* to get on board the *Evangiel* and the ship to jump away. If we didn't hear from them, we were under standing orders to detonate no matter what. If they were ready to jump before then, they'd tell us.

Several uncomfortable minutes passed while Kaiden and Toran completed the equipment preparations.

"This rock thing is weird," Toran observed while he worked. "I've never seen a material like this."

"My pendant is glowing like crazy," Kaiden said.

"Must have some connection with the crystals," I suggested.

Kaiden stared at it pensively. "I wonder if this is some sort of ultra-dense crystal—like a diamond is to coal."

"I could see how that would be a significant energy source, assuming it maintains a direct connection to the crystalline network," Toran said.

My stomach twisted. "Too bad we have to blow it up."

"It will endure," Hoofy said, appearing before us for the first time on the world. *"But they are coming."*

The viewing-sphere turned black beneath Toran's hand. "How do we stop it?"

"You can't. They have been waiting, building their forces. You must detonate now."

"Kaiden, Toran, get back," I instructed. After a momentary hesitation, Toran removed his hand and ran to stand near me with Maris. "Shield!" I instructed.

Maris waved her hand, and a purple shell appeared around

the spatial disruptor and viewing-sphere. "How are we supposed to get to them to do what we need to do with these shields up?" she asked.

"Still working on that." I assessed the scene. "Wait! I've got it. Shrink the shield."

Maris gave me a quizzical look.

"If it's tight enough against the sphere, we might be able to prevent them from transitioning completely," I explained.

"Ah, yes!" She made the necessary adjustment, positioning the outer boundaries of the shell just beyond the crystal sphere's surface.

"All right, if this can hold, we can drop it at the moment of detonation," I continued. "Stars, is the *Sanctum* back to the *Evangiel* yet?" With the way things were going, I didn't know if we'd be able to wait until the agreed upon detonation time.

"Something's coming through!" Kaiden gripped his staff, ready to act.

Dark forms pressed on the inside of the shield, flexing the shimmering purple outline.

I stepped closer, prepared to slash them if they broke through. "How long until our detonation time?"

"Three minutes twenty seconds," Toran replied.

There was no way we'd make it that long. The purple shield was already starting to stutter as the creatures pressed against it. I estimated less than a minute before Maris wouldn't be able to hold it any longer.

"Maybe I can force them back." Kaiden's staff electrified, and he shot a lightning charge toward the sphere. The energy danced along the surface.

"I can't loosen the field enough to allow it to pass through," Maris said. "I can barely hold it as it is."

"You're doing great," I encouraged her, my mind racing

for another tactic. "Maybe—"

"Dark Sentinel team, you're clear to proceed," Colren said in our earpieces. "Jump commencing in fifteen seconds." The commlink cut before I had a chance to reply.

"Okay, set seventeen seconds on the detonator," I instructed Kaiden. "Maris, on my mark, drop the shield and then we all make contact." I ran to the sphere and surrounded it with my friends. Kaiden finished setting the timer and joined us, each of us hovering one hand over the sphere and Hoofy alongside us with his horn poised.

With one second left on the detonator, I gave the order. "Now!"

The shield collapsed, freeing the beings waiting to emerge inside. Before they could fully materialize, we touched the sphere.

Reality unfolded around us, turning to blackness. With a flash, the eighth-dimensional window maze came into focus. Hundreds of window facets shined in the corridor, all displaying the energy core site spanning the dimensional planes. The viewing-sphere floated between us.

I immediately raised my sword, blade pointed down several centimeters above the sphere's surface. "Stay focused," I told my friends. They wrapped their hands around mine on the hilt, and Hoofy touched his horn to our hands.

The disruptor detonated.

Its wave of destruction spread throughout the innumerable window facets. It accelerated through the hyperdimensional energy connections to the farthest reaches of the Saps' domain, sucking everything it touched into a new dimensional pocket within the disruptor field.

The disruption around the new dimensional bubble continued to expand, pushing through to the higher planes. It was coming for us.

"Focus!" I shouted as the bubble broke through.

My sense of reality warped as the windows disappeared around me. They unfolded and expanded, each of the facets becoming a crystal. The crystals stacked on one another, forming endless fractals spanning as far as I could see. Somehow, we'd been pushed into the ninth dimension, the domain of the crystalline network itself.

I wanted to wonder at its beauty, overcome with pure joy. But, the dimensional pocket was collapsing beneath me. I was falling back to the lower planes.

The branching crystals collapsed into single facets and the windows returned to focus. The dimensional pocket we'd created was folding back, moving toward one of the windows. This was the moment we'd been waiting for.

I thrust my sword into the viewing-sphere while directing our combined magical energy toward the dimensional pocket. We focused our energy to force the pocket into that single window. I cried out with exertion as the energy channeled through me.

The sphere shattered, throwing my friends and me to the ground. I landed hard on my back, stunned.

I propped up on my elbows. "Did we do it?"

Inside our targeted window-facet, the disruptor wave dissipated, leaving only darkness. The other facets around it were now filled with light.

Kaiden grinned. "I think we did!"

Hoofy bowed his head. "*You have succeeded. The Overlords are now confined within the dimensional pocket, and this is the only exit.*"

Toran rose to his feet and went to inspect the window. "Amazing."

I stood up and joined him next to the window. "A single exit point is one too many."

"Not sure we can do much about that," Kaiden said.

"There is," Hoofy stated. *"You can fold it so it will never be found."* He trotted to the facet's location and pointed his horn toward it. *"Elle, your sword is part of the crystalline network itself. It has the power to reform this plane of reality."*

"How do I—"

"Follow your instincts," he told me. *"The power is within you."*

I examined the area around the facet. I knew what I needed to do.

Trusting my gut, I traced the tip of my blade down the outer edges of the facets adjacent to the darkened section where the Saps were trapped. The two vertical lines glowed bright white. I then held my open right palm toward them, sending the same telekinetic energy commands I would to collapse matter. The two lines glowed brighter for a moment and then started to draw together, folding the dark facet backward and trapping it in a now-hidden fold between them. No one would ever find it unless they knew where to look.

"Wow," Kaiden murmured.

I let out a surprised laughed. "Did not know I could do that."

"Now that you have mastered your abilities, you can create a doorway to anywhere you wish," Hoofy revealed. *"This is a power to rival the Ancients."*

I stared at my sword. "Seriously?"

"You wield great power, I told you," Hoofy said. *"You have only scratched the surface of your potential. I would be honored to have the chance to join you in your future endeavors."*

"Except, we're about to go back to our regular old selves,"

I muttered. At least, I assumed as much. I honestly had no idea what to expect from the upcoming universal reset.

"*May I join you?*" Hoofy asked, ignoring my comment.

"Of course!" Maris exclaimed. "I mean, five-year-old me would be furious if I turned down a unicorn companion."

I laughed. "Our families are going to have us committed if we breathe a word about what's happened."

"All the more reason to get the team back together as soon as possible," Kaiden said.

"Very true." I paused. "So, back to the *Evangiel*?"

"Actually, if you can make a doorway to anywhere, do we even need to go back to the *Evangiel* in order to get to Crystallis?" Maris asked.

"Everyone will be wondering where we are," Kaiden replied.

Maris shrugged. "But if we're about to do a universal reset, does it matter? They won't remember any of this, anyway."

Kaiden looked at me with longing. "That doesn't give us any time to celebrate our success."

My heart ached as I thought about the different ways the next several days we could go. One option was to return to the *Evangiel*—to celebrate, receive the thanks of the Hegemony, and share final moments of friendship and love, all the while knowing we were about to say goodbye. Or, we could return to the Master Archive now while the victory was fresh and get to our new futures that much sooner.

As much as I wanted more time with Kaiden, I couldn't bear the thought of growing even closer before it would all come to a sudden end. I wanted to save something for the reunion I had to believe was coming.

"I've never been one for long goodbyes," I said at last. My gaze met Kaiden's, and I saw the understanding in his eyes.

"Returning to my family is all I've ever wanted," Toran said. "The sooner, the better."

Maris frowned. "I wish I had something I was looking forward to back home. What I used to think was a pretty good life is now…" She faded out, shaking her head.

"We remembered before, we can remember again," I said. "We can find each other."

Kaiden took my hand. "We better."

Maris held up one finger. "Wait, what about the crystal shard? Don't we need that for a universal reset?"

"Not if we're in the Master Archive, I wouldn't think," Kaiden replied.

"What'll happen to that shard, then?" I asked.

Toran shrugged. "I'm not sure. But, that might not be a bad thing to have floating around somewhere. It's not like the average person would know how to use it or have access to a viewing-sphere."

"True, I guess you never know when something like that might be needed." I took a deep breath. "Okay, so we're decided?"

When my friends had nodded their assent, I took my sword in both hands and traced it through the air, picturing a doorway to the crystal cavern deep within the Master Archive. The air glowed bright white where the blade passed. After I had completed a full rectangle, the entire shape flashed white and then dissolved, leaving a gateway to our destination.

"I've gotta say, this is a *way* more convenient way to travel," I said.

Kaiden sighed. "Figures we'd learn about this trick *after* we complete our task."

Maris shrugged. "Who knows? Maybe we'll be called for future missions—or maybe even some adventures!"

"I will find you then," Hoofy said. *"Your next stop is a place I cannot go."* He faded from sight.

"Well, he seems confident enough," I said.

"Assuming we can ever find these artifacts again," Kaiden replied.

Toran flexed his hands in his gauntlets. "I imagine that if these items truly have become a part of us, and us of them, that reunion is inevitable."

"I hope so." I smiled, looking through the open doorway to the darkened Archive. "For now, let's put everything back how it should be."

26

IT WAS BITTERSWEET stepping through the passageway into the Master Archive on Crystallis. I hated the fact that our mission's success meant our time together was coming to an end—at least for now. We'd become a surrogate family in our weeks together, living through experiences no one else could possibly understand.

"I'm gonna miss you guys," I said, my heart heavy.

Toran nodded. "Likewise."

Maris started to tear up. "I'm not sure if I'm happy to be going home or sad this is over."

I gave her a hug and she squeezed me back. "Whatever future you want, go out and get it," I told her.

She nodded, pulling out of the embrace. "Same with you."

We walked slowly down the rock pathway leading to the crystal column for the Archive's interface. Having witnessed the crystalline network in our brief touch with the higher plane, I had even more reverence for this place.

"I have to admit, I wasn't sure this day would come," Kaiden said.

"Things were looking pretty bleak at a few points," I agreed. "There were times when I wasn't sure we'd make it through."

"Yeah, seriously." Maris shook her head. "The only thing that kept me from losing hope was Colren's assurance that there are future entries in the Archive, so I knew it would all work out."

"No," the mysterious voice in the Archive stated.

My heart skipped a beat, surprised by the sudden interjection. "Sorry, 'no' about what?"

"There are no records from the 'future'," the voice clarified.

Kaiden's brows drew together. "There aren't? Then what did the Hegemony observe to make them think they were seeing records of future events?"

"They misinterpreted the layered progression. No records exist beyond the furthest point of physical progression in spacetime." That didn't clear up matters in the least.

"I don't know what you mean," I admitted. "But why base everything around spacetime? There are so many other beings in the higher planes. Why is everything centered around us?"

"Because that is where we began, before we ascended," the voice replied.

"What did I tell you!" Toran looked rather pleased with himself.

"All right, that confirms it." I nodded. "And the 'Overlords'?"

"We encountered them when we first began to expand our consciousnesses. We sought to share with them, to stand as equals, but their spirits were too driven by greed for them to ascend."

"That explains the city ruins," I concluded. "Did everyone ascend?"

"Those who could did. Others ventured out from their home planet—you could consider them your ancestors who were brave enough to leave their oppressors behind. Much of the technology they brought with them was lost until recently," the voice explained.

"Stars..." Kaiden murmured.

"The ascended just let the Overlords take over their former world?" Maris asked.

"It wasn't ours or theirs. We resided in the same place on different planes. One could make no more claim to it than another. After ascension, many no longer cared about their roots. Others wished to maintain a connection to the corporeal realm, so we developed technology to allow our consciousness to take physical form when we desired."

Toran came to attention "The bioprinters! Those were originally used to enable the 10D pure-consciousness beings to take physical form?"

"That was their original purpose, yes," the voice confirmed. "You have found a... creative new use for them, which was needed in this time of crisis."

"No wonder we had so much influence over our attributes," Kaiden mused. "I guess the original design was quite literally to form a body based on the innermost desires of our consciousness, from the sound of it."

"Yeah, I guess so," I realized, absently running my fingers through my fuchsia hair.

"And what are *you*?" Maris asked. "Are you one of the ascended?"

"I am a... copy. A preservation of one of our leaders who has since moved on, just as those who guard the artifacts were created to endure beyond natural life."

"If you're already ascended, what's next?" Maris questioned.

The voice let out a musical laugh. "Words could never describe."

"Back to what you were saying before..." I said slowly. "Why do some of the records in the Archive look like they are future events, but you said they're not?"

"This place is the result of the physical cause and effect—the chain of the events—transpiring in your plane," the voice explained. "New records cannot be created until that path progresses, only previous states are overwritten."

"But there are records beyond the reset point," I protested. "How could those exist?"

The musical voice chuckled again. "These progressions don't have to happen at the same pace. The hours elapsed have not yet reached the point of a previous universal reset."

Suddenly, everything clicked for me. "Stars, that's it! We *did* win this battle against the Saps, but we hadn't lost yet after this amount of chronological time in another previous-future timeline."

"Ow, my head," Maris moaned.

Kaiden perked up. "Damn, you're right."

"There was never a 'bright future' ahead... it was only evidence of another reset loop where we waited longer before initiating a universal reset," Toran said.

Maris stared at him blankly. "I'm still lost."

Kaiden crouched down and traced his finger along the stone floor over the cavern, leaving a glowing, golden trail behind wherever he touched. "Okay, this is the timeline." He drew a narrow rectangle. "It goes on forever, but physical reality can be altered. Say some corn is growing and is almost ready for harvest." He filled in most of the box. "But then we reset back two weeks—that corn is now immature again." He drew a horizontal line through the shaded part of the box at the one-quarter mark. "Now, the corn needs to grow for two more weeks and then a little more until harvest," he traced his finger up the shaded area, "but it's only after it completes the growing cycle that it will be ready." He shaded in the remaining area of the box. "Up until that final stretch, it's just growing back to the growth point it achieved before the reset."

"And anything could happen to it after the reset," I chimed in. "There's no guarantee it will ever grow as well as it did that first time because the environmental conditions might change—or it might do better. But as far as any records in the Archive are concerned, everything up to the reset point already happened, and that same amount of time must elapse before new records are formed, versus adding a layer when looping over the same timeframe."

Maris thought for a few seconds. "Okay, so, if we were the corn, we grew faster than we did on one past loop leading up to the universal reset. The events from that old loop now *look* like the future only because we got to 'here' faster."

"Exactly," Toran said. "Just because we grew more efficiently, the overall rate that time passes isn't any different; planets will still orbit at their natural pace, cells will age. It's been, what, a little over a week since we sealed the Master Archive?"

Kaiden nodded. "Yeah, something like that."

"Well, a previous iteration may have taken two weeks, or a month. The future we thought the crystals showed was really just us being terrible on a previous loop."

I smiled. "Damn, this version of us is *good*."

Toran chuckled. "I suppose we are."

"After we catch up with that longest duration loop, it's back to etching untouched crystals, no more layering," Kaiden concluded.

I shook my head. "All this time when we thought the records showed a future of victory, but it was actually a record of failure."

Kaiden took a shaky breath. "But without that, we might not have believed we'd make it through."

"Maybe that's why we finally gave up and reset that first time," Maris said.

"Perhaps," I agreed. "And every time since, we've been trying to achieve the bright future we were convinced we must have—taking less and less time with each reset as our confidence grew, believing that victory was possible."

"That's pretty crazy when you look at it in those terms," Kaiden said.

"Yeah, it really is." I fell into quiet reflection. The hyperdimensional beings weren't beholden to the constant of time, but we still were—as strong as we had become. Despite all our abilities, hope remained one of the powerful most tools are our disposal.

"This next loop will be different," Maris said, breaking the silence. "No more Darkness."

"How long do we go back? Four months?" Kaiden questioned.

"Sounds about right." I shrugged, then groaned. "Ugh, I'll still be in school then."

"Hey, if our memories are as bad as they were on the other loops, you won't remember you've done it before," he pointed out.

"No, instead I might just have a frustrating case of déjà vu—as if senioritis isn't bad enough as it is." I chuckled. "Except, remembering all of the answers on my finals would be handy."

"Do you think we *will* remember anything?" Maris asked.

"We've never done a reset that far back, as far as we know," Toran replied. "I can only imagine that duration will exacerbate the recall issues we experienced with other universal resets. However, perhaps the Duzies in us will give us enough of a boost to retain some memories."

"Memories or not, our physical upgrades will be gone." I'd be going back to my injured self, but perhaps I could look into a corrective surgery on another world. The time for self-pity was far in my past.

"I would value the chance to reconnect, even if our magic is no longer present," Toran said.

"Yes, absolutely," I agreed.

We exchanged details about where each of us were residing before the Darkness came and how we could be reached on the Net. I didn't know how many details we'd retain after the universal reset, but it was worth a shot.

"What about the Hegemony?" Kaiden asked. "We saved civilization, and no one will ever know."

"Is it possible to leave a note somewhere?" I wondered.

"The Hegemony references the Archives' records," the mysterious voice offered. "This place will not be affected by the reset."

"Can you make some sort of entry about our team and what we did?" I asked it.

"Yes, but the Archive must be un-sealed for such modifications to be made."

Kaiden came to attention. "Oh, right! Almost forgot about that part."

"We'd like to unseal the Archive now. The threat has been neutralized." I grinned. "Always wanted to say that."

"Your intentions are pure," the voice replied. The crystal at the center of the platform flashed and then began to glow brightly. "The Archive is now active."

I nodded. "Please make a record that the four of us are the Dark Sentinels, and we—"

"Highlights from your memories will annotate the record," the voice replied. "It is done."

Maris looked taken aback. "Not sure I want everything in my mind, you know, hanging out there for anyone to look at."

"Yeah, I hope those 'highlights' are focused on the battle-y things and not… private stuff." I glanced at Kaiden and he gave me a knowing smile.

"The record will convey the necessary information," the voice stated.

"I guess that will have to do," Toran said.

Maris bit her lip. "Is that everything, then?"

I looked around at my friends. "Yeah, I guess it is. Everyone ready?"

"No. One more thing." Kaiden took me by the waist with one hand cupped the other around the back of my head, drawing me in for a kiss.

I felt awkward at first with Maris and Toran standing right there, but I blocked them out. Nothing could be allowed to ruin that moment, knowing this would be our last together in… I had no idea how long.

We parted, and he leaned his forehead against mine. "This isn't goodbye."

I fought back the lump my throat. "I know."

When we turned back to Toran and Maris, I saw they had wandered away to give us some privacy. "Okay, the grand romantic moment has passed," I said.

Maris turned around, flashing a smile. "I would have been disappointed if there wasn't one."

Toran chuckled. "Time to go home?"

Kaiden nodded. "Yeah, it is."

We gathered around the column at the center of the platform.

"We'll find each other," I emphasized, as much for myself as them.

Kaiden gave my hand one last squeeze. "We will."

Toran smiled. "We really did it. We stopped the Darkness and now everything will go back to how it was."

"Not everything," I replied. "We'll be different."

He nodded. "Yes, I suppose we will be."

"Well, it's been great," Maris said with a grin. "Terrifying and maddening, but great."

"Couldn't have had a better team." I smiled back. "See you around."

EPILOGUE

TWO MONTHS BEFORE the end of school, I started to remember.

It was just flashes at first, no more than fragments of a half-remembered dream. But, as the weeks passed, the images became vivid—previous-future memories of another life. I had been a warrior, a partner, and a leader. I had fulfilled my aspirations and become a hero in a way I never imagined was possible.

With the thrill of the discovery came the harsh realization that I couldn't tell anyone. Unless the Hegemony managed to uncover our message in the Master Archive, there would be no documentation for what the Dark Sentinels had done to save our worlds. My memories were of a reality that would never come to pass, at least not as it had unfolded before the universal reset. The only people who would believe me were my teammates. We'd vowed to reunite, in whatever bodies we now possessed, and I intended to keep that promise.

I was nervous about meeting them again—for them to see me in a damaged body, unable to move in the ways I had before. I knew they would be different, too, but I'd always taken comfort in the knowledge that they'd gotten to know me in a form that matched how I'd always viewed myself on the inside. Except, as I came to accept that there was nothing I could do about it, I started to transform.

The changes came slowly. First, my injured shoulder ached less in the morning, and I didn't get winded as easily during gym class at school. As time went on, I continued to feel more vibrant, stronger. By the time graduation rolled around, others had started to notice I was different.

I brushed off the observations for as long as I could, but when my hair began growing fuchsia at the roots, my parents insisted I visit our family doctor for a full physical. Scans revealed that my shoulder had completely healed, and I was as physically conditioned as a seasoned athlete. Defying all conventional medical explanation, the doctor justified it as a delayed 'growth spurt'. I played along, but I knew the truth: the Duzies were still inside me. They were a part of me, and I was forever changed.

The reset had rolled me back to a base state, but the zepto-exotic singularities had been gradually recharging my body, allowing me to return to the state that my higher dimensional consciousness longed for me to have. I had no way to be certain if my magic-casting abilities would also return, but I was compelled to find my friends like we'd agreed, to see if we still shared the kinship we'd developed during our time together.

Through some careful sleuthing on the Net, we made contact and set our rendezvous for Falstan II, where Kaiden was in the middle of a research study that required his presence.

I broached the topic with my parents in terms of a post-graduation trip, making the case that interstellar travel would broaden my horizons and help me decide on a career path.

Adrianne and Jiro had asked to come, eager to get away from our remote world and see the rest of the Hegemony. I let them down as gently as I could, explaining that this was something I needed to do on my own. In the fashion of true friends, they wished me well and promised we'd get together as soon as I returned. I didn't tell them that I might not come back, at least not for a long time. As much as I loved my family and friends, my experience in the previous-future had fundamentally altered my life outlook. Erusan was no longer my home; I belonged among the stars.

Seasonal work for the month following graduation allowed me to scrape together enough money to fund a ticket off my homeworld. I wasn't sure what to expect on Falstan II when I arrived, but I promised myself to take everything in stride.

After a grueling slog aboard a budget civilian transport ship, I finally arrived at my destination. Falstan II was a small world, relatively barren in appearance from space, with only a handful of green patches where industrious settlers had set up agricultural operations. I boarded a shuttle headed for a port on the small northern continent.

I stepped off the shuttle into the quiet port, tended only by an elderly man who seemed content to read the news and nap while on his shift.

"Can you direct me toward Holloway Farms?" I asked him, hoisting my backpack onto my shoulders.

He cracked open an eye. "Holloway? It's up Route 7 to the northeast. Not much reason to head up to those parts."

"I think I'll find what I'm looking for." I smiled to myself. "Is there any public transport headed that way?"

"You can take the Number 2 bus as far as Independence. You can walk from there," the old man replied.

"Thank you."

I located a stop for the bus number he'd indicated and rode it to the town twenty kilometers away. Independence was little more than a fueling station and grocery store, but the locals were able to direct me toward the road that led the rest of the way to Holloway Farms.

I took a leisurely pace on the three-kilometer walk, enjoying the warm sun and the dirt road beneath my feet. The quiet was a welcome change from the tight quarters and constant mechanical hum during the previous part of my journey.

Eventually, I reached a sign marking the official facility entrance. My stomach fluttered, knowing I was only minutes from seeing my friends again.

Three structures—a large house, a cabin, and an industrial lab—were positioned along the access road. A man in his late-fifties emerged from the house as I approached.

"Can I help you?" he asked.

"Hi," I greeted. "I'm here for the reunion—a friend of Kaiden's."

"Yes, yes! Welcome. I'm Bill Holloway." The man extended his hand.

I shook it. "Happy to meet you, Bill. I'm Elle. Thank you for hosting us."

He smiled. "Our pleasure. The farm's been too empty and lonely since the kids moved out. Susie always loves to cook for a group."

"Sounds like we came to the right place." I looked around. "Where is—"

"Elle!" a high-pitched voice called out, followed by rapid footsteps on wooden stairs.

I turned to see Maris barreling toward me. "Hi!"

She wrapped her arms tightly around me as soon as she

was close enough, almost knocking me off balance. "I can't believe we're finally back together!"

"I know, this is surreal." I pulled back so I could examine her at arm's length. She looked almost identical to the last time I saw her in my previous-future memories—same wavy, dark hair, curvy figure, and bright eyes, though it was strange to see her in normal street clothes.

Maris gently ran her fingers along a length of my hair. "You weren't kidding about the fuchsia hair coming back! That's wild."

I grinned. "I know! Freaked my parents out."

"How'd you explain it?"

"I didn't. Not well, anyway." I glanced at Bill, not wanting to say too much in front of him. "You know how it is."

"Yeah, I got off easy. Wait until you see Toran." Maris nodded toward the house.

The door opened a moment later, and a large man stepped outside—not quite the behemoth I'd traveled with, but formidable nonetheless. "Stars!" My jaw dropped.

"Hello, Elle," he greeted. "I'm glad you made it."

"Toran, wow!" I gave him a hug as soon as he jogged over, my arms barely wrapping around his torso. His muscular physique was a scaled-back version of how I remembered him, but seeing him with dark hair threw me off.

"How was your trip?" he asked, his voice still deep and warm.

I smiled. "I have to say, it was kind of nice being put under for the hyperspace jumps. Budget travel, but it wasn't all bad. The food was better than on the *Evangiel*!"

He laughed. "It doesn't take much to top that bar."

"I'll, uh, leave you to your pleasantries," Bill interjected. "Would you like me to take your pack to your room for you?"

"Oh, that would be great, thanks." I slid off my backpack and handed it to him. "Thank you again for having us."

He nodded. "Dinner will be in an hour."

"Great, see you then." I smiled.

We waited for Bill to enter the house.

"Talk about a transformation!" I said as soon as Bill was out of sight.

Toran chuckled. "Caught me by surprise when it first started to happen. Fortunately, the memories had started to surface, so at least I had some idea about what was going on."

"How'd your wife react?" I asked.

"Shocked and concerned, at first." Toran shook his head, his eyes sparkling. "I had no choice but to tell her what had happened. Took a little convincing, but," he gestured to himself with both hands, "I had some good physical evidence to back up my story. Once she got used to the idea, she wanted to come meet all of you, but she couldn't get time off from work. And then there's Leia's school, of course… But, we'd love to have the three of you come for a visit on Dunlore, if you're interested."

"That sounds great, Toran. I'd love to meet your family," I said.

"We'll need to decide if we should reveal ourselves to the Hegemony," Toran stated.

I shrugged. "Maybe they'll find that message we left. But, for now, I'm happy all of the worlds are safe."

Maris shook her head. "It's like it never happened—except, we know it did."

"Brought us together!" I said.

Toran smiled. "Whoever would have thought we'd all end up as friends?"

Maris laughed. "*Not* me! I still can't believe we're all here."

I looked around. "Speaking of which, where's Kaiden?"

"Ah, right!" Toran exclaimed. "I'm sure you're anxious to see him. He's still out in the fields."

Maris smirked. "We'll give you two some privacy."

"You should be able to find him out that way." Toran gestured to the west.

"Thanks." I took a slow breath. "I'll see you in a bit."

"Elle." Maris gave me another hug. "It's great to see you again."

I smiled. "You too."

"I'm looking forward to getting to know this other version of you," Toran said.

"Likewise. I knew we'd find our way back to each other."

He patted my shoulder. "Things are now as they should be."

With a renewed wave of nerves, I headed toward the western field. The crop was still young, barely reaching my knees. Despite the clear visibility across the flat field, I didn't see anyone at first. After a minute of fighting the glare from the afternoon sun, I finally spotted the back of a young man with medium-brown hair crouched down, collecting a sample.

"Hey," I called out, approaching him.

He straightened and turned around. Instant recognition filled his sky-blue eyes, and his lips spread in a warm smile. "Hey yourself."

I smiled back, trying to play it cool as I strolled toward Kaiden. He was just as handsome as I remembered in my previous-future memories. "Nice place you have here."

He surveyed the field. "It's been fine for the past few months."

"And now?"

He stepped forward to meet me. "Now, you're here."

We ran the last several paces and embraced. He scooped me up in his arms and held me close.

I buried my face in the crook of his neck. “I missed you.”

“I missed you, too,” he murmured into my hair.

Our lips met in a passionate kiss, as comfortable and familiar as two longtime lovers after a prolonged separation.

Breathlessly, we pulled apart, laughing with joy to be back with one another. I entwined my fingers in his, never wanting to let go again.

“What now?” I asked, looking into his eyes.

“Well, I’m not sure how long Toran and Maris intend to stay, but I’ll need another month to finish this research study. After that…”

I nodded and squeezed his hands. “I have nowhere else I want to be.”

Kaiden turned so his back was to the farmhouse. “Good, because things could get interesting.” He pulled his right hand free from mine, and electricity danced across his fingertips.

I grinned. “Oh, this is going to be fun.”

THE END

AUTHOR'S NOTES

Thank you for reading *Masters of Fate*!

Wow, this series has been a wild ride to write! When I first conceptualized this trilogy, I thought it was going to be pure space fantasy. As you can tell, it evolved to be much more than that. However, I can't talk about how it got an infusion of hard sci-fi without talking about Jim.

Now, Jim and I had an interesting start to our relationship—in that we met online via him leaving a one-star review on the first book in my Cadicle series. Contrary to some popular writerly advice, I will occasionally respond to one-star reviews, and I did in this case. I addressed each of his criticisms and explained some aspects of the Cadicle series that aren't evident in the opening chapters. Jim graciously replied and said he'd give the book another chance. As it turned out, he rather enjoyed the series and went on to be interested in my future writings. I always value a critical eye on my books, so I invited him to be a member of my beta reader team.

Fast forward to the beta review stage of *A Light in the Dark*, the second book in the Dark Stars trilogy, Jim started asking me about some of the universe mechanics in Dark Stars. This sparked a number of long, in-depth conversations. I had a lot of ideas and knew how I wanted things in the universe to work, but I didn't have the science background to put the right vocabulary to those concepts. Working together, we documented the dimensional hierarchy and how different aspects of the crystalline network functioned. I'm incredibly thankful for the amount of time Jim spent talking through all aspects of this story and lending his expertise to help me fill in the gaps. This story wouldn't be what it is without him!

With that said, there are several assumptions about the story universe that are touched upon but didn't get fully explored in the book's narrative. If you're curious about the universal mechanics, read on :-).

Q: What is the dimensional hierarchy, and what's in each dimension?

3D – normal physical reality

4D – time

5D – telepathy/thought

6D – Toran's gauntlets artifact; Saps/Overlords

7D – Kaiden's circlet; Hoofy and other 'mythical' beings (unicorns, dragons, etc.)

8D – Maris' shield artifact; window maze; nimbuses (nimbuses also have a 7D component)

9D – Elle's sword artifact; crystalline network connections/storage

10D –Consciousness

11D –Duzies

Q: How does the 'magic' work?

A: The 11D dimensionally ubiquitous, zepto-elemental singularities ('Duzies') enable the apparent magic. The team's hyperdimensional artifacts concentrated and intensify Duzie energy. Kaiden's circlet functions like a magic antenna that allows his non-magical staff weapon to become super-saturated with Duzies, making it a concentrated director of magic. As the team's bodies become saturated by Duzies, they are more readily able to cast their own magic without their artifacts.

Q: Why could only 'viewing-spheres' be used for dimensional transitions and not normal crystals?

A: Crystals only exist in 3D spacetime while viewing-spheres span all dimensions. Crystals are Duzie-saturated normal matter. Viewing-spheres are Duzies in pure solid form.

Q: Do all planets that exist in spacetime also have extended existence in higher dimensions in some form or another?

A: The planets have a distinct physical presence in 6D, 7D, and 8D. In 5D, 9D, and 10D, all mass is amorphous 'dark matter' which supports thought channeling and network storage. In 11D, all matter is pure Duzie-plasma.

Q: Why do Darkness planets have reduced-gravity in normal spacetime?

A: The anomaly-related, Duzie-powered Darkness draws power from transmutation of planet's mass, reducing its density but not disturbing its magnetic field or geologic underpinnings.

Q: Why did the anomaly site in space where the aliens first appeared have excess gravity but no apparent mass?

A: The dimensional-rift anomaly channeled and concentrated normal matter and dark matter gravity from nearby systems across extended dimensions into 3D spacetime at a central point. The 6D aliens used this unique site as a staging ground for their intended invasion from their home plane.

I hope you enjoyed this story and found it to be a satisfying blend of sci-fi and fantasy. I've loved both genres for as long as

I can remember, and I'm excited to have been able to merge the two in what I hope was a fun, unique way.

I'd also like to give shout-outs to the rest of my fantastic behind-the-scenes team who helped polish the book and get it publication-ready: Kurt, Randy, Troy, John, Eric, Pam, Charlie, Leo, Diane, and Nick. You are all amazing! Thank you for your continued support and for donating your time to helping me turn dreams into reality.

Special thanks to my husband, Nick, for always keeping me fed and for putting up with my weird work hours. I couldn't have a more perfect life partner!

Thank you again for reading the Dark Stars trilogy! Readers like you are who enable me to be a full-time author, and I'm so thankful to you for making that possible. If you'd like to see future stories in this universe, please let me know in your review or send me a message via the contact form on my website. In the meantime, look for other new books in the coming months :-). Happy reading!

ALSO BY A.K. DUBOFF

Dark Stars Trilogy
Book 1: Crystalline Space
Book 2: A Light in the Dark
Book 3: Masters of Fate

Cadicle Space Opera Series
Book 1: Rumors of War (Vol. 1-3)
Book 2: Web of Truth (Vol. 4)
Book 3: Crossroads of Fate (Vol. 5)
Book 4: Path of Justice (Vol. 6)
Book 5: Scions of Change (Vol. 7)

Mindspace Series
Book 1: Infiltration
Book 2: Conspiracy
Book 3: Offensive
Book 4: Endgame

Troubled Space
Vol. 1: Brewing Trouble
Vol. 2: Stealing Trouble
Vol. 3: Making Trouble

ABOUT THE AUTHOR

A.K. (Amy) DuBoff has always loved science fiction in all its forms—books, movies, shows and games. If it involves outer space, even better!

Now a full-time author, Amy can frequently be found traveling the world. When she's not writing, she enjoys wine tasting, binge-watching TV series, and playing epic strategy board games.

To learn more or connect, visit www.amyduboff.com.

www.ingramcontent.com/pod-product-compliance
Lightning Source LLC
LaVergne TN
LVHW091113080826
845145LV00008B/1901

* 9 7 8 1 9 5 4 3 4 4 1 8 1 *